HAPPY INDEPENDENCE DAY

MICHAEL RUPURED

DSP PUBLICATIONS

Published by
DSP Publications

5032 Capital Circle SW, Suite 2, PMB# 279, Tallahassee, FL 32305-7886 USA
www.dsppublications.com

Happy Independence Day
© 2016 Michael Rupured.

Cover Art
© 2016 AngstyG.
www.angstyg.com
Cover content is for illustrative purposes only and any person depicted on the cover is a model.

ISBN: 978-1-63476-987-7
Digital ISBN: 978-1-63476-988-4
Library of Congress Control Number: 2016901925
Published July 2016
v 2.0

First Edition published by Dreamspinner Press, 2014.

Printed in the United States of America
∞
This paper meets the requirements of
ANSI/NISO Z39.48-1992 (Permanence of Paper).

ACKNOWLEDGMENTS

FIFTY YEARS ago, nobody talked about gay marriage. Why would they? The American Psychiatric Association considered homosexuality a mental illness until 1974. Homosexual acts were illegal across the United States (Illinois decriminalized sodomy in 1962—ten years ahead of any other state). Coming out of the closet often resulted in job loss, eviction, and disownment by family and friends. Homosexuals who didn't kill themselves or get beaten to death faced "cures" like electroshock therapy, lobotomy, or castration.

Things were especially bad in New York. Serving alcohol to homosexuals was an invitation for the state regulatory authority to revoke an establishment's liquor license. Ongoing campaigns to clean up Greenwich Village through police raids and undercover sting operations were common.

In late June of 1969, some of the most disenfranchised men and women in America—the gayest of the gay—stood up for their rights after the police raided a tiny, Mafia-owned and operated establishment called the Stonewall Inn. I was eleven years old and heard nothing for another fifteen or twenty years about the uprising considered by many to be the birth of the modern gay liberation movement. My mother hadn't heard of the Stonewall Riots until after I mentioned them while working on this book.

Happy Independence Day is a work of fiction set around the Stonewall uprising. Long before I finished writing *After Christmas Eve*, I knew Harold Clarkson and Terrence Bottom would be present for the riots. Cameron McKenzie came into being when I learned about the Mafia's ties to the Stonewall Inn and an international extortion scheme. Two incidents of resistance to police brutality—one involving a lesbian and the other a drag queen—ignited the crowd's rage to start the riots and served as the inspiration for Kreema Dee Kropp and Kelsey Ryan.

The characters may be fictional, but every effort was made to stick to the events comprising the early hours of the riots. For a factual and more detailed account, I highly recommend David Carter's *Stonewall: The Riots that Sparked the Gay Revolution*. My battered, dog-eared copy contains highlighted phrases, sentences, and paragraphs on just about every page.

Thanks to my beta readers (Amy, Misty, Tali, and Jennifer), the wonderful folks at Dreamspinner Press, and the patrons of the Stonewall Inn who made this story possible.

CHAPTER ONE

Tuesday, June 24, 1969

TERRENCE BOTTOM tapped a sandaled foot on the linoleum-tiled floor and bit his lip. Speaking his mind at a Mattachine Society meeting was a waste of time and energy. But watching the older members of the homophile organization nod their heads in agreement as the speaker droned on about homosexuality being a mental illness had been more than he could take. As the uptight men and women nearby glared at him, he rolled his eyes at Kelsey Ryan and whispered, "You ready to blow this joint?"

Before she could answer, the esteemed speaker concluded his remarks. After a polite round of applause, the well-dressed men and women filled the aisles and chatted as they made for the door of the Columbia University lecture hall where the meeting had been held.

Kelsey and Terrence merged into the slow-moving mass creeping toward the exit. Between reed-thin Terrence's curly blond hair and Kelsey's height—never mind that she was built like an offensive lineman for the Washington Redskins—the unlikely pair stood out in the crowd. Rather than the suits worn by other men in the lecture hall, Terrence had on faded bell-bottomed jeans embroidered with flowers, a tie-dyed T-shirt, and a wide white belt with a peace-sign buckle.

"The old guard just doesn't get it," Kelsey said, rolling up the sleeves of her oxford shirt to her elbows as she walked. "Working behind the scenes to change the world hasn't gotten us anywhere."

"I don't know about that," Terrence said, falling in beside her. "Legal challenges to alcohol regulations have helped to crack open the door here in New York."

"How?" Kelsey shoved her hands into her pockets. "The police have raided every gay bar in town at least once in the last two weeks. Legal victories haven't stopped them from harassing us every chance they get."

"Philip and George—"

"Are just like the other men their age working for change." She shook her head. "They think we should be patient, but my patience has run out. We need new tactics so the world stops seeing homosexuals as mentally ill, morally bankrupt freaks who can't be trusted to work in the government or around children."

Terrence nodded. She was on her soapbox now. He didn't bother reminding her he agreed with her. She was too wound up to stop until she'd said her piece.

"The white men in power aren't going to give us our rights. We need to stand up and fight for equality, like the Black Panthers or Students for a Democratic Society." She punched her open palm with a fist. "They didn't get anywhere until they stood up to the cops. What a fight!"

Despite Kelsey's pleas, Terrence hadn't gone uptown with the students in his sociology class last year to show support when the SDS had staged a protest over Columbia University's backing of the war in Vietnam. The students had been beaten with nightsticks and bombed with tear gas. The sight of his bruised and bandaged classmates afterward had flipped the switch for Terrence. If he hadn't learned anything else on the streets, he'd learned you fought force with force.

Terrence and Kelsey descended the steps into the subway station to wait for the next train to Greenwich Village. Businessmen, sweating in suits, loosened ties and glared at them. Terrence knew they made quite a pair. He'd toned down his flamboyance some, but next to Kelsey— sturdy, stocky, and rumbling, like a Mack truck—he was the picture of femininity. Despite her efforts to conceal them, her impressive breasts might have been attractive on another woman, but on her masculine frame, they just looked out of place.

"Want to grab a drink at the Stonewall Inn later?" Terrence asked, spotting a headlight moving toward the station.

Kelsey snorted. "And would the reason you want to go have something to do with that high-class callboy you've been watching?"

Terrence punched her arm. "You don't know he's a callboy." He tossed his hair and smiled. "And he's watching me. I just happened to have noticed."

"Who wouldn't?" She paused, waiting for the noisy train to come to a stop. "The man is gorgeous, and for me to notice is saying something." They stepped onto the car and the doors squealed shut behind them. "But he's a hustler, trust me, and he's working for the mob. I've seen him talking to Frankie Caldarone too many times, and he ain't shining the man's shoes."

Terrence led the way to the back of the subway car, and they settled onto the last seats on each side of the aisle. "Frankie Caldarone? The bald-headed goon at the Stonewall Inn?" Terrence crossed his legs and adjusted the forty-inch bellbottoms to cascade in folds above the sandals he wore. "He's just a bouncer."

"More like the enforcer, at an unlicensed private club, owned and operated by who?" She spread her legs wide, leaned back, and wove her hands together behind her head.

"Wouldn't that be whom?" Terrence didn't want to admit Kelsey could be right. Trading sexual favors for money didn't bother him so much. Hustling was a dangerous, dead-end job he'd managed to escape more than two years earlier, thanks to Philip and George. Hustling for the mob, however, was a death sentence with no chance for parole, pardon, or escape.

"Either way, the answer is the same." She shook her head and leaned forward, dropping her hands to her knees. "You'd be smart to stay the hell away from that one."

"Come on, Kelsey." Terrence fluffed his hair and adjusted his headband, feeling the embroidered peace sign with his fingers and shifting the band a bit to center the emblem over his nose.

She laughed and punched his arm. "You say that like going out with him is the furthest thing from your mind."

Terrence gazed at her, wide-eyed. "You know me better than that."

"Oh, you are so good." Kelsey shook her head and folded her arms. "I know you all right. Hearing you can't have something just makes you want it that much more."

Terrence sat up, turned to her, and put his hand on her knee. "All we have is right now, this very minute. Two minutes from now, this train could crash, killing us both."

"Shit, Terrence." She shuddered. "You know I hate the subway."

His gaze shifted to the window behind her. He stared, seeing remembered faces in the passing blackness. "When you want something, you gotta go for it—before somebody snatches it away from you and it's gone forever." He brushed a fist over his eye and shook his head. "Besides, I've never even talked to him."

"Maybe not, but the way you two look at each other is enough to make me blush." She chuckled. "I'm just jealous. Hell, I'd pay a year's tuition to have a pretty girl look at me like that."

Terrence reached over and tousled her short brown hair. "You're a good person, Kelsey. If I was a lesbian, I'd be proud to be your girlfriend." He leered at her and grinned. "Even without those big titties of yours!"

She laughed and reached for her top button. "Careful now, or I'll turn 'em loose on you."

CHAPTER TWO

PHILIP POTTER opened the door and smiled, delighted to see his first guest had finally arrived. He'd fussed around his Washington, DC apartment all morning to make sure everything was ready for the party. Nervous energy had collided with a dish of chocolates around noon, forcing a last-minute trip to the store to replenish a bowl that seemed to empty of its own volition.

"Lieutenant White!" Philip clasped his hands together. "I'm so glad you could make it."

"Oh come on, Philip. Must we be so formal?" A dazzling smile lit up her face, the bright red lipstick drawing attention to the contrast between her pearly whites and ebony skin. "Call me Shirley—at least when I'm not in uniform." She threw her arms around his shoulders and squeezed. "I wouldn't miss Harold's graduation party for the world, never mind the chance to see you again. Where's George?"

"He took the guest of honor out to lunch and has strict orders not to arrive back here a moment before three o'clock." He glanced at his watch. "There's coffee. Would you like a cup?"

"Like you read my mind…."

As they turned toward the kitchen, the apartment door burst open. A smiling redheaded boy beelined for Philip. "*Zio!*" He flung his arms around Philip's waist, his feet leaving the floor.

"How about I just help myself to a cup of that coffee?" Shirley smiled. "While you greet your guests."

Philip nodded and then grabbed the precocious child to keep him from falling, holding him close. "My goodness, who is this young man?"

Jade-green eyes peeked out from under blond lashes and rusty bangs as an enormous smile, minus several teeth, spread across his freckled face. "I'm Thad Parker, your nephew, silly!"

Philip set Thad down and ran a hand through his silky hair. "Good grief! You've grown a foot since I saw you last week. Dear child, where are your glasses? I don't suppose you've outgrown them too?"

"Here they are," said Mary Parker, giving Thad his glasses as she came through the door and handing Philip a gift wrapped in white paper and topped with a silver bow. "For the graduate." She hugged Philip and kissed his cheek. "How's my little brother?"

"Delighted to see you, as always." Philip placed the package on the table with several envelopes. "Where's your husband?"

"He's coming." She poked her head out the door. "Hurry up, Alex, we're letting out the air-conditioning!"

A bespectacled man stumbled into the apartment behind her, juggling a thick brown briefcase and half a dozen short, square boxes. He glanced at Philip, and one of the boxes fell to the floor. "I brought the slides from our trip to Italy."

"Wonderful!" Philip retrieved the fallen box. "Why don't you set that up in Harold's bedroom? I'll send anyone back who wants to see."

A disappointed Alex headed down the hall. "But I was thinking…."

"Yes, Alex, I know." Philip frowned. "But remember how awful everything looked on that dark green living room wall?"

He gave Philip a sheepish nod.

"I think you'll be much happier with the white walls in the bedroom," Mary said. "Thad, run along with your father and get everything set up before Harold and George get here." She hooked Philip's elbow with her hand and whispered, "Well done."

"Avoiding another grand viewing of the slides from your trip has become a priority of late," Philip said, pulling a monogrammed handkerchief from his pocket to wipe his brow.

She laughed. "You've only seen them three, maybe four times. What about me?"

"I'm sure we'll treasure them, years from now." Philip returned the folded handkerchief to his pocket and steered her to the kitchen. "Lieutenant White, er, I mean Shirley, allow me to introduce my sister, Mary Parker."

Shirley stood and extended her hand. "Pleasure to meet you!"

Mary grasped Shirley's hand in both of hers and smiled. "I feel like I know you! Nice to finally meet the woman Philip wrote so much about in his letters."

During Alex's two-year deployment to Manila for the State Department, Philip had missed them even more than he'd imagined he would. Except for when he and George had gone to Italy for a visit, Philip had written long, chatty letters to Mary every week while they were abroad.

A series of knocks on the apartment door drew his attention. "Excuse me, ladies. That must be the Dombroskis." Philip hurried to the living room to greet them. "Mrs. Dee! I'm so glad you could come."

A pudgy, middle-aged woman in a homemade dress pushed past him, a Tupperware cake carrier in one hand and a well-worn shopping bag in the other. Philip clasped his hands together and smiled at a willowy teenage girl with short blonde hair plastered to her head, darkly rouged cheeks, and enormous, mascara-ringed blue eyes. She held a box wrapped in psychedelic paper with several matching bows. "And look at you, Abigail!"

"Hi, Mr. Potter." She blushed and looked at the floor.

Mrs. Dee lifted up the shopping bag. "I brought you a few jars of the bread-and-butter pickles, green tomato relish, and blackberry jam I put up last week." She handed the bag to him. "When the strawberries come in, I'll bring you some preserves." She lifted the cake holder to eye level. "And this is jam cake with boiled caramel icing. Harold's favorite. Which way is the kitchen?"

"This way, Mom," Abigail said, pointing down the hall. "Where's Harold?"

Philip glanced at his watch. "He should be here soon. Come on back and say hello to everyone."

The crowd in the little kitchen spilled over into the living room. Philip did a quick head count as his guests chatted and caught up with each other. "All right, except for Harold and George, I believe everyone is here."

"Isn't Terrence coming?" Shirley asked.

"No." Philip shook his head. "He wanted to be here, but he's taking classes this summer at Columbia University."

"He's come so far." She patted Philip on the back. "You should be very proud of him."

"I am. He's turned into a fine young man." He cleared his throat and waited a moment for everyone to quiet down. "Thank you all for coming today to celebrate Harold's high school graduation." He paused, glancing at the familiar faces around the room. "As you know, the last few years haven't been easy for him. Holidays and special occasions have been particularly difficult—"

"But not nearly as bad for him as they would have been without you," Shirley said. Heads around the room nodded in agreement.

"And the love and ongoing support of everyone here." Philip glanced around the room. "Thank you, for everything you've done for us."

"When do we yell surprise?" Thad asked. A sheepish look came over his face when everyone laughed. "Mommy said I couldn't have any cake until after we yell surprise."

Philip glanced at his watch again. "Any minute now, Thad. Okay everyone, into the living room."

"If he hears us, he won't be surprised." Thad put a finger over his lips. "Shhhh!"

CHAPTER THREE

Cameron McKenzie walked through Central Park, wondering how he'd landed in such a mess. Trading sex for money was supposed to have been a short-term solution to a temporary cash-flow problem. Now he was trapped.

Pigeons scattered out of his way as he walked. His jeans and T-shirt clung to him in the humidity and heat of high summer, and he resisted the urge to wipe the sweat from his brow with the still-dry shirt slung over his shoulder. He glanced at his watch and quickened his pace.

The cash he'd brought with him from Kentucky had run out in two days—much faster than he'd expected. His experience on the farm didn't translate into any kind of job in the city. A chance encounter with a kind man who'd stopped to offer him a ride had launched his career. Having sex with men wasn't so bad, and the money was good. After that, rather than starving to death, Cameron had done what he had to do to get by.

Cameron wasn't queer. Couldn't be. He wasn't the least bit effeminate, had no desire to dress up like a woman, and would never touch a child of either gender. If he ever managed to find a way out of the mess he was in, he wanted a wife, children of his own, and a little dog to keep in a spacious, fenced-in yard somewhere. If women got horny enough to pay for sex, he wouldn't even be here. But they didn't. Sex was sex, and though some of his clients were disappointed, they accepted that kissing wasn't part of the deal.

The point of no return came with his first run-in with the law. The officer had talked with Cameron about his career choice and, because he liked him, had given Cameron another chance. Rather than taking him to jail, the crooked cop had introduced him to Frankie Caldarone, the man he now hurried to meet.

At first Cameron had thought he'd found the perfect gig to tide him over until he landed a breakout role in a big Broadway show. Hustling for Frankie came with a tiny room in a dilapidated boarding house, a free meal from Guiseppe's every day, a little spending money, and protection from harassment by local police. Instead of walking the streets in all kinds of weather, he hung out in nice, dry hotels with heat in the winter and air-conditioning in summer. Unlike the self-employed hustlers he saw getting tossed out every night, nobody bothered him. Bellhops and front-desk clerks on the mob's payroll sent johns his way.

The downside hadn't become apparent right away. Rather than free, Frankie's deductions for the shabby little room and free meals ended up consuming almost all the money he made. Skipping meals didn't increase his income either.

Handing over all the money he made was bad enough. Submitting to Frankie's sexual demands was worse. Whatever he wanted, anytime, wherever they happened to be. But that paled in comparison to what Frankie made Cameron do to his customers.

Frankie sat alone on a bench overlooking the lake. The very sight of his bald-headed employer repulsed Cameron, a feeling that had intensified in the months since he'd tried to quit hustling for a star-making supporting role in an off-Broadway musical comedy. Frankie had laughed, saying Cameron already had a job, and the next day had sent his goons to retrieve Cameron from rehearsals.

Cameron slid onto the opposite end of the bench and waited for Frankie to speak. By the lake, two little boys pulled boats on strings. Cameron saw the way Frankie eyed them and shuddered. His sadistic employer liked them young and was likely responsible for the disappearance of more than a few missing boys.

"Whaddya got for me?" Frankie said, with an accent Cameron had come to identify with the Jersey Shore.

He reached into his pocket, pulled out three wallets, and slid them across the bench with a wad of crumpled bills.

Frankie stuffed the cash into his pocket and then picked up the wallets. "Just three?" He glanced at Cameron. "You used to bring me five or six." He flipped through the contents, adding any cash he found to the bills in his left pants pocket before dropping the wallets into a brown paper bag on the ground between his feet. "Getting old?"

Cameron watched the dirty old man check him out, looking for signs he'd lost value. He had an extra wrinkle or two, but he hadn't gained any weight or lost any hair. They wouldn't be fitting him for concrete wading boots anytime soon. But Cameron knew sooner or later his day would come.

Frankie pulled a ten-dollar bill from his wad of cash with thick fingers and handed it to Cameron before shoving the rest back into his pocket. "The photos of you and that john you picked up at the Hilton Hotel last week turned out to be worth a fortune."

Cameron wondered which unlucky bastard he was talking about. At first he'd thought stealing the wallets was a crime of opportunity, since the victims were unlikely to tell anyone. But Frankie used the information in the wallets to blackmail the men who'd paid for the privilege of being robbed. The ones who didn't kill themselves always paid. The alternative was just too costly.

"Come around the club before dark. I need your help." Frankie retrieved the bag at his feet and stood. Despite his girth, he was solid muscle. Cameron had heard he'd been a small-time professional wrestler known as "The Bull" before he'd hooked up with the mob. "A little birdie told me the police will be dropping by for a surprise visit tonight. I wanna make sure they don't find anything illegal-like on the premises, *capisce?*"

Cameron nodded and then watched as Frankie strolled up the sidewalk and stopped to chat with the boating boys before continuing around a curve and out of sight. He got up and, tossing his shirt over his shoulder, strolled alongside the lake in the opposite direction.

Most of the bars he'd frequented in search of clients had closed. The police often raided the few that remained open. With an election in November, the mayor wanted to call attention to his record for ridding Gotham of vile homosexuals. The police raids were never a surprise and didn't happen without Frankie's prior approval. He paid the local precinct captain twelve hundred dollars a month for protection that included advance notice of any plans to drop into the Stonewall Inn. On at least three occasions, Cameron had counted the money into a White Owl cigar box for Frankie, only to see Frankie hand the very same box to the captain an hour or so later, who just happened to pop into the illegal club to make sure everything was okay.

The homosexuals hadn't gone anywhere either. In fact, sissies from across the eastern half of the United States continued to flock to Greenwich Village in droves. They fled the isolation of small towns and cities, leaving behind the bleakness of inconspicuous obscurity. The newcomers were often surprised by the state of affairs in New York City. Various and sundry laws and regulations had pushed the gay scene underground, which, like Prohibition, created an opportunity for the mob to cash in on an unmet need. The Stonewall Inn, thanks to the jukeboxes and dance floors, was the most popular of several Mafia-owned establishments catering to homosexuals.

Although he wasn't gay—he was sure of it—Cameron had fallen head over heels in lust the first time he'd seen the lithesome man with the curly blond hair at the Stonewall Inn. Since that first night Cameron had seen him dance, the pretty young man had become prominent in the fantasies he thought about to keep his dick hard for clients he didn't find attractive. In his mind's eye, he curled his fingers into the blond curls as the pretty boy sucked his dick.

He adjusted his pants, glancing up at the benches as he passed to see if anyone had noticed. An old man leered at him over his newspaper, licking his lips when Cameron caught his eye. Cameron winked, out of habit as much as anything else, and if the creep had looked like he had a good job, would have stopped to chat. Turning perverts like him over to Frankie was a pleasure.

But his victims—most of them, anyway—were nice guys who tried hard to do everything right. Most of the time, they succeeded. But once in a while—perhaps 1 percent of the time—a desire for the company of handsome young men was their undoing. Cameron would assure them he wasn't a cop, thinking they'd probably be better off if he were.

Letting the nice guys go wasn't an option. Cameron never knew when he was being watched. Holding out on the Mafia wasn't an option either. Frankie checked up on him often enough to keep him honest. Cameron knew the rules and valued life too much to risk his for a stranger's sake.

But it didn't keep him from hoping that one day he'd find a way out.

CHAPTER FOUR

HAROLD CLARKSON knew Philip was up to something. Had known, in fact, for weeks. Whispered telephone conversations and talk of the weather when Harold entered the room were dead giveaways. His legal guardian—up to Harold's last birthday, anyway—was a lot better at keeping a secret than concealing the fact that he had one to keep.

Whatever he was up to, Harold thought today's outing with George Walker, Philip's attorney, was somehow connected. Mr. Walker had requested a late lunch meeting to discuss provisions for Harold's continuing education. Harold thought they'd covered all the bases at a similar meeting back in April when he had turned eighteen, about registering for the draft and his options for avoiding a stint in Nam.

"Have you given any thought to what you'd like to do, now that you've finished high school?" Mr. Walker touched a linen napkin to his lips and placed it across his lap before looking over a carnation-filled bud vase at him. Understated, elegant, and timeless in his tailored suit, crisply starched shirt, and narrow silk tie, Mr. Walker fit right in with the staid, conservative décor of the dining room at the Mayflower Hotel.

Harold poked at his salad and avoided Mr. Walker's gaze. "Some."

"I see." Mr. Walker patted his lips again with his napkin. "Well, between grants, scholarships, and the foundation's support, you can go to college just about anywhere you want."

"Yes, sir, I know." But Harold didn't want to go to college. He'd explained to anyone who'd listen his desire to learn everything he could about hair and makeup before moving to California to open a little boutique catering to movie stars and models. Beauty school was a better choice for him, but Philip wanted him to go to college first.

"Philip is very proud of you for finishing high school." Mr. Walker shifted in his chair. "I know you hit a few rough spots.…"

Harold wondered what all Mr. Walker did know. Terrence had told him he and Philip were lovers, but Harold had met Mrs. Walker and played with her little dogs. The bond between husband and his well-dressed wife was obvious. She'd been just as nice to Philip—hardly the way Harold imagined she'd treat her husband's lover. Besides, sleeping with a married man was wrong. And yet, he'd seen the way Philip and the man seated across the table looked at each other. Harold wasn't sure he believed only foundation work forced them to spend so much time together. "Nothing I didn't bring on myself," Harold replied. "Philip tried to warn me, but I wouldn't listen."

Coming to a new school the first day dressed in a beautifully tailored suit, modeled after one he'd seen on Jackie Kennedy, with his hair teased, a little makeup, and the longest fake lashes he could find hadn't gone over at all the way Harold had expected. But Philip had allowed him to dress up, knowing what was going to happen, in spite of Harold's assurances that everything would be fine. Before the first bell rang, a bunch of mean boys had forced him to seek refuge in the girls' bathroom.

Philip had appeared out of nowhere, making Harold fix his face and repair the damage to his hair before leading him by the hand from the bathroom, down the hall, and out the front door while everyone in the school stared at them. On the way home, Philip had explained that Harold had the right to be whoever he wanted to be, but the less like everyone else he appeared, the more likely he'd be to encounter people who'd want to hurt him for being different.

Changing schools had given Harold a chance to practice what he'd learned, with better results. He still teased his long hair and never left home without at least a little eyeliner and mascara, adding blush and lipstick for special occasions. But the inevitable run-ins with bullies and the sparring sessions with Terrence had taught him how to protect himself, toughened him up, and tempered his desire to stand out in the crowd.

"He loves you very much," Mr. Walker said, glancing at his watch. "Are you about ready to go?"

Harold thought about stalling. He could ask for the dessert menu and linger over each and every delicious bite, watching Mr. Walker fidget and play with his watch like he was waiting for a bomb to explode. But he was curious and anxious to move on to the next phase of Philip's secret operation. "Yes, sir."

MR. WALKER paid the cab driver, and they walked up the sidewalk to the entrance of the building where Harold shared an apartment with Philip. Until he'd gone away to New York for college, Terrence Bottom had been Harold's roommate and, next to Abigail Dombroski, the best friend he'd ever had.

"After you," Mr. Walker said, smiling as he held open the door to the three-story apartment building.

Sensing he was about to find out the big secret, Harold bounded up the steps two at a time and waited outside number 203 for Mr. Walker to catch up with him. His pulse raced, as much from excitement as from his rapid ascent up the stairs. He wasn't sure, but he thought he'd heard shushing coming from inside—like Thad's "shhhh!" when anyone dared to talk during one of his television shows.

As Mr. Walker reached the second floor, Harold turned the knob and opened the door.

"Surprise!"

Harold jumped back at the loud chorus of shouted greetings and bumped Mr. Walker, who had to grab the rail to keep from falling backward down the steps. Harold raised a hand to his open mouth and gaped around the living room at the smiling crowd. "Abigail!" He ran to his friend and threw his arms around her. "You were in on this too?"

She nodded and hugged him back, her large eyes almost disappearing beneath the long false lashes she wore.

"How could we have a party without the guest of honor's best friend?" Philip beamed. "Won't you stay for some cake and coffee, Mr. Walker?"

"Show him Mrs. Dee's cake," Shirley said. "That should be enough to persuade him."

"Harold and I did skip dessert." Mr. Walker glanced at his watch. "If you insist."

Mrs. Dee served cake and Philip brewed more coffee as Harold opened gifts. Thad and his parents gave him a silver pen-and-pencil set with his name engraved on them in a fine script.

"For writing thank you notes," Thad suggested, over his second piece of cake.

Abigail's psychedelic box contained a pink corduroy newsboy hat like they'd seen Twiggy, a high-fashion model and the most beautiful woman in the world, wearing on a television talk show. Lieutenant White gave him a keychain with his initials engraved on the silver whistle attached to it.

Philip handed Harold an envelope. The card inside contained a long note he didn't read, knowing it would make him cry. He'd save it for later, when he was alone. Also in the envelope were tickets of some kind. Harold picked one up for more careful study and gasped. "Tickets for *Hair*? On Broadway?"

"The very same," Philip said. "For you and a friend." He put his arm around Abigail and gave her a hug.

She looked at Harold, her dark-ringed eyes amplifying the concern on her face. "Mom said I could go. That is, if you want me to come with you."

Harold could hardly contain his excitement. "Of course I want you to come! There's nobody I'd rather have with me in New York than you."

Mr. Walker pulled an envelope from his coat pocket and gave it to Harold, who stared at it for a moment, his hand shaking with excitement. Ever since he'd ridden up to New York in the rented van to help Terrence move into his Greenwich Village studio apartment, Harold had wanted to return. And now, to be going with Abigail…. Harold ripped open the envelope and skimmed through the words on the card, trying not to stare at the two, crisp hundred-dollar bills it contained.

"Since you're going to New York, Mrs. Walker and I thought you might need a little spending money, in case you want to shop."

"Thank you all, so much," Harold said, trying to maintain his composure. "I'm so excited! When do we go?"

"Mr. Walker and I have to be in New York for foundation business," Philip said, glancing at his attorney. "We've booked rooms at the Hilton Hotel. We're taking the train up Thursday morning and coming back Sunday afternoon."

Harold couldn't decide what excited him most. Seeing Terrence? Exploring New York with Abigail by his side? Shopping on Fifth Avenue? Seeing a Broadway show? He'd just have to wait and see. No matter what, the trip promised to be an experience he'd never forget.

CHAPTER FIVE

Kreema Dee Kropp couldn't wait to go to the Stonewall Inn to show off her new dress, fashioned from the curtains she'd stolen after her john had passed out in his room at the Taylor Hotel. She slapped both palms on her vanity and laughed, leaning forward to adjust the water-filled balloons that gave her chest the extra *ooh la la* she needed, at least until she was cleared to take hormones for the operation to make her a real woman. "Mm-hmm. Yanked them bitches down and wrapped 'em around my ass like they was fine mink or sumpin'."

She clapped her hands together and laughed again. The dark brown of the thickly brocaded fabric nearly matched her skin tone. With a chuckle she tilted her head back and polished off another shot of whiskey.

Born Robert Clayton Taylor, thirty-five-year-old Kreema Dee Kropp—the most recent and enduring of many assumed identities—had abandoned the name and gender assigned to her at birth in her early teens. Despite her muscular build and the enormous penis the good Lord had blessed her with, Kreema would cut anyone who dared to suggest she was anything but a lady. "Mm-hmm. Miss Franklin got it right. R-E-S-P-E-C-T."

Though she didn't really want the damn thing, Kreema was too smart to let her endowment go to waste. "Long as I still got a dick and you got ten dollars, I'll fuck you up your tight white ass. Black ass. Yellow ass. Red ass. Shit." She rocked forward with a snort and slapped the vanity again. "I don't care. Your money's still green, ain't it?"

She reached over and filled her shot glass with another couple of fingers of whiskey. "Mm-hmm. I like the color green." She chuckled, checking her eyes in the mirror one last time, certain nobody would notice her false lashes didn't match.

Rising from the dainty stool she'd been perched on, Kreema paraded across her boudoir, looking back over her shoulder, studying her reflection in the badly chipped mirror. "Mm-hmm, looking good, Miss Thing." She spun and sashayed back to the vanity, checking herself out from head to toe to make sure she was ready for an evening on the town.

Until she had her operation and her driver's license matched the person she really was, she had to wear at least three articles of male apparel to avoid arrest—hence the wide leather and studded belt, man's tank-style T-shirt fashioned into a bra of sorts, and combat boots. Though dainty slingbacks would be more appropriate for the dress, for a fine lady such as herself who often ventured out without an escort, the steel-toed boots were far more practical.

To go with the boots, she decided on her black bag. She dumped the contents of the red purse she'd carried the night before onto the bed. First into the bag were the men's slacks and dress shirt she kept folded up in the bottom for emergencies, followed by an enormous pair of scissors, a nail file with an unusually sharp point, a fifteen-inch length of heavy steel chain, two baseball-sized rocks, a gold cigarette lighter with KDK engraved in block letters on the side, a crumpled pack of Virginia Slims, and her wallet, containing exactly four dollars, her lucky penny, and a dime—just in case she had an emergency and needed to use the pay phone.

She'd carry a knife if it weren't against the law. As she'd explained to Betty Badge any number of times, no self-respecting woman would ever leave home without a nail file. The scissors were in case she wanted to snatch some curtains down off the wall or something. "Mm-hmm, like what I have in my bag is any of Lily Law's damn business."

She gave herself another long look in the mirror and shifted the hairpiece she'd fashioned into a bouffant a smidgen to the left. "What this dress needs is a damn hat." She knew where she could find one too. Over at Saint Mark's A.M.E. come Sunday morning. But mugging some old lady wouldn't be right. "The good Lord will provide."

Closing and locking the door behind her, she slung her bag over her shoulder and clomped down four rickety, garbage-filled flights of wooden steps to the street. On the sidewalk she stopped, yanked her dress into place, adjusted the balloons in her T-shirt, and then dug in her purse for a cigarette and the engraved lighter she'd stolen from some john. Admiring her finest possession, she lit her Virginia Slim and wondered, as she often did, what that sucker's name had been.

She exhaled a thick cloud of smoke, glancing up and down the street where she stood, because a lady never walks with a cigarette in her hand. She assumed her most seductive pose, leaning back against the masonry exterior with her left arm crooked over her head, elbow pointing skyward, her right leg bent at the knee with the foot flat against the wall. Tilting her chin just so, she took a big draw and thought about what to do with her evening.

Lowering her arm to fan herself and to clear the smoke from the heavy air around her face, she ruled out going down to the waterfront. "Too damn hot for that shit." Climbing into the back of an empty truck and joining the pile of sweaty, masculine bodies grunting in the dark interior could be hours of fun. But a romp on the docks would destroy the look she'd worked on most of the afternoon. Nobody would see her new dress either. She hadn't spent all that time perfecting her look for nothing.

She dropped her cigarette on the sidewalk and ground out the glowing ember with the toe of her boot. A tan car passed with its windows down, and Kreema heard her favorite Supremes song coming from the radio. "Mm-hmm, set me free, baby."

Snapping her fingers and, though she could no longer hear the radio, singing along as she walked, Kreema made up her mind. She'd head over to the Stonewall Inn, have a few cocktails, and check on her pals in the back room. She shook her head. Poor boys. She looked after them as best she could. "Mm-hmm, better than their sorry, no-count mommas done."

An attractive window display in a little dress shop caught her eye. She put her hand to her brow and pressed her nose to the glass for a clearer view. "Just like I always say, the good Lord provides."

Catching her reflection in the window, she reached up and shifted her bouffant back into place, glancing up and down the street for any bubblegum machines—the domed red lights centered on the roofs of police cruisers. "No sense getting my ass arrested this early in the evening."

Pulling the bag from her shoulder, she reached in and pulled out a rock. After another quick look around to confirm nobody was watching, she drew her arm back and flung the rock, shattering the plate-glass window. When the glass stopped falling, she kicked the remaining shards out of her way and then reached in to retrieve a peacock-feathered cap and her rock.

A trio of nuns stopped and gaped at her.

After securing the hat on her head at a dashing angle with bobby pins dredged from the bottom of her purse, she turned and stomped her foot at them. "What the fuck you lookin' at?"

They stared at her, speechless.

She glared back at them and pulled the chain from her bag. "Ain't you supposed to be in church or sumpin'?"

After another stomp of her steel-toed boot, the sisters scurried off. Kreema dropped the chain into her bag, tugged on her dress again, and continued toward Christopher Street. She stopped before another window to check out her reflection. "Mm-hmm." She adjusted the hat so the feathers rose over her head rather than trailing down her back. "Just what this dress needed."

CHAPTER SIX

TERRENCE WALKED from his Charles Street apartment in Greenwich Village down Seventh Avenue South, wishing he had brought his camera along. On occasion he ventured into different parts of the city to take pictures, usually when the sun was low in the sky—after sunup or before sunset—for the interesting light. Otherwise, his camera stayed tucked away in the top of his closet. Carrying books back and forth to class was challenge enough, and dancing with a camera on one shoulder and a bag of accessories over the other really cramped his style. Besides, now that he'd made up his mind to become an attorney, photography had become more of a hobby than the obsession it had been throughout high school.

He turned left on Christopher Street and, less than a block away, saw Kelsey standing outside the Stonewall Inn. She looked fiercely butch in a man's light blue cotton dress shirt with the sleeves cut off at the shoulders and the hem tightly tucked into khaki pants, accessorized with a wide brown belt fastened with a sturdy silver buckle and a well-worn pair of brown loafers.

The rusted sign jutted out from the brick façade of the two-story building, extending from the top of the first floor up to roof in a giant T.

RESTAURANT
S
T
O
N
E
W
A
L
L
INN

The Stonewall Inn had indeed operated as a restaurant for many years, until extensive fire damage had closed the place down. But as far as he knew, the two-story brick building had never provided overnight accommodations. Not for people, anyway. He suspected the place had been cleaner back in the early 1900s when horses had been stabled there.

Terrence stopped to take in the spectacle of Kreema Dee Kropp, parading down the street toward Kelsey. Drag queens were nothing new to him. DC was full of them. But none compared with the wildly eccentric legend of Greenwich Village.

Having long grown accustomed to her muscular physique, the combat boots Kreema always wore, and her tendency to apply excessive amounts of garish makeup to her oversized features, the first thing Terrence noticed was the trio of four-foot long peacock feathers rising from a combination hat/bouffant atop her head, then the unusual brocaded fabric of her dress, cinched like a burlap sack at the waist by a belt at least six inches wide, covered with studs the size of lug nuts.

"Mm-hmm," she said as the three of them came together on the sidewalk. "Ain't you lookin' fine this evening." She ignored Kelsey as she walked around Terrence, giving him a very thorough once-over. "That vest is nice. Mm-hmm, bet it'd look even better against my ebony skin." She reached over and stroked the fringe on Terrence's suede vest, combing it with her thick, ring-adorned fingers. "But I'd have to wear me a nice blouse or sumpin' under it instead of going shirtless like you." She traced a finger down the middle of his chest and over his belly, stopping at his peace-sign belt buckle. "Mm-hmm, wouldn't want my big ole titties floppin' all over the place."

"You're looking mighty fine yourself tonight, Miss Kropp," Terrence said, lifting her hand from his belt to give it a squeeze. Something wasn't quite right about her eyes. He took in the dress and the elaborate chapeau. "Where did you find that gorgeous outfit?"

"You really like it?" She twirled, sending her bag in an arc, causing it to strike Kelsey's head with a jangling thud. "Baby, I'm sorry!" She patted Kelsey on the shoulder and returned her attention to Terrence. "Just sumpin' I got from Lord & Taylor."

"Magnificent." Terrence looked her over again and realized her false lashes didn't match. The left was thicker and longer, giving her the impression of a permanent wink. He bit back a laugh. "If you're gracing us with your presence, I'd consider it a privilege to pay the cover charge for you and buy you a cocktail."

Kreema gave an awkward curtsy, forcing Terrence to dodge the peacock feathers the tilt of her head propelled in his direction. "I'd be honored. Give me a dime and tell me your momma's phone number. I'm gonna walk over to that pay phone right this very minute and call her to tell her she done raised a fine chile."

Terrence fingered the dime in his pocket and thought about giving her Philip's number but decided against it. "Thanks, Miss Kropp, but she's working tonight."

"Mm-hmm, I know that's right. Gotta pay them bills." She fanned her face with a giant palm. "Damn it's hot. If I don't get me a cold cocktail soon, I'm gonna die of thirst."

The windows of the two brick storefronts, merged into a single building more than thirty years earlier, had been boarded up from the inside with plywood and painted black. Terrence rapped his knuckles on one of the twin giant oak doors inside the brick arch below the misleading rusty sign that teetered over the entrance.

A small door at eye level opened, revealing iron bars and a pair of bloodshot eyes.

"Mm-hmm, Kreema Dee Kropp has arrived, honey, with guests. Open up and let us in before the cops run us off."

The heavy oak doors were the only way in or out of the building. Keeping out hotheads who might inflict harm on customers was less of a concern than preventing a speedy entry by law enforcement. The extra security provided sufficient time to hide anything illegal. Terrence heard bolts sliding, and after a moment, one of the doors opened. "Ladies first," Terrence said, gesturing toward the door.

Kreema stepped through the doorway, knocking her hat and bouffant loose. "Shit!" She stopped, both hands flying to her head. The owner of the bloodshot eyes gave her a baleful look as she struggled to repair the damage before signing the membership book.

Terrence gave the brute the dollar admission for each of them and then signed under the shaky KD Kropp, claiming to be Vincent Bradbury. Knowing the risk of extortion by the mob, and with the police confiscating the book every few weeks, nobody signed their real name. Kelsey signed Annie Oakley, and they proceeded down the short hallway past the coatroom and turned right across from the office, where Terrence saw Frankie Caldarone smoking a cigar, and then down a step to the front room.

Perhaps half a dozen patrons in shirtsleeves with loosened ties—men Terrence thought might be around Phillip's age—sat on round stools in front of a long wooden bar. Patsy Cline wailed from the jukebox, but the dance floor in the back of the club's largest room and the cages for go-go dancers on either end of the bar were empty.

Kreema led them through a door to the left into the darker, smaller back room where a group of teenage boys did a choreographed dance in a line with their elbows hooked together to Jackie DeShannon's "Put A Little Love in Your Heart." She sashayed past them, smiling and waving, and stopped at the little bar in the very back, across from the restrooms, to wait for Terrence and Kelsey to catch up.

The plumbing left much to be desired, and the aroma was overwhelming. As far as he knew, the urinals and toilets contained the only running water in the whole building. Terrence would rather die than set foot in either restroom, especially in sandals.

"Three whiskeys, no ice," Terrence told the surly, muscle-bound bartender. Whether gin, vodka, rum, or whiskey, straight up was the way to order. The booze was so watered down, especially the clear liquors, that getting drunk was just about impossible. The higher concentration of alcohol in a drink without mixers or ice also increased the chance of killing the germs picked up in the bucket of water the glasses were rinsed in after each use.

He paid for the drinks—a jaw-dropping buck apiece—handed Kreema hers along with three quarters from his pocket, and nodded at the jukebox. "I know you came here to dance. Go pick out your favorites."

"Mm-hmm, you got that right," she said, sliding a quarter into her bag as she turned and headed for the jukebox.

CHAPTER SEVEN

Cameron took another swig of his watered-down whiskey, hoping to wash away the taste of Frankie Caldarone. He'd come to the Stonewall Inn just before dark to help the bartenders and waiters, also on the mob's payroll, to prepare for a not-so-surprise raid by the police. His job had been to label the bottles that hadn't already been removed from the club with names from the guest book.

Compared with other gay hangouts, the Stonewall Inn was different, both better and worse than the bars that had opened and closed before it. Nothing was up to any kind of code. Elevating the décor to seedy would have taken some doing.

Cameron had been called in to help ready the place for opening two years earlier. For the renovation of the burned-out interior, they'd used cheap plywood to build a bar and a few shelves in each room, and bench seating along the walls. Black lights had been added, and more boarding had been nailed over the windows spanning the front of the building. The only things to have changed since opening night were the songs available in the jukeboxes and the people who worked there. Yet even with overpriced, watered-down drinks, from midnight until three when they closed, the place was packed every single night.

Dancing set the Stonewall Inn apart from anyplace else in New York. Cameron had heard tales of couples stealing an illegal dance now and then in homosexual hangouts. But here, the two jukeboxes, one in the front room and one in the back, never stopped. Cameron liked hanging out in the darker, edgier back room where Motown hits played and the dancing was raw and suggestive. He preferred country music and had never danced himself, but he sure liked to watch—especially the guy with the amazing blond curls.

Cameron had finished his part in the raid preparations and taken the membership book to Frankie's office. The moment Frankie closed the door behind him, Cameron knew what was coming. "Come over here, boy." He rubbed his crotch and leered at Cameron.

Frankie liked to play rough, but either through genetics or decades of steroid abuse, possessed the tiniest dick Cameron had ever seen. He struggled to keep the little pecker in his mouth as Frankie grunted and thrust his hips. Cameron felt the fingers gripping his hair tighten, holding his head in place as Frankie climaxed. Then he let go of Cameron's hair and fell back into his chair.

Cameron got up off his knees. He wanted to spit, but instead he swallowed and wiped the back of his hand across his mouth, trying not to glare at the boss he hated with every fiber of his being.

"There's a big Defense Department gala at the Hilton tonight," Frankie said, fastening his pants. "I've got a room there for you." He slid a metal key and ten dollars across the desk. "Make sure you look nice."

Three watered-down drinks had succeeded in washing the vile taste from his mouth, but hadn't made a dent in the despair Cameron felt for having landed in such an impossible situation. Leaving tiny Paris, Kentucky had been the right thing to do. After his parents had died in a fiery crash when he was fifteen, he'd gone to live with his grandmother. He'd found work at nearby Claiborne Farm, mucking stalls, mending fences, and helping out with other chores however he could. When she had died, Cameron had sold what he could of her possessions and still hadn't had enough money for another month's rent.

He'd pondered his future and had seen no reason to remain in Kentucky. He could be homeless anywhere. The freedom to go wherever he wanted had been exhilarating. Cameron had listed his options, noting what he liked and didn't like about each destination. The list had been short. Having never left central Kentucky, he didn't know much more than the names of many places on his list, much less what they might or might not have to offer.

In the end he'd picked New York City over Hollywood. People often said he looked like a movie star. He decided, since it was closer, to go to New York. The Great White Way would provide the acting career he desired.

He'd dropped out of college, packed what he could into a bag, and hitchhiked to New York City. The eight-hundred-mile trip had taken nearly a week as he'd zigzagged across the map through Ohio, Pittsburgh, Baltimore, Philadelphia, and finally, across the Hudson River into Manhattan.

Where he was now trapped, doomed to keep doing the same thing forever. Well, probably not forever. Only for as long as men found him attractive enough to be worth the money and the risk of arrest. And the worst part—the part he couldn't let himself think about—was that he had nowhere to turn. Except for Frankie, whose interest was entirely financial, nobody in the world cared if Cameron lived or died.

The boys dancing in the back room didn't even see him. He just faded into the background—like a light switch or electrical outlet.

He finished his drink and was about to leave for his apartment to get cleaned up when he saw the curly blond, with the mannish dyke he was often with and the most outrageous drag queen in New York. The blond of his fantasies had on a fringed suede vest that riveted Cameron's attention to his flat stomach and the wisp of a happy trail that disappeared behind the peace-sign belt buckle. The belt was more for decoration than to keep his pants up. The jeans he wore looked to have been painted on, accentuating his narrow waist. Cameron imagined placing his hands on each hip and having his fingertips meet on a back hidden by the long fringe of his vest. He wanted to bury his face in that mass of loose blond curls, wrap his arms around him, and claim him like a prize.

The nelly boys' dancing came to an abrupt stop as the song ended, their line fragmenting as the young men dispersed across the room into smaller groups. A few headed for the bathrooms, paying no attention to signs denoting boys or girls, as others waited to be served watered-down drinks at the bar.

Unlike bars and clubs in New York that catered to a particular segment of the ever-expanding gay population, the dance floors at the Stonewall Inn attracted a diverse crowd. Queers of all ages, from all walks of life, and in every imaginable flavor came and went. But the back-room dance floor belonged to the flame queens—flamboyant, largely homeless teenagers who, for the dollar cover, could stay inside until the place closed rather than wander the streets in rain, snow, and cold weather. They reminded Cameron of the barn cats back on the farm in Paris, playing together one minute and trying to scratch each other's eyes out the next.

Cameron recognized the opening refrain coming from the jukebox and watched as the gorgeous blond, swaying in time to the music, led the top-heavy dyke onto the dance floor. The lithe young man closed his eyes, and the gentle swaying in his hips spread slowly up to his shoulders, reaching his fingertips and even his hair with an explosion of movement as his eyes opened and he launched into the chorus.

Half the queens in the room sang along. Cameron knew many saw "Aquarius" as an anthem. On Friday and Saturday nights, the tune played once or twice every hour, with the chorus never failing to incite a rousing rejoinder from the crowd. The blond danced with passion, steps of his own choosing and design—spontaneous, free, and wildly erotic. He couldn't look away. The rhythmic movement of the beautiful man's hands called attention to every part of his lean and graceful body.

A wink accompanied by a flash of gleaming white teeth in his direction made Cameron realize he'd been caught staring. His face grew hot and he looked away. He checked his watch and was shocked to see it was already after ten o'clock.

CHAPTER EIGHT

TERRENCE SQUEALED as the first bars of "Aquarius" played and grabbed Kelsey's hand. "Come on, girl. We gotta dance!"

"Have you seen *Hair*?" Kelsey asked, following him onto the dance floor. "I finally saw a matinee last week."

"Yes," Terrence said, his eyes closed as he swayed with the music. "Four times."

"Do you know the Greek myth behind Aquarius?" Kelsey shifted from her left foot to her right, twisting her shoulders and arms with each step, now and then in time to the music.

Terrence shook his head and, out of the corner of his eye, saw him. He was dressed in scruffy blue jeans and a red-and-blue striped shirt. The way he stood against the wall made Terrence think of cowboys. He possessed a rugged masculinity more in line with wide-open spaces than the closed-in urban bohemia of Greenwich Village. His tanned, ruddy complexion made him look like he'd spent hours on the high plains on a horse, tending his cattle.

"Zeus kidnapped the most beautiful boy in the world, made him his water bearer, and loved him so much, Hera got jealous," Kelsey said, repeating the same movements to a beat only she could hear. "When he died, Zeus turned him into the constellation Aquarius."

"Really? I had no idea." He joined the regulars, yelling more than singing. He threw himself into the familiar music and, seeing the man he'd been crushing on for weeks was watching his every move, flashed his best smile at him and winked.

His handsome cowboy reacted like he'd seen a ghost, or worse. He turned his head away, glanced at his watch, and then dashed to the front room like he'd been shot from a cannon. Terrence wanted to run after him, but chasing men—even a guy as gorgeous as this one—had never been his style. He saw the concern on Kelsey's face and knew she'd seen the exchange. "Shy," Terrence said, forcing a weak smile.

Terrence surrendered to the rhythm. He pushed the studying he needed to be doing, the overdue letters back home to Philip and Harold, and the horrified eyes of the man he desired from his mind to focus on the moment, to enjoy just how damn good losing himself in the music made him feel.

Kreema—not a girl to stay in one place for long—had vanished, probably hitting up patrons in the front room for cocktails.

He knew some of the other guys, at least by sight. Whether he knew them or not didn't matter. The ragtag collection of misfits and outcasts were a family of sorts, closer to each other than to the blood kin who'd abandoned them, united by a trait the rest of the world saw as a sin, a crime, and a mental illness. But here, at the Stonewall Inn, the people who'd always rejected them were out of place. G-A-Y was A-O-K. Sure, divisions abounded. Old versus young, butch versus femme—within both genders—and numerous differences related to various preferences, fetishes, and compulsions. The only taboo, aside from the namesake perfume many wore, was to be like everyone else.

The song ended, leaving the room silent except for the mechanical sounds coming from the jukebox. Before Kelsey could reach the refuge and relative comfort of a seat along the wall, Terrence's favorite song came on. He grabbed her arm. "Come on, you can be Marvin Gaye and I'll be Tammi Terrell."

But before Terrence got a chance to sing one word, the lights came on, eliciting a loud groan from the patrons. He saw uniformed police behind the bar and knew the Stonewall Inn was being raided. Though wary of the cops, he wasn't too concerned. Police raided gay establishments so often everyone knew the drill. Since he was old enough to drink and not in drag, they'd check his ID and let him go.

Like a school of fish he'd seen in a Jacques Cousteau television special, people went this way and that, but the mass moved toward the exit to have their IDs checked and then out the door to the street. The captain laughed with Frankie Caldarone as the police herded the departing patrons outside.

They walked across the street to Christopher Park. "So much for dancing," Kelsey said with a shrug. "Want to wait a couple of hours until they reopen or is there someplace else you want to go?"

Terrence shook his head. He knew where Kelsey would like to go. But as much as he loved her, the idea of sitting around drinking beer with a bunch of women he didn't know had no appeal. No more than Kelsey would want to go with him to the Checkerboard, his watering hole of choice. Although there were never many lesbians there, the Stonewall Inn was the only place where they both felt equally at home.

The mass of departing patrons dispersed into smaller schools heading in different directions. Terrence and Kelsey fell in with a small group heading up Christopher Street toward Greenwich Avenue. The sticky wet heat, even approaching eleven o'clock, made Terrence glad he'd chosen not to wear a shirt. Worried sweat would stain the suede, he slid out of the garment and hooked a finger in an armhole to carry his vest.

An image of his rugged callboy popped into his head. The frightened look Terrence had seen in the split second their eyes had met stabbed like a knife. He expected that kind of reaction from men on the street or classmates who caught him looking them over. Enjoyed it, even. But in a gay bar, and from a presumed homosexual…? The honest-to-God truth was rejection wasn't part of Terrence's life experience. He'd been abandoned more than once, through no fault of his or the dearly departed who'd left him behind. Except for Philip and George, nobody gay had ever out-and-out spurned his advances. Not even once. Terrence couldn't decide whether his pride or his heart was more hurt.

"So you're going to just tuck your tail between your legs and slink away?"

Terrence stopped. "Am I that obvious?"

Kelsey wiped the back of her hand across her forehead and grinned. "Considering the most talkative man at Columbia hasn't said a word for a good five minutes and that you were hoping he'd be there, yeah."

He shrugged, shifted the vest to his other hand, and ambled forward. "It's crazy to feel the way I do about him when we've never talked. I don't even know his name."

"But…," Kelsey prompted.

"But that's how I feel." Terrence shrugged again.

She put her arm around his shoulder and matched his stride. "We've been friends for, what, two years now? And in all that time, I've never seen you look twice at another guy. What's so special about this one?"

Terrence shook his head. "I don't know. There's no explaining feelings. They just are."

She squeezed his shoulder. "A wise man once told me I should go after the things I want before someone snatches them away."

He draped his arm across her shoulder. "You know what, Kelsey?" He pulled her close to him. "You're absolutely right. Next time I see that handsome devil, I'm going to have a few words with him, even if I have to chase him down and hogtie him to get him to listen."

CHAPTER NINE

ANY OTHER time, Cameron would never have allowed a john to tie him up. But the bartender had seen him leave and would have called the photographer who waited in the connecting room to let him know they were coming. Cameron knew he watched through a peephole, waiting for the right moment to jump into action.

Pictures of the fully clothed gentleman admiring Cameron on his back, spread eagle with his extremities securely anchored to the bedposts with silk ties, weren't the kind of shots the man behind the camera wanted. He'd wait for something more incontrovertible, preferably with the john disrobed, ideally with Cameron's cock somewhere inside him. But that was just Cameron's preference. The photographer didn't care. It wasn't his ass.

His client had an air of authority about him. He sat upright in the armchair with his legs crossed, in his shirtsleeves, smoking a pipe. Fearing the smoke might mess up the pictures, Cameron coughed.

"Would you like me to open the window?" The man uncrossed his leg, leaning forward to peer at him.

Cameron nodded. The portly man rose from the chair, placed his pipe in the crystal ashtray on the coffee table, and moved toward the heavily curtained window. He pulled back the drapes and raised the sash, stopping for a moment to take in the Central Park view. He turned, rubbing his hands together, and returned his attention to Cameron's supine form, naked and helpless in the room's double bed.

He removed his shirt, draping it with care across the back of the armchair before stepping out of his trousers. Cameron saw he didn't remove the wallet or anything else from the pockets as he placed his pants on the chair. Still in his T-shirt, boxer shorts, and black nylon socks pulled high on his calf with garters, he approached the bed.

Something about his expression frightened Cameron—a glint in his eye, or maybe the curl of his lip. Cameron struggled to move his arms but was too securely tied to do more than raise his elbows an inch or so from the bed. He wanted to draw his knees up, to protect his exposed groin as the man reached over and placed his hand on Cameron's stomach, caressed his belly, trailed his fingers slowly upward, and skimmed his palm lightly over Cameron's chest up to his throat.

Cameron had never been so terrified. The grip on his throat tightened, then relaxed as the man's hand continued upward to grasp his chin, tilting Cameron's head toward him. He felt the other hand on top of his head, holding him in place as the man lowered his lips to Cameron's. He tried to kiss him, but Cameron resisted until the man bit his lips. Cameron cried out, only to be cut off by the foul-tasting tongue that filled his mouth. The hand on his head moved down his face to pinch his nose, and Cameron couldn't breathe as the man rammed his tongue deeper into Cameron's mouth.

The sadistic man let go and Cameron gasped for air. The man's erection poked through the slit of his boxers. Glaring, he spat out his words. "That's so you understand who's in charge. I make the rules, not you. Understand?"

Cameron nodded, keeping his eyes on the man, wondering what was next and how much longer the damn photographer was going to wait. Doubt entered his mind. What if the bartender hadn't called? Or maybe he'd called, but the photographer had stepped out for some fresh air. The old fart could have even had a heart attack or a stroke or something.

The man sat on the edge of the bed, cracking his knuckles as he studied Cameron. "I have to say, you have about the prettiest body I've ever seen." He traced his fingers across Cameron's belly. "All that marvelous fur…." He placed his hands on Cameron's pecs, gripping the hair and pulling, watching Cameron's eyes for a reaction. Again, with no warning, he released his grip, sliding his hands down to Cameron's rigid cock. "So you like it rough, I see."

Cameron closed his eyes, unwilling to admit he enjoyed the firm grip of the man's hand on his balls and the gentle pumping motion on his rock-hard erection.

The man tightened his grasp on Cameron's balls, causing him to cry out. The man stood, rubbing his hands together before stripping down to his socks and garters.

Now, Cameron thought. *Please!*

"Hungry for some cock, boy?" He sounded angry and had become even more menacing. He stroked his cock as he talked, glaring at Cameron. "Yeah, I bet you can't wait to get your fucking pretty mouth on my cock." He slapped Cameron's cock with his open palm before grabbing both nipples and twisting hard.

Cameron cried out in pain again. *Damn. Where's that fucking photographer?*

The man climbed onto the bed and crawled on top of Cameron, coming to rest with his fat ass planted firmly on Cameron's chest. He folded his arms across his chest and glared down over his cock at Cameron.

"Lick my balls, boy."

The weight on his chest prevented Cameron from breathing. The stubby cock throbbed, and a drop of precum glistened on the mushroom head. The man eased forward, and Cameron caught the musky aroma of sweaty balls.

He raised his hand and swung it hard, striking Cameron's left cheek. "Don't make me tell you again, boy. I said lick my balls." He fisted his hand into Cameron's hair and yanked, pulling his head up into his crotch.

There was no photographer. Cameron was alone. Nobody cared what happened to him, one way or the other.

He lapped the salty scrotum and heard the low groans of his captor. Adrenaline coursed through his veins, and he arched his back, pushing as much as he could with his shoulders and legs, hoping to knock the man off-balance.

The man raised his hand and struck him again, harder this time. Enraged, he got up on his knees, forced his cock into Cameron's mouth, and pulled him by the hair as he fucked his face, grunting with each thrust.

Cameron fought for his breath as the man plunged his cock harder and deeper into his mouth. The choking and gagging sounds he made seemed only to spur the man on, and his grunts became staccato as he pounded, steering Cameron's head with his hands in his hair, like Cameron held the mane when he rode a horse without a bridle.

The pounding escalated and Cameron knew the man was going to cum. He braced himself, fighting for air and hoping he wouldn't drown.

"Smile, you're on Candid Camera."

The room exploded into brilliant white light as the man shot his load into Cameron's mouth. The man slid off the bed and stood onto still-shaking knees as the photographer snapped more photographs.

Another of Frankie's goons came through the door. He pulled something out of his pocket and flicked a switch, causing a six-inch blade to shoot from the end. He sliced the ties binding Cameron to the bed and motioned for him to get dressed.

Cameron rubbed his jaw. His cheek still smarted, but he didn't think anything was broken. He sat up, glared at his captor, and as he slid from the bed to his feet, slammed his fist into the man's tear-stained, frightened face, earning a "Hey!" from the goon who'd cut him loose.

The goon emptied the man's pockets as Cameron dressed. The photographer helped himself to a shot of whiskey from the bottle the man had brought with him to the room. He raised the glass and nodded at Cameron. "Good work."

The bastard had been there the whole time. Cameron drew back and punched him in the nose, sending him backward to the floor. The goon who'd cut him loose nodded at Cameron and smiled.

CHAPTER TEN

Thursday, June 26, 1969

TERRENCE STIFLED a yawn as he surveyed the crowded, smoke-filled bar. He and Kelsey had hopped the subway after class to meet up with friends for dinner, ending up at the Sea Colony, on the corner of Eighth Avenue and Horatio Street near Jackson Square. Though he wasn't 100 percent certain about a few of the patrons, Terrence believed he was the only man in the building.

He stood shoulder to shoulder with Kelsey, who argued with Carrie, a black woman sporting an Afro even bigger than Terrence's, about the relative importance of equal rights for women, blacks, immigrants, and homosexuals.

"We're all women." Kelsey shouted to be heard above the noisy crowd. "Until we have the same rights as men, whether we're lesbians, people of color, or immigrants won't make any difference."

"Said the WASP." Carrie shook her head. "Tell that to any black man in the South."

As the debate continued, Terrence tried to figure out what was going on at the bathroom door. A steady stream of women waited in line while a short, square woman stood guard, handing each person something before letting her go in and then closing the door behind her.

"Mark my word," Carrie said. She leaned toward Terrence so he could hear. "We'll have a woman president decades before a Negro gets elected."

Kelsey shrugged. "The race is definitely between women and blacks. The Constitution bans immigrants from running for president, and hell will freeze over before a homosexual can get elected."

"Maybe we've already had a gay president," Terrence interjected. "James Buchanan never married."

"Good point," Carrie replied. "And if he was, then at least one vice president had to have been gay too. The man Buchanan lived with for more than ten years was Pierce's VP."

Terrence looked at Carrie and, behind her, could now see the bathroom guard handed the women pieces of toilet paper from a roll she held before letting them into the loo. "Want to tell me about the potty guard?"

"Sis?" Kelsey glanced over her shoulder toward the bathroom. "She's really nice."

"Yeah," Carrie agreed. "Been here forever."

"But what's the deal with the toilet paper?"

"Well," Kelsey said, folding her arms across her chest, "she makes sure only one lady goes in at a time—to keep the police happy."

"From what I've been told, the toilet-paper thing came later." Carrie lit a pink clove cigarette and exhaled. "Girls used to flush all the paper down the toilet, and then slip somebody in for some action when Sis went to get another roll from the back room."

"Nobody minds. The line moves faster and the toilet almost never backs up anymore," Kelsey said.

Kelsey had admired Carrie from afar for months, and they seemed to be hitting it off. Terrence didn't want to get in the way. Besides, he wasn't really in the mood for company. Unless, of course, a certain rugged cowboy came along—highly unlikely given his current location. Never mind said cowboy's adverse reaction to Terrence's flirting.

He hugged Kelsey. "Darling, I'm going home. Good luck." He kissed her on the cheek and turned to Carrie. "Nice to meet you. Take care of my friend. I'm heading out."

Carrie smiled and shook his hand. "My pleasure." She winked at him. "And it was nice to meet you too."

Terrence left the Sea Colony and, deciding to skip the subway, headed up Horatio Street to Greenwich Avenue. The walk would do him good and give him a much-needed chance to think.

Confusion was not something Terrence knew how to handle. Certainty was his game, and had been for as long as he could remember. Focusing on what he didn't know or wasn't sure about had never gotten him anywhere. When life got complicated, Terrence grabbed onto what he knew for sure and acted accordingly.

What Terrence knew, beyond any doubt, was he had never been so enamored of anyone. The more he saw of the quiet cowboy, the more he liked. Or at least, up until that horrified reaction to Terrence's wink.

If he did work for the mob, Terrence suspected he made big money for them. Unlike the flame queens and cross-dressers who worked the streets, the ruggedly handsome man looked straight, without the threatening air of the straight hustlers Terrence had known. They didn't call them "rough trade" for nothing.

He cast a long shadow on the sidewalk from the nearly full moon. The traffic noise, the rotten garbage, and the scampering rats reminded him of Washington, and not in a good way. The street might be a nice place to visit, but he hoped he never had to live there again.

Handsome as the cowboy was, Terrence figured his boss kept him off the streets for the more lucrative hotel trade. A guy like him could attract the upscale clients who'd pay more—a lot more—to avoid the risk of entrapment cruising the streets entailed. He was an asset, and as long as his value exceeded the cost of taking care of him, he was a source of revenue the mob would protect.

Maybe Terrence was getting all worked up for nothing. He'd never even talked to the man. He might discover the guy was a real asshole—a total jerk. He was definitely a loner. Terrence had never seen anyone with him or even talking to him.

But then, working for the mob probably wasn't conducive to friendships. He knew too much for his employer to allow him to have friends he could confide in. Terrence didn't think he was Italian. From everything he'd heard, blood ties were required for entry into the mob. Without kinship, whether he lived or died hinged upon his usefulness. Until he stopped bringing in the bucks, he'd live.

A dark-colored, four-door sedan slowed to a crawl, creeping along beside him. "Give you a lift?"

"No thanks." Terrence kept walking without so much as a glance at the car.

"I'd make it worth your time," the man said, clearing his throat.

Nervous, Terrence thought, ignoring him. At least he's not a cop. He thanked his lucky stars each and every morning he didn't have to hustle any longer, especially in New York. DC was a relative Utopia, with cops like Shirley White, whose efforts to rid the force of bad cops at least gave him hope for a better future.

"I'll give you twenty dollars to blow me."

Big spender. But Terrence had left that life behind. Never mind his promise to Philip. The man could offer him a thousand dollars, and he'd still keep walking.

"I'll make it thirty…."

Terrence stopped. "I said no thanks. Now fuck off."

"You little shit," the man said, his tone menacing. "I oughta get outa this car and teach your pansy ass a lesson."

"Oh yeah?" Terrence said, folding his arms across his chest. "Getting out of that car would be a big mistake."

The man laughed and opened the door. "What you gonna do, sissy?"

"Take one more step and I'll show you." He was about Terrence's height, maybe forty, and might have played sports in high school.

He leered at Terrence and cracked his knuckles. "This is going to be fun."

Terrence smiled. "You have strange ideas about fun."

The man raised his foot to take a step, but before it hit the ground, Terrence grabbed him by the throat and rammed his knee into the man's groin. When he doubled over in pain, Terrence jammed his elbow downward into the guy's neck, sending him face-first into the sidewalk.

As the man rolled on the concrete, groaning and clutching his crotch with both hands, Terrence said, "Now that was fun!"

CHAPTER ELEVEN

THE MOMENT for which Philip had spent weeks preparing had finally arrived. The talk. George had suggested the idea when they'd first discussed bringing Harold and a friend to New York. Since then, Philip had discussed his concerns with schoolteachers, guidance counselors, a child psychologist, Lieutenant White, and finally, Mrs. Dombroski, who'd signed off on the plan.

Philip eyed his charges, holding hands across from him on the love seat in the living room of their suite at the Hilton. He leaned forward, resting his elbows on his knees with his chin on his knuckles. Niggling doubt plagued him, and he almost abandoned the plan. *Could they be trusted?* He thought so, but what if he was wrong?

He cleared his throat, dropping his hands to his knees and looking back and forth from the boy he'd come to love, surely as much as any parent loved a child, and pretty little Abigail. Her enormous and heavily mascaraed eyes, surrounded by several sets of false lashes, stared back at him. "You're not children any longer." Even if they still looked like kids playing dress-up, it was true. "Now that you're eighteen, you can buy alcohol, serve our country, get married...." He glanced at Harold and then turned to Abigail. "In short, you're old enough to do whatever you want."

"Mom made me promise I'd follow your rules, Mr. Potter." Abigail smiled. "I'm too excited to be here to mess up." Her face grew serious. "Besides, Mom said she'd ground me for the rest of my life."

Philip fought back a smile. "I have a few ground rules, for your safety. Violate them, and the consequences could be far more serious than getting grounded." He could see his words hit home from the looks on their faces. "I don't want to frighten you, but New York can be a very dangerous place."

"No worse than Washington," Harold said.

"True," Philip agreed, realizing he should have set new ground rules the day Harold turned eighteen. "Okay, so here's the deal. Unless you give me reason to do otherwise, I'm going to treat you like adults."

Their faces lit up. Harold squeezed Abigail's hand. They sat rapt, waiting for him to continue.

"You're free to come and go as you please while we're here in New York—" He paused, hoping they'd heed his advice. "—with these rules." He folded his arms across his chest and gave them his sternest look, wanting them to know just how serious he was, to understand the importance of the rules he'd agonized over for weeks. "You will stay together at all times, keep me informed of your plans, and if you can't reach me…." He handed them each a packet of matches he'd picked up from the hotel bar with the telephone number printed beneath the Hilton logo. "Leave a message here at the hotel."

"Yes, sir," Harold said, sliding the matches into his pocket. "Is that all?"

"Stay on the main streets, and if you're going far, take the subway, or better yet, a taxi. If you get lost or someone makes you uncomfortable, go to the police. Remember, they're here to protect you." Philip offered a silent prayer to Saint Michael, patron saint of police, to protect his charges from bad cops. He reached into his pocket and fished through his change for the coins he desired. He handed them each several dimes. "Keep these in your pocket—for the phone, in case you need to call me."

He looked at them for a long moment, thinking about how very young they were, remembering how grown-up he'd believed himself to be at the same age. If anything happened to either of them, Philip knew he'd never forgive himself. "One more thing." He paused, hoping he wasn't making a big mistake by opening the door, but he trusted his instincts. "Since you're in an unfamiliar city and for countless other reasons, I'd rather you not, but if you must have wine, beer, or a mixed drink, please consume at least three nonalcoholic beverages before you have another."

"I don't think you need to worry about that," Harold said.

"Yeah." Abigail nodded in agreement. "Everything we've ever tried tasted horrible."

Part of him wanted to go down that road. He was more than a little curious to find out what they'd done, how, and if he had any culpability. But instead, he decided to focus on the positive outcome of their experimentation. "Well, that's one less thing for me to worry about."

"Anything else?"

Philip didn't know if he'd ever seen Harold so happy. The nights he'd lain awake, wondering if taking the boys in had been a mistake, fearing he was doing more harm than good. Terrence's success at Columbia University and Harold's obvious improvement had convinced him his instincts about taking care of the boys had been correct. "Other than everything else I've ever told you, no, that's it. You're free to go."

Abigail and Harold jumped up from the couch. But instead of bolting for the door, as Philip had expected, they threw their arms around his neck, hugged him tight, and kissed his cheek.

"Thanks, Mr. Potter. You're the best!" Abigail stepped back. "We won't let you down."

"She's right, you know," Harold said, hugging him close. "You're the best thing ever to happen to me, that's for sure."

Relief flooded over him. He'd imagined hundreds of different reactions, but nothing like this. Mrs. Dee had been right. "I feel the very same way about you, Harold." He draped an arm around the neck of each of his charges and walked with them to the door connecting their rooms.

Harold looked at Abigail. "How do you feel about going to Greenwich Village before we hit Times Square for the show? We can stop someplace along the way for dinner."

"Sounds great to me," Abigail replied. "I can't wait to see *Hair*!"

"We'll probably come back to the room right after the show," Harold said, his hand on the door. "I was too excited to sleep last night, and it's already been a long day."

"If you change your mind, call me here at the hotel to let me know. I might go out for a bit, but I won't be gone long."

"Will do!" Harold closed the door.

Philip closed the door from his room and slid the deadbolt in place. Then he walked across the living room to a similar door on the opposite wall. He slid the deadbolt back, opened the door, and rapped twice. A pang of guilt washed over him for his subterfuge. With the federal ban on hiring homosexuals, his relationship with George put Philip's Smithsonian job at risk. Absent a major scandal, the likelihood he'd ever lose his job was slim. Still, considering he was having an affair with a married man and a prominent Washington attorney, caution was in order. He heard the jiggle of the deadbolt in the connecting room and the door opened.

"Well," George said. "How did it go?"

Philip took a step back. "Much better than I expected. I'll tell you all about it, but let me look at you first." He let out a low whistle as George did a slow turn to model the short black silk robe he wore.

George smiled. "I'm glad you like it." He threw his arms around Philip's neck so they stood nose to nose. "Alone at last."

CHAPTER TWELVE

CAMERON NEVER wanted to get out of bed again. His face hurt from the punches he'd taken, his bruised throat was sore, and his fist throbbed. But staying in bed wasn't an option. He had to pee like a racehorse, and the community bathroom he shared with everyone else on his floor was all the way at the other end of the hall.

He'd dreamed about the blond again. Only this time, rather than the erotic images that sustained his career, the beautiful man had come to his rescue, showing Cameron a way out of the trap he was in that he hadn't seen before. He wanted to return to his dreams, where hope still lived.

His feelings confused him. He couldn't explain his attraction. Feminine men repulsed him, making them his most-dreaded and difficult clients. But this one, rather than the lisping, fawning, limp-wristed faggots Cameron encountered, exuded self-confidence with a decidedly masculine flavor. *He wasn't feminine so much as*—he struggled for the right word—*feline.*

Yeah, feline, but not like some domesticated tabby. More like a sleek jungle cat, with a glorious mane of blond curls. He looked like the kind of guy who always landed on his feet, and Cameron suspected he wouldn't hesitate, when push came to shove, to bite, kick, and scratch. Whatever it took to come out on top.

He closed his eyes, and the image of the gorgeous man dancing in that suede vest popped into his head. Freed from the fear of detection, he studied him with his mind's eye, lingering over the flat belly behind the maddening fringe. In his imagination, instead of bolting when the man had winked, Cameron had smiled back and nodded.

Each and every tick of the windup alarm clock beside his bed jarred his nerves. Most of the time he didn't even hear the damn thing, and in fact, he had trouble falling asleep without the monotonous sound. But at this moment, the metallic ticking grated on his nerves, like fingernails on a chalkboard.

He wrapped the pillow around his head and squeezed his eyes closed, shutting out an ugly reality for the refuge of his fantasy. In his imagination, where he controlled the way things turned out, he'd walked right over and asked him to dance. Rather than a gay anthem, something slow and romantic played on the jukebox. He held the young man close, swaying against him in time to the music, enjoying the weight of his head on his shoulder, burying his nose in the fragrant mass of soft curls, caressing the silky skin of his lower back as the suede fringe tickled his arm.

His desire, Cameron rationalized, stemmed from the guy being so very different from any of the men who'd paid him for sex. He was younger—by decades, in most cases—and judging from what he'd seen under his suede vest, in much better shape. In stark contrast to the beer bellies and sagging flesh of his clients, the narrowness of his hips and his slim waist appealed to Cameron. He imagined himself picking him up and being amazed by how light he'd feel in his arms.

In his mind's eye, they danced alone, barefoot and shirtless in a rolling meadow of Kentucky bluegrass, surrounded by whitewashed fencing that gleamed in the moonlight. In the distance a mare stomped her hoof and whinnied, nudging the foal standing on shaky legs beside her. Cameron nuzzled the top of his dance partner's ear with his nose, kissing his earlobe before leaving a trail of tender kisses down the hollow of his neck to his throat.

He wanted to kiss his chest, flick a brown nipple with his tongue, and nibble that sexy little happy trail. He imagined himself having his way with him, bending him over, taking him from behind as the mare and her foal looked on. He wanted to dominate the fragile man, claim the beautiful boy, and make him his own.

"Stop!" He sat up in bed, the motion causing his head to ache. He willed his erection to go away. Jacking off hadn't been an option for longer than he could remember. The less he got himself off, the easier getting off was with a client. Holding back was never the issue. Staying hard, however, was a job requirement, and jacking off made that more difficult.

So he didn't.

Usually.

He lay back and closed his eyes, sliding his hand down over his belly to his throbbing erection. His jungle cat danced for him, tossing his mane as he swayed, bending his body in graceful, seductive moves, leering at Cameron with an enticing smile.

Ouch!

Squeezing his cock with his bruised right fist wasn't an option. He'd never understood clients who wanted him to hurt them, whether with belts or whips or riding crops, for pleasure. Pain was not his thing. Though he knew it would never work, desperate times called for desperate acts. He switched to his left hand.

Shit.

The moment had passed.

Cameron sighed and flung his arms down beside him—in his single bed, in a tiny room, in a flophouse. And this was it—the sum total of his accomplishments. His life would never get any better than it was at that very moment. In fact, given how he had to rely on his looks and the inevitable consequences of aging, he wondered how much longer he had before the Mafia decided he'd outlived his usefulness.

His Italian coworkers would take pleasure in dumping him in the Hudson River. They treated him like dirt and didn't care if he was queer or not. Having sex with men, even if only for money, earned him nothing but abuse from the goons who worked for Frankie.

He'd looked up to the older hustlers and even befriended a few. But now he was about the oldest one around. He'd worry less if he knew where any of his old pals were today, or even if they were alive. But one by one they'd disappeared. Some died in accidents—hit by cars, falling in front of the subway or from a tall building, or drowning.

Leaving the mob's employment wasn't an option. He'd never have the freedom to do what he wanted to do and live a life of his own. If there really was no way out, he was doomed no matter what he did.

He rolled out of bed, slid into his jeans, and gathered up the personal items he'd need for a shower. His mind was made up. He was going to talk to Frankie Caldarone that very afternoon. Tell him he was finished. He'd done his time and had earned a fortune for the Mafia. Now he wanted out.

What did he have to lose?

CHAPTER THIRTEEN

Spending an hour or two most afternoons in the park across from the Stonewall Inn gave Kreema Dee Kropp an opportunity to keep tabs on her boys. With no place else to go, they hung out between the park and Grove Street, begging for change, joking around with each other, or napping. Cooling her face with a fan she'd fashioned out of newspaper salvaged from a nearby trash bin, she lowered herself onto a shady bench that provided an unobstructed view of the park as she chatted with her old friend, General Philip Henry Sheridan.

"Yes, sir, Mister General, sir." She pulled a cigarette from her bag and lit it, crossing her legs and smoothing the pleated plaid skirt she'd found in the backseat of an unlocked car across her lengthy thigh. "I wish you'd tell me where you got them damn boots. I've looked all over New York for a pair that comes up over the knees like that."

"Are you talking to me?"

She turned toward the voice. "Mm-hmm, handsome, I sure am." She patted the bench next to her. "Come sit down here and visit with me for a spell."

"I'm kind of in a hurry," he said, shoving his hands in his pockets.

"In a hurry?" She stomped a booted foot and snorted. "Somebody about to die or sumpin'? Sit your ass down here." She patted the bench again. "What's your name?"

"Cameron," he said, sitting down beside her but leaving as much distance as he could between them.

"I ain't gonna bite." She slapped her thighs and laughed. "Miss Kreema Dee Kropp, at your service." She offered her hand.

"Nice to meet you." He gave her hand a reluctant squeeze.

"The pleasure is all mine." She squeezed back and gave his hand a vigorous shake. "I seen you around here for some years, working up in them fancy Midtown hotels. Mm-hmm. Nice to finally make your acquaintance."

"Yeah, it's been some years." He pushed his hair back from his forehead and wiped his brow.

She dropped her cigarette and ground it into the sidewalk, then looked him up and down. "Who won?"

"I beg your pardon?" He looked confused.

"You, or the dude who smacked your pretty face?" She glanced at his right hand. "Looks like you got in a few good licks."

Cameron grimaced and rubbed his knuckles. "Work-related injury."

"Mm-hmm. I hear that." She studied him for a long moment. "Did your dog get hit by a car this morning?" She rested her hand on his knee. "Sumpin' bad had to have happened to make you look so sad."

He looked at her, startled, and shook his head. "No, ma'am. I just have a lot on my mind."

"Like what?" She waited, but he didn't answer. "Give me an example."

He shrugged. "Just thinking about making some changes, that's all."

She nodded. "Mm-hmm. Changing things up sure can make a difference." She'd seen the sagging shoulders, empty eyes, and glum expressions before on countless hopeless and defeated young men. Too many believed when life got hard, death was the only solution. "What kind of changes?"

He leaned back against the bench, tilted his head back, and sighed. "I don't know."

"Yes, you do." She jabbed his arm with her finger. "You just don't want to tell me." She shrugged, crossed her legs again, and studied her plaid skirt. "I've seen a hundred like you come and go."

He raised his head and looked at her.

"You think they got you by the balls and they ain't gonna let go until they throw your tired ass in the river." Seeing she had his full attention, she looked him in the eye and shook her head. "You done gave up before the fight even started." She saw the hope in his eyes and placed her hand on his knee. "Honey chile, you're in some deep shit, for sure, but you ain't as trapped as you think. Breaking loose ain't easy, but it happens."

"How?"

She looked around, nervous. Fucking with the Mafia was serious business. Her life was hard enough without having the mob on her back. "You gotta know the right people and be one lucky son of a bitch."

He sighed. "Then I'm doomed. I've got the worst fucking luck in the universe."

"I don't know." She shrugged. "You look pretty damn lucky to me. Pretty boy with those blue eyes, and I love the way your eyebrows stand out against your tan skin." She looked down his sturdy physique. "Mm-hmm, the good Lord done blessed you, honey chile."

He didn't say anything, just stared at the ground between his knees.

She felt sorry for him and reached a long arm behind his back to hug him. "How old are you?"

"Twenty-three."

"Shit. Just a baby." She shook her head and fanned herself. "You got a boyfriend?"

He turned to her, angry. "I'm not queer."

"Honey chile, you suck dick for a living." She rolled her eyes. "It don't get much more queer than that."

He pushed her away. "But I-I don't have any choice."

She shook her head. "Baby, you always got a choice. Be a victim, if that's what gets you off." She studied her nails, wishing she could quit chewing on them so they could grow long enough for polish. "People think I'm fucked up. Mm-hmm. Crazy even." She smoothed her skirt down again. "Everybody is some kind of crazy." She winked at him. "Mine's just a lot more noticeable than most."

A smile flickered across his face and disappeared. "Yes, ma'am, I'd say that's true."

"My life ain't all roses and carnations, for damn sure." She slung her purse off her shoulder and onto the bench. "But it's mine—thorns and all. Nobody calls the shots for Kreema. Mm-hmm. I'm in charge of me." She pulled a crumpled pack of Virginia Slims from her purse. "Cigarette?"

He shook his head. "Thanks. Don't smoke."

She dropped her lighter back into the bag and blew smoke at the pigeons. "You got any friends?"

He didn't answer for a while. She could see the wheels turning, and then he spoke. "No ma'am." She'd seen that look before, the minute she became a real person instead of a cartoon.

"I'll be your friend, baby." She patted his leg. "Now, where was you in such a hurry to get to?"

He looked at her, taking her measure, wary like the little kittens she sometimes found in the alley. "I was on my way to see Frankie, to tell him I quit."

She smacked the side of his head. "What the fuck are you thinking? You *trying* to get your ass killed?"

He rubbed his head where she'd struck him and looked at her, stunned.

"Mm-hmm. I know you ain't that damn dumb." She folded her arms across her chest and looked at him. "Are you on drugs?"

He shook his head. "No, ma'am. I drink a little. Not enough."

"Here's what you gonna do." She pointed a finger at his chest and gave him a stern look. "You gonna get up from this bench, walk your fine ass home, and forget you even thought about having that conversation with Frankie."

"Yes ma'am." His face fell.

She reached across and lifted his chin. "Then you gonna get down on your motherfucking knees and pray to God."

He gaped at her.

"Mm-hmm. Pray." She raised an eyebrow. "'Cause what you need is a miracle, and praying is the only way I know to make that happen. You know how to pray, don't you?"

"I don't know any prayers."

"You just tell the Lord what's in your heart." She smiled. "He don't need no fancy words."

CHAPTER FOURTEEN

HAROLD AND Abigail got off the subway at the Christopher Street station, emerging onto a sidewalk shimmering with heat. He glanced at his watch. "Almost four o'clock. That gives us a bit more than three hours to walk around Greenwich Village, grab something to eat, and hop the subway to Times Square for the show."

"Being in New York is so cool. I love the subway!" Shielding her eyes from the sun with a raised hand, Abigail looked around. "The subway system DC is building won't be open for years." She pulled a map from her purse and pointed to a small park with a statue of a Civil War-era military figure and several benches. "Let's sit over there and get our bearings."

They were halfway to the bench when Harold saw....

He stared, unsure how to refer to the tall, dark-skinned person sitting on a bench smoking a cigarette. He decided, based solely on the clothing, to go with feminine pronouns. She had on an ill-fitting tube top that fell loosely over a pleated plaid skirt like the uniforms Catholic girls wore to school, more costume jewelry than Harold had ever seen on one person, and combat boots that hadn't seen polish since at least the Korean War.

Abigail sat on a bench across from the exotic creature and studied the city map. Harold sat next to her, holding a corner of the map, unable to look away from the spectacle across from them. He'd seen a few drag queens in DC, but nothing like this one—and certainly, never in broad daylight. Despite the garish makeup and unflattering clothing, she was magnificent.

His stomach rumbled. "We should eat first, then we'll know how much time we have to explore."

Abigail pointed across the street to a rusted sign attached to a two-story brick building. "How about the Stonewall Inn Restaurant?"

"That's where Terrence is taking us to dance tomorrow night," Harold said. "He didn't say anything about eating there." The boarded-up windows offered no clue and made him wonder if the place was still open.

"Did you say Terrence?"

The masculine voice came from the exotic creature on the bench across from them. Harold smiled and nodded. "Yes. Do you know him?"

She dropped her cigarette, ground it into the sidewalk with the toe of her boot, and then exhaled a cloud of smoke. "Curly blond hair?"

"Yeah," Abigail said. "That hair is definitely his most distinguishing feature."

"Yes, ma'am," Harold replied. "That's him."

"Mm-hmm," she said, smiling. "Terrence is a fine young man. One of my very best friends." She nodded. "We were out on the town just the other night." She rose from the bench and extended a giant, ring-laden hand. "Any friend of his is a friend of mine. Miss Kreema Dee Kropp, at your service."

"Pleasure to meet you, Miss Kropp." He shook her hand. "Harold Clarkson. This is Abigail Dombroski, my best friend."

"You can call me Kreema." She turned to Abigail. "Miss Thing, who does your makeup? You're beautiful—like a damn model or movie star or sumpin'."

Abigail blushed as her little hand disappeared in Kreema's grasp. "Thank you." She nodded at Harold. "He does my makeup. He's great!"

Harold's face grew hot. He had no training—just tips gleaned from thousands of beauty magazines and a lot of practice. He and Abigail had been putting makeup on each other and anyone else who'd let them for as long as he could remember.

Kreema bent over until her nose was inches from Abigail's and stared at her eyes. "I ain't never seen eyes like yours in my whole life. Girl, how many sets of lashes you wearing?"

"Three pairs," Harold answered. "Two on top and one on the bottom."

"On the bottom?" Kreema slapped her thighs. "I never woulda thought of that in a million years." She put her thumb on Abigail's chin and turned her head to study each side. "Beautiful." She dropped her hands and straightened, the giant black bag slung over her shoulder clanking against her side.

Abigail shot him a furtive glance. The meaning was clear: fashion emergency.

"If you like...." He hesitated, not wanting to imply the garish makeup she wore was anything less than stunning. "I'd love to do your makeup for you."

"Would you?" She clasped her hands together and her face lit up. "I been thinking about changing up my look."

Harold got up to study the features and contours of her face. Everything about the makeup she wore was wrong. The palette clashed with her ebony skin, accentuating rather than concealing her masculine brow, nose, and jaw. Her tattered bouffant only added to her clownish appearance. He checked his watch. "We've got tickets for a show at eight on Broadway, and we need to eat. Do you live near here?"

She shook her head. "No, honey. My penthouse is up on Park Avenue."

"Well," Harold said, disappointed. "That's too bad."

Kreema put her index finger to her lip and chewed on the nail. "Wait a minute." She yanked the bag off her shoulder and dug through it, handing Harold a length of heavy chain and a change of clothes. "Hold this a second." She renewed her search, burrowing deep into the cavernous bag. "Mm-hmm!" She held up a key, triumphant. "I knew it was in there somewhere. Friend of mine lives just a few blocks up the street. The place is a dump, but it will do."

Harold looked at Abigail and could see she was as excited as he was. "Is there a store along the way? I'll need to pick up a few things."

She nodded. "The thrift store or the five-and-dime around the corner should have everything you need."

"What about food?" Abigail asked. "I need to eat something."

"This y'all's first trip to New York?"

"I've been once before," Harold replied, "but Abigail has never been here."

"Mm-hmm, just as I thought." She snatched the chain and clothes from Harold, jammed them back into her bag, and motioned for them to follow as she marched up Christopher Street. "What y'all need is some gen-u-wine New York pizza."

Harold handed the map back to Abigail. "Guess we won't be needing this tonight."

CHAPTER FIFTEEN

Cameron's walk back to the boardinghouse passed in a blur. Fragments of his conversation with the eccentric drag queen popped in and out of his head in rapid succession—too fast to focus on the words, much less their implications.

One thing he knew for certain. Stopping him from talking to Frankie had saved his life. What had he been thinking? If quitting the mob had been an option, he'd be a big Broadway star by now, maybe with a Tony under his belt.

Kreema was right. He did have choices, and when push came to shove, Cameron wanted to live. Only now, unlike this morning or yesterday or last week, his new friend had given him a glimmer of hope.

Escape was possible.

Was he homosexual? He shoved his hands deeper into his pockets as he made his way along the crowded sidewalk. He didn't know what to think. Did the fact that he'd never been with a woman matter?

He thought about the married men whose lives he'd ruined. They'd been driven to seek his company by urges they couldn't ignore. Wouldn't those same urges impel him to seek the comfort of a woman's arms?

The opportunity had presented itself often enough. His gentle rebuffs of the ladies who came on to him were many a time what encouraged a john to approach him. Until this moment, he'd attributed his lack of interest in the women who wooed him to shortcomings on their part. Now he wasn't so sure.

Cameron had often dreamed of a wife and children. But in his dreams, they slept in separate beds, like Ozzie and Harriet or Lucy and Ricky, exchanging chaste kisses when he left for or returned from work. Lust never entered the picture. The appeal, he had to admit, was a deep-seated need for something more normal than his life had been since the fiery deaths of his parents.

He tried to recall a woman who'd captured his attention the way the lithesome blond had as he danced in that fringed suede vest. None of the pretty faces he recalled came close. He'd admired and respected many women but felt nothing like desire for even the most beautiful among them.

Awareness settled over him like heavy saddlebags on his shoulders as he climbed the steps to his fourth-floor room. He didn't meet any of the known criteria, but that didn't change the fact that he was homosexual. Focusing on what he was not had obscured his vision, preventing him from seeing who he was.

With a conviction that surprised him, Cameron knew he'd always been more interested in men. Male images from his past flooded his brain. He'd lusted after shirtless movie stars, handsome classmates, and sweaty farm workers for as long as he could remember. How could he have been so blind?

The goons had seen him for what he was from the start, laughing at his insistence that he was straight. Refusing to kiss the men who paid him for sex had kept his delusions alive in the face of overwhelming evidence to the contrary. What a fool he'd been.

He slunk into his room, closed the door behind him, and fell onto his unmade bed to stare out the dingy window at the brick wall a few yards across the alley. If he stepped out and leaned over the rail far enough, he could look up and see a sliver of blue sky through fire escapes and hanging laundry. Instead of sooty bricks and mortar, he longed to see something alive, like a tree, or better yet, horses grazing in a rolling pasture. He couldn't remember when he'd last heard a cardinal's whistle or the call of a red-tailed hawk.

The filthy, bedraggled sheers hung still over the open window. Spending as much time as he did in the relative comfort of air-conditioned hotels had spoiled him. He got up, shed his sweaty clothes, and switched on the tabletop fan he'd bought his first summer in New York. Moving the hot air around made him feel like he was doing something, even if it made no difference in the temperature.

Blaring horns and the occasional siren interrupted the steady ticking of the clock on the dilapidated bedside table. He stood before the fan, closed his eyes, and, with his arms raised over his head, turned in slow circles. Rivulets of sweat trickled down his neck and chest.

Okay, he was homosexual. So what? The men who paid him for sex lived in terror of being discovered. He'd seen what happened when word got out. How many lives had he ruined? How many suicides could be laid at his feet? Cameron didn't want to know.

He didn't need to worry about his family abandoning him because he didn't have any. He wasn't going to lose any friends because of his sexual preference either. Kreema didn't care. Nor would the revelation endanger his employment. The thought made him laugh.

Nothing about Cameron's life would change as a result of his discovery. Not one thing. He was the same person today as he'd been yesterday and the day before that—before he'd become aware of his lack of interest in women. Nobody cared one way or the other if Cameron was queer. Not a single, solitary soul.

Finding Kreema when he had was downright miraculous. His one and only friend had already made a difference. At least for now, he wasn't alone. Were it not for her, he might at this very moment be wearing concrete boots and watching the fish swim by from the bottom of the Hudson. She was right. They would have killed him. Cameron knew too much for them to ever allow him to walk away.

She was right about something else too: a miracle was his only hope. He dropped to his knees before the fan and tried to pray, but could find no words. Turning to God now, after all Cameron had done, couldn't be right.

He clenched his hands together and stared at the ceiling. Sorrow at the pain and suffering he'd caused overwhelmed him. Tears mingled with the sweat that ran down his face, caught in the hair on his chest, and slid down his belly and over his thighs to the floor.

Cameron didn't deserve any miracles. Since leaving Kentucky, he'd thought only of himself. The lives he'd destroyed along the way were collateral damage in his battle for survival—a cost of doing business. Feeling guilty about what he'd done hadn't changed anything. So he'd stopped feeling much at all, going out night after night to ruin still more lives.

"I'm sorry," he sobbed, repeating the words again and again, thumping his chest with his clasped hands as bitter tears of regret streamed down his cheeks. Asking God for anything—much less a miracle—invited a lightning bolt to strike him dead on the spot.

He brought his clenched hands up to his brow, squeezed his eyes shut, and again tried to pray. Words failed him. His parents might have taken him to church a few times when he was little, and he'd gone to Vacation Bible School once, but he'd never learned any prayers. He whispered the closest thing to a prayer he could remember: "Jesus loves me, this I know." He repeated the phrase after a moment because he couldn't think of anything else to say.

Cameron's naked body glistened with the sheen of sweat and tears. His knees ached from the hard wooden floor. The tears had stopped, but his heart felt heavy. A siren wailed above the gentle whir of the fan.

"You just tell the Lord what's in your heart. He don't need no fancy words."

Cameron opened his eyes. Forget about the miracle. He needed something far more important. He knew just what to say.

"Please, God, forgive me."

CHAPTER SIXTEEN

PHILIP LISTENED to the slow, steady thrum of his lover's heartbeat, his head rising as George inhaled and falling with each scalp-tickling snore. He didn't know how long they'd slept. The air conditioning had chilled the sweaty sheets and Philip too. He snuggled closer, purring when George squeezed him tight and kissed his forehead.

"You know I consider those little noises of yours to be an invitation," George said, his voice husky from sleep. They shifted position, ending up nose to nose and chest to chest in a tangle of arms and legs.

"You don't say." Philip slid his hand over George's hip, caressing the silky-smooth skin and the little patch of hair in the small of his back. "My door is always open," he said with a lascivious smirk.

"Yes, I know." George laughed and rolled on top of him, placing his elbows on either side of Philip's head and resting his chin on his palms. "Do you have any idea how much I appreciate your gracious hospitality?" He kissed the tip of Philip's nose.

Philip smiled. "No, but I've got a few hours to kill if you'd like to present your case." He ran his hand through George's hair. "I know how you lawyers like to talk."

"Oh?" George leaned down and kissed him again, teasing Philip's lips with his tongue. "If it's evidence you want, allow me to introduce Exhibit A." He ground his hard cock into Philip's thigh.

"Ah yes," Philip said, shifting his weight, wrapping his arms around George's neck, and raising his knees. "We've met."

"Yes, you're right, on numerous occasions." He buried his face in Philip's neck, tickling the soft skin of Philip's throat with his flickering tongue.

Philip reached down and stroked the head of George's cock with the tips of his fingers. "Such an impressive… instrument." He traced his index finger down the underside. "I'd know it anywhere."

"Could you pick it out of a lineup?" This time George's kiss was more demanding.

Philip responded with slow, lazy thrusts of his tongue, relishing the weight of George's body on top of him and the dreamy state of ecstasy induced by their languid, all-consuming kisses. Philip rolled him onto his back. "I think so, but I'd better take a closer look, just to be sure." He lowered his head, lifted the sheet, and, kissing his way over George's collarbone, stopped to tease his nipple, rigid from the chilly air.

George moaned and then jumped when the telephone on the bedside table rang. "Let it ring," George growled.

"I can't," Philip said, pushing away and reaching for the phone. "What if Harold and Abigail are in trouble?" He lifted the handset from the cradle. "Hello?"

"How was the trip up?"

"Terrence! Good to hear from you," Philip said, swinging his feet to the floor and sitting up on the edge of the bed. George sighed and rolled onto his side. "Hot but uneventful. Are you here at the hotel?" He looked around, eying the clutter left from an afternoon of lovemaking, and hoped he'd have enough time to straighten up the room. A quick shower would be nice too.

"No, I'm at my apartment," Terrence replied. "Just checking in to make sure you made it okay."

Philip tried to conceal his relief. He offered a quick prayer to whichever saint was responsible for such things and vowed to confine their intimate relations to George's room for the rest of their stay. "We did, thanks." He glanced at George, curled up beside him with an expectant look on his face. "Harold and Abigail have already left for the evening. We're staying close to the telephone until they get back."

"We?"

"Uh, yes. George is here too." Philip felt his face grow hot. "Foundation business."

"Cool. Tell him I said hello."

"I certainly will," Philip said. He glanced at the clock. "Did you want to meet for dinner?"

George made faces at him and shook his head.

"Would you mind too much if I passed?" Terrence paused. "I've got a big test tomorrow morning and I really need to study."

"Of course," Philip said. "I don't mind." He really needed to find out who was the patron saint for good luck. George nodded his approval, then shifted position. Philip felt warm breath on his lower back and tried not to moan when George began to lick and suck along the base of his spine. "School comes first."

"Thanks, Philip. I knew you'd understand. When are you going back to DC?"

Philip could tell Terrence was just as relieved and wondered what was up. "We're taking the train back Sunday afternoon." Warm, wet heat climbed up his back as George continued kissing his way toward Philip's neck. "Other than tickets for Harold and Abigail to see *Hair* tonight, we haven't made any plans."

"Cool," Terrence said. "My exam is at ten o'clock. I'll call you when I'm done and we'll go from there."

Philip found himself sandwiched between solid thighs. He leaned back onto George's chest and felt hot breath on his earlobe as George's arms wrapped around him and pulled him close. "Sounds like a plan." He gasped as a throbbing Exhibit A prodded his lower back. "Good luck on your test."

"Thanks. With a few more hours of studying, I shouldn't have to rely on luck."

George pinched Philip's nipples, rolling them between his thumb and forefinger. He continued teasing the left nipple as he lowered his right hand to stroke Philip's erect cock.

"I'm so proud of you." Philip tried to keep his voice normal. "See you tomorrow."

"Okay. Bye!"

Before Philip could respond, the call ended. He leaned forward and hung up the phone. "Looks like we've got the rest of the evening to ourselves."

"Good." George pulled Philip onto his back and rolled on top of him. "Now, where were we?"

Philip smiled and looped his arms around George's neck. "I believe you were about to present evidence and closing arguments about how much you appreciate my hospitality."

"I'm afraid that will have to wait," George said with a teasing grin. "I need to break a few laws first."

CHAPTER SEVENTEEN

TERRENCE HUNG up the phone and laughed. Philip's lack of focus and distracted demeanor suggested Philip and George were in the middle of some important "foundation" business. The foundation was real enough, providing Terrence with a generous stipend and covering the gap between the scholarships he'd received and tuition at the college of his choice. But there wasn't any foundation business. Beyond meeting with the occasional donor, the foundation more or less ran itself. The executive director handled the foundation's day-to-day operations. The same beautiful and talented woman also ran the business side of George's law firm.

Terrence understood the need for the ruse. As Philip and George were both too honest to sneak around behind Maxine Walker's back, Terrence figured she had to know about their relationship. And if she knew, she not only didn't care, but from what Terrence had seen, seemed to have given them her blessing. She turned up on George's elbow for fundraising galas and the occasional cocktail party, greeting Philip like an old family friend anytime they ran into each other. George and Maxine were too old-fashioned to divorce but modern enough to find happiness anyway.

Terrence tried to concentrate. Although he was interested in the theories behind social movements and how they applied to homosexual rights, tonight the words in the political science textbook failed to hold his attention. His mind wandered to the leaders of the Mattachine Society and their resistance to new, more radical approaches to changing the system. The old guard preached patience, a trait Terrence had never pretended to possess.

Society had to change—to stop viewing homosexuality as an immoral and subversive mental illness. Terrence was tired of being the butt of queer jokes, which had a lot to do with homosexual men being the frequent target for verbal and physical abuse. Two women sharing an apartment were lucky to have each other, but two men doing the same thing were nasty homos to be driven from the community before they ate the children or something.

Flamboyant and campy stereotypes didn't help. Sure, lots of queer guys he knew—himself included—stood out. The absence of other types among the men who danced at the Stonewall Inn didn't mean they didn't exist. Terrence had run across lots of men who showed no outward indication of their proclivity and were turned off by more obvious types.

Homosexuals had to change too. Getting along better would be a step in the right direction. The different factions, however they were defined, would accomplish more by working together instead of bickering back and forth. Acting fearful and ashamed wasn't going to change anything, either. Instead of hiding in closets, shirking in the shadows, and running from confrontations, gay people needed to stand up and be counted so the world would see homosexuals weren't so very different from everybody else.

He slammed the book closed and rubbed his eyes. With luck, essay questions would comprise the biggest part of the test. Terrence could bullshit with the best of them about collective action, relative deprivation, and value-added theories. But deciding if a confusing phrase was true or false, or selecting the correct answer from several similar options was tricky, especially given his tendency to overthink simple questions.

His stomach rumbled, and Terrence realized he'd forgotten to eat dinner. He glanced at the clock on his bedside table. Almost nine o'clock. He stepped across his one-room apartment to what Kelsey called the kitchen unit—a stainless-steel behemoth against the opposite wall consisting of a stove, oven, refrigerator, two cabinets, two drawers, and a sink. Opening the door to the miniature fridge, he leaned down and saw catsup, mustard, Worcestershire sauce, a bottle of milk he was afraid to open, and a jar of strawberry jelly sharing the solitary shelf with a moldy chunk of cheese and an aluminum foil packet, the contents of which he could no longer remember.

After retrieving the jelly, he closed the refrigerator and pulled peanut butter and a bear-shaped jar of honey from the cabinet. He didn't need to unwrap the loaf of bread to see it wasn't any good. Rather than his own rendition of Philip's signature peanut butter and jelly sandwich, he opted to eat the honeyed, strawberry-tinged peanut butter blend he'd mixed in a coffee cup with a spoon. On the plus side, he didn't have to cut off the crusts.

He washed out the cup and spoon and, leaving them in the sink to dry, changed into a loose-fitting tie-dyed T-shirt and Bermuda shorts with a white vinyl belt and his favorite sandals. The shirt and shorts clashed, and the belt didn't really go with the shoes, but Terrence didn't care. Given the heat and humidity, comfort trumped style.

What I should do, he thought as he sauntered down Charles Street to Greenwich Avenue, *is return to my political science textbook for another hour or two and then hit the sack*. But that wouldn't do. Besides, his test wasn't until ten o'clock. He had plenty of time to study before class.

Any other night he might have stayed home. But Terrence was more likely to run into his midnight cowboy on a Thursday night than Friday or Saturday when there was money to be made hustling busy hotels. Besides, with Philip and Harold in town, he wouldn't have another chance to go out on his own until next week.

The horrified reaction to Terrence's wink flashed through his memory. What had scared him? The question repeated itself in his mind like a stuck record. He had to know.

Ignoring the men who cruised him as he walked down Greenwich Avenue, Terrence wondered what he would do when he saw him. He had no idea. All he knew was this time he wouldn't get away without talking to him.

His already-voluminous hair had doubled in the humidity by the time he turned onto Christopher Street. Sweat trickled down his temples and sides. The streets and parks were filled with sweat-soaked bodies seeking relief from apartments and boardinghouse rooms made unbearable by the relentless heat.

"Terrence!"

He looked back and stopped, stunned by the vision before him.

"Mm-hmm, it's me!"

Terrence recognized the voice, but if it hadn't been for the familiar combat boots peeking out from beneath the mermaid hem of her dress, he never would have recognized the rest. "Why, Kreema," he stammered, amazed. "I don't know what to say. You've been… transformed."

"Yes, sir, I have." She beamed a radiant smile and gave a graceful turn. "It's a miracle!" A mountain of loose curls cascaded over her shoulders. The enormous wig deemphasized her oversized features, accentuated now by an ingenuous application of makeup featuring luxuriant, extralong lashes over and under her eyes with astounding quantities of mascara, foundation, and lipstick. Rather than clownish, the effect was stunning. The simple red gown she wore fit tight, creating the impression of ample curves where, Terrence knew, Kreema had none.

Terrence let out a low whistle. "Gorgeous. Did you do this yourself?"

She shook her head and smiled. "No. Two friends we have in common."

"Mutual friends?" Terrence scratched his head, trying to recall if he knew anyone capable of rendering such a complete and total transformation. "Sonny and Cher?"

Kreema exploded into laughter, slapping her thighs with her lacquer-tipped hands. "You don't know Sonny and Cher."

"I give up. Who?"

She tucked her arm under his and led the way. "I'll tell you, but first you have to buy me a drink."

CHAPTER EIGHTEEN

CAMERON FLEW down the stairs, left the shabby tenement house, and hit the sidewalk with a spring in his step he hadn't realized had been missing. Whether the result of an afternoon of tearful prayer, a long nap, his newfound friend, or the possibilities created by the epiphany about his homosexuality, he couldn't say. Pondering the cause was looking a gift horse in the mouth. Better not to know. Maybe he'd take a closer look after the new wore off.

He stopped to admire a basket of tomatoes.

The grocer nodded and smiled. "They were still on the vine this morning."

"Oh yeah?" Cameron remembered his father growing tomato plants in pots on the kitchen windowsill, nurturing and protecting the tender seedlings until the weather warmed enough to plant them outside in hopes of a ripe tomato by the Fourth of July. His mother would slice the much-anticipated first tomato into thirds, sprinkle the thick slices with salt and pepper, and then place each slice between two pieces of white bread slathered with mayonnaise. They'd sit around the table, wiping juice from their chins with paper napkins, remarking between bites about the difference between store-bought and homegrown tomatoes.

"Yes, sir." The grocer picked up a dark red fruit and handed it to Cameron. "My brother keeps his plants in a greenhouse until almost June."

Cameron dug into his pocket and pulled out a crumpled bill. "Any chance of getting a couple of slices of bread and some mayo?"

The grocer chuckled. "You'd have to buy a loaf of bread and a jar of mayo. Sorry."

Any other day, Cameron would have returned the tomato to the basket and walked on. Letting food go to waste was against his nature. He didn't have a refrigerator and could never eat a loaf of bread before it went bad. Come to think of it, before today, despite the colorful baskets of produce arranged before the window, he'd never even noticed the little grocery store. He reached into his pocket and pulled out another crumpled bill. "Sure, with three tomatoes."

Cameron carried his purchases to the bench where he'd met Kreema Dee Kropp. Several young men he'd seen dancing in the back room at the Stonewall Inn laughed together two benches away. "You guys ever had a 'mater sandwich?"

A thin young man with heavily mascaraed eyes, sallow skin, teased hair, and black bangs approached him, leaving his friends on the bench. "What the hell is a 'mater sandwich?"

Cameron reached into the brown paper sack and pulled out a tomato. "Best thing you ever ate."

"Oh, I get it. 'Mater." The boy smiled at him. "Where are you from?"

"Kentucky." Cameron pulled out his pocketknife. "You hungry?"

"I could eat," he said, his dark eyes never leaving the pocketknife.

"What about them?" Cameron nodded at the young man's friends, staring at them from the park. He waved them over. "You guys want a sandwich?"

The way they ran to him made Cameron wonder how many hours had passed since any of them had eaten. He pulled out the loaf of bread and opened it. "Hold your hands out with your palms up." The hungry waifs obeyed, and Cameron dropped a slice of bread onto each grubby hand before him. Then he opened the mayonnaise and used his pocketknife to smear a bit on each slice of bread. After wiping the blade clean on the paper sack, he cut into a tomato and placed a couple of slices on the piece of bread in each boy's left hand. "Bring your hands together and you got yourself a 'mater sandwich."

The boys inhaled the summer delicacy, and Cameron offered seconds. As he dropped the last slice of tomato on the heels of the loaf, he realized, other than the tomato ends he'd dipped in mayo, he'd been the only one not to get a sandwich.

RATHER THAN pissing on the campfire of his good spirits, checking in with Frankie had been almost pleasant. He'd shown no interest in having sex, making Cameron think he must have found a new little boy—another gift horse he declined to investigate. He'd hit the hotel bars after midnight just like Frankie wanted. Only tonight, Cameron had no intention of adding yet another name to the long list of men whose lives he'd ruined.

Breaking bread with some of the participants made watching the dancing in the back room at the Stonewall Inn more enjoyable. Cameron laughed and shook his head when the dark-eyed young man—Marty, he'd learned—had beckoned him over to join their high-kicking chorus line. The camaraderie was a nice change.

He didn't miss the no-man's-land he'd occupied before. Fearing the predilection might rub off, Cameron had kept his distance from the queers. Frankie and his goons had rejected Cameron's company for the same reason. Funny how different things looked with the shoe on the other foot.

Despite the odds against him, Cameron had decided to act as if the miracle he needed and had prayed for was just around the corner. Focusing his concern on *when* rather than *if* was a show of faith that, at the very least, made him feel like he was doing something. He wondered if maybe praying in church would make a difference and, figuring it would, decided to attend services somewhere on Sunday morning.

A tall, beautiful woman with a mass of dark curls cascading over her shoulders shuffled toward him as fast as the hem of her tight red dress would allow. Though in keeping with the enormous black bag slung over one shoulder, the combat boots she wore seemed an odd choice for the dress. Her face lit up when their eyes met. "Cameron!" she gushed. "How you doing?"

The glass slipped from his hand and shattered upon impact with the floor. "Kreema?"

She smiled and put her hands on her hips—hands free of all but one enormous ring and sporting long red nails. "Mm-hmm, it's me, baby." A thousand-kilowatt smile lit up her artfully painted face. "How do I look?"

Cameron walked around her, feeling the crunch of glass beneath the heels of his boots as he searched for some sign of the woman he'd met in the park. The hair made her look taller and, somehow, smaller. He wondered who had transformed the big ugly duckling into the beautiful black swan now beaming at him.

"You gonna say sumpin' or just keep staring?"

"I don't know what to say," he said, figuring that sounded a lot better than unbelievable, amazing, or synonyms emphasizing how… eccentric she'd looked just hours before. "You look like a movie star."

"Yes, she does, and I'd say the same is true for you."

Cameron turned toward the voice and gasped. He hadn't seen the blond come in. Seeing him hand Kreema a drink shocked Cameron.

"You two know each other?" Kreema said, looking back and forth between them.

"No, I don't believe we've met," the blond man said, extending his hand. "Terrence Bottom."

Cameron froze, staring at the offered hand, unable to move. For the only two people in the world he cared about to be at the Stonewall Inn together scared him. Was he one of Frankie's spies? Could this be a setup?

The room closed in on him as the possibilities ran through his mind. The longer he stood there looking from her face to his, the more awkward he felt. Confusion struck him dumb, and he watched as Terrence withdrew his hand, noting the pained expression on his face too late to do anything different.

Cameron needed air. The moment for a normal response had long passed. Fearing he might vomit and anxious to avoid the foul-smelling bathrooms, he bolted for the exit.

CHAPTER NINETEEN

Terrence watched in stunned silence as his cowboy disappeared through the door into the big room. What had he done this time? Nothing to provoke that kind of response—he was sure of it.

"Go after him," Kreema said.

The worry on her face surprised him. "Why?" Terrence shrugged and shook his head. "I don't even know his name."

"Cameron." She put her hand on his shoulder. "Now go on, before you can't find him."

Terrence shook his head. "He runs every time I so much as look at him. For some reason I scare the hell out of him."

"Mm-hmm, he's scared all right, but it ain't you he's afraid of, honey." She pushed him toward the door. "Talk to him." She pushed again. "Cameron needs a friend more than just about anybody I know."

"Why should I?" He stood firm, glaring at her with a drink in his hand and his arms folded across his chest, resisting her efforts to move him toward the door. "Is he in some kind of trouble?"

"Ain't my place to tell you that boy's troubles. He'll tell you, if you give him a chance." She folded her arms across her chest and glared back. "Go on now. Hurry."

Terrence didn't care if he ever saw the guy again. Cameron had made quite clear his lack of interest in talking with Terrence. Were it not for her obvious concern for the young man, he'd have given up and just walked away. "Okay, I'll go after him."

Relief flooded her heavily made-up face. She touched his shoulder and looked into his eyes. "You're a good man. Thank you."

Terrence chugged his watered-down drink, set the glass on the bar, and made his way through the dancing young men to the front room, past the office and coatroom and out the door to Christopher Street. He saw Cameron disappear around the corner and, determined not to let him get away, ran after him.

Kreema's interest in the hustler and her apparent knowledge of his plight surprised and intrigued him. Terrence had figured Cameron for a loner. Other than the bouncer, he'd never seen Cameron talking to anyone. Her concern piqued his curiosity. She knew dozens of men a lot younger than Cameron in dangerous situations, forced out of or running away from homes where they'd felt unwanted, unloved, and too often, unsafe. Why did she worry so much about Cameron?

"Cameron!" Terrence shouted as he ran. "Wait! I need to talk to you."

He didn't stop or turn, but Terrence could see he didn't walk quite as fast. He slowed to a jog, panting from the exertion, as he closed the distance between them. Cameron was a tad bowlegged, but Terrence focused his attention on the slim hips and the motion of his muscular ass as he walked.

"Come on, man. Stop!"

Without so much as a backward glance, Cameron kept walking, his hands thrust deep into the pockets of his skintight jeans.

Terrence's anger grew as he neared. The heat did little to improve his mood, and by the time he caught up to Cameron, he was furious and dripping with sweat. Grabbing Cameron's shoulder, Terrence spun him around and pushed him up against the wall, clenching Cameron's shirt in both hands to hold him in place. "Stop running from me." When Cameron offered no resistance, Terrence let go of his shirt and took a step back. He didn't say anything as he studied the handsome face for some clue about what he was thinking.

"I'm sorry," Cameron said, his voice deeper than Terrence had expected.

They stood, faces inches apart, for a long moment. Up close, he was even better looking—more masculine and rugged, like a guy in a cigarette ad. Staring into his blue eyes, Terrence's anger dissipated. He searched for something in the line of his stubble-ridden jaw that would reveal his thoughts.

Cameron's expression was guarded, but Terrence could see he wasn't afraid so much as curious and at least a little defiant. Sweat ran in rivulets down the sides of his face, disappearing into the hair jutting from the neck of the T-shirt he wore under a now badly crumpled short-sleeved shirt. Terrence saw the challenge in his eyes—and something else.

Desire.

His heart skipped a beat and his mind reeled as he absorbed this surprising piece of information. After a quick glance around to see if anyone was watching, Terrence steered him backward into the narrow, trash-can-filled alley. Cameron offered no resistance, backing away from the well-lit sidewalk into the forgiving darkness. Terrence stopped and slid his hands up Cameron's chest to his shoulders.

Cameron met his gaze, defiance evident in the tilt of his chin. "What did you need to talk to me about?"

Terrence couldn't remember, any more than he could tear his eyes away from Cameron's gaze. He leaned in close and kissed him.

Cameron kept his mouth clenched shut and his arms by his side but offered no resistance as Terrence caressed his lower lip with little kisses and nibbles. Undeterred by the heat or his passivity, Terrence pulled him close and continued his tender assault, expanding his ministrations to a salty cheek, a stubbly chin, and his furrowed brow, returning now and then to steely lips that refused to open.

Cameron met his gaze. He didn't shake as much, his lips weren't clenched quite as tight, and his stance had loosened. Terrence trailed kisses over his chin and along his neck and, encouraged by Cameron's gasp, ravaged the hollow of his throat, relishing the way Cameron's arms felt around him and the sound of his low, breathy moans against Terrence's ear.

Hands in his hair turned Terrence's head as Cameron launched his own assault on the tender flesh of Terrence's neck. Terrence moaned and, placing a palm on each of Cameron's cheeks, kissed him again, groaning with pleasure as Cameron's mouth opened, now eager for the kisses he'd been resisting.

The flashing red light of a passing police car reminded Terrence of the risk they were taking. He pushed Cameron away, keeping his hands on his shoulders. "We have to stop. This isn't the place."

Cameron ran a hand through his hair. "I have to… go to work." He brushed his hand through Terrence's curls. "I'm glad we… talked, but I've got to go."

Terrence didn't need to ask where. He knew. But he couldn't let Cameron walk away again without asking him the one question that now burned. "Hey!"

Cameron stopped and turned to face him.

"Can I see you again?"

The pained expression on his face surprised Terrence, even as it prepared him for his response. "That wouldn't be a very good idea."

Terrence wasn't willing to accept his answer, but the street wasn't the place to continue the discussion, especially with Cameron anxious to get to work. He pulled out his wallet and retrieved one of the calling cards he kept there. "Take this." He handed the lavender card to Cameron. "Call me if you change your mind."

CHAPTER TWENTY

Friday, June 27, 1969

CAMERON SAT at the bar, sipping his fourth bourbon and water, wondering how many of Frankie's goons were watching him. None, he hoped. Otherwise he was going to have some explaining to do. Rejecting polite inquiries from potential customers about their desire for company wouldn't have gone unnoticed.

Earlier, on the subway from Greenwich Village to Midtown, he'd thought more about the surprising alliance between his only friends and decided he'd overreacted. He'd accused and found them guilty of a setup—a crime he should be committing at that very moment. Beyond the way he'd come to see the world, his only evidence for any conspiracy was the two of them happening to know each other. If Kreema and Terrence were in cahoots about anything to do with him, Cameron would be surprised. But if they were, well… they weren't looking to do him harm. His gut said to trust them.

He blamed overexcitement, general paranoia, and stress-induced panic for his outsized reaction. The day had certainly been eventful. Meeting Kreema and following her advice had changed his life. Confessing and asking for forgiveness made a bigger difference than he ever would have believed possible. The relief he'd felt—still felt—surprised him. He didn't know much about God, but Cameron figured his confession would hold more water if he didn't run right out and repeat the same transgressions.

Being queer was supposed to be a sin too. But Cameron figured God wouldn't hold against him something he couldn't help. Any involvement in prostitution, extortion, and other crimes, however, was a different matter. Those days were over, he'd decided, knowing he couldn't continue hurting other people and expect a miracle to fall his way.

Kreema Dee Kropp had saved him from himself at the last possible moment. Until it no longer mattered, Cameron would keep praying for the miracle he needed. He just hoped his prayers would be answered before Frankie noticed he wasn't producing any income.

He should get while the getting was good. The sooner he left New York, the better. But where would he go? In his dreams, Terrence had shown him the way. In the alley, Terrence had ignited a flame Cameron didn't think he could live without. The way Terrence had taken charge and pushed him against the wall had shocked him. His aggressive demeanor had thrilled him and turned him on. Cameron had resisted the test of his kisses for as long as he could. But he'd failed, succumbed to desire, and submitted. His response to Terrence's kisses had removed any lingering confusion. Beyond any reasonable doubt, he was, in fact, homosexual.

A bald-headed man with a paunch settled into the barstool beside Cameron. "The bellman said maybe you could use some company." He pulled out his wallet and rifled through a thick wad of cash before pulling out a hundred-dollar bill. "Buy you a drink?"

Cameron turned and glared at him. "Fuck off, faggot."

The man's eyes grew wide, and he stood up fast, retrieving his money from the bar. "Fuck you, asshole." He moved around the corner, where Cameron couldn't see him. After believing he'd been straight for more than twenty years, pretending to be so now that he knew he wasn't struck Cameron as funny.

Three times already he'd gone to the lobby pay phone to call Terrence, without ever spending his dime. The first trip he'd only dialed two digits before hanging up. The last time he'd made it all the way to the final number before his nerves got the better of him.

What would he be doing right now if he'd stayed with Terrence instead of coming to the Hilton? He'd been really turned on in the alley. Now he wondered what the sex acts he'd been paid to perform with clients would be like with someone whose kiss he desired.

Part of him had wanted Terrence to take charge and drag him back to his apartment. Cameron would explain his plight, Terrence would take him someplace far away from New York where none of Frankie's pals could ever find him, and they'd live happily ever after.

The miracle could be justified as a necessity. But Cameron knew the fairy-tale ending fell squarely in the "wants" category. Needs had to come first. Besides, if he got his miracle—not if, when—involving Terrence in his mess was the last thing he wanted to do.

He studied the lavender card, examining the blocky print. Terrence Bottom was centered over the telephone number, with a peace sign replacing the first *o* in his last name. The dime Cameron had used for the previous calls burned in his pocket, but he resisted the overwhelming urge to go to the pay phone again. Calling Terrence would be a mistake. He didn't think anyone had seen them together, and he wouldn't endanger Terrence by seeing him again.

Turning over a new leaf wouldn't be easy. He hadn't thought about anyone but himself for so long, he'd about forgotten anything else was possible. But he had no choice. Before he could have the life he wanted, he had to leave behind the life he'd made for himself and now despised.

But how? Walking away was no better than telling them he wanted out. They'd find him, sooner or later, and when they did, they'd kill him.

The bartender pointed to Cameron's empty glass. "Another bourbon and water?"

Cameron shook his head. He didn't need another drink. He couldn't remember the last time he'd allowed himself to drink so much. His eyes burned from all the cigarette smoke as he pushed past the men crowded around the bar. Fearing he'd fall asleep on the subway, Cameron decided to walk home. The fresh air would do him good.

Outside the air-conditioned hotel, the heat hit him like a steamy wet blanket. The cotton slacks he wore were cooler than the jeans he preferred, but the boots were hot on his feet and his short-sleeved dress shirt was soon soaked with perspiration. An ever-changing stench hung thick in the humid air—a mix of exhaust and rotting garbage interspersed with blasts of garlic, unwashed bodies, and urine.

He could walk the fifty-three blocks down Avenue of the Americas in an hour if he hurried, but Cameron had no need to rush. The electric fan at home—his only worldly possession aside from the alarm clock and his clothes—would be his only relief from the heat. Nope. No reason to rush.

Crossing Forty-Second Street reminded him again of why he'd come to New York. How foolish and naïve he'd been to think he'd hit the big time. The city drew young men and women with similar dreams like moths to a flame. The blinding light of certain success had kept him from seeing the pile of tattered wings and carcasses at the candle's base.

By the time he'd crossed Broadway and Thirty-Third Street, he'd abandoned his dream of a career on stage. He should have gone to Hollywood. Things couldn't have turned out any worse there. Even had he not become a star, at least he'd be free to do whatever he wanted.

Whatever that was.

Anything would be better than his current occupation. He'd trade places with anyone, no matter what kind of work they did, for the chance to be free again. Trying to imagine a job he would turn down occupied his mind through the Twenties, and by Sixteenth Street, Cameron had determined there wasn't a job in America he wouldn't swap for hustling if it got him out of his current predicament.

The one thing Cameron wanted more than anything—to run away with Terrence Bottom—was out of the question. He couldn't put another life at risk. A block shy of Greenwich Avenue, he stopped by a pay phone and pulled the badly crumpled lavender card from his pocket. He dug around his other pocket until he found what he wanted. He struck a match and set the card on fire, holding the corner until the flames burned his fingers.

He ground the smoldering ashes into the sidewalk, shoved his hands back into his pockets, and tried to put Terrence out of his mind as he headed to his room.

CHAPTER TWENTY-ONE

HAROLD SPRAYED his teased hair and then retrieved the Colony Records sack from the pile of shopping bags on the floor between the two double beds in the hotel room he shared with Abigail. "Too bad we didn't bring that old portable record player," he said. He hopped onto the bed, tossed the empty sack on the floor, and arranged the three new additions to his meager album collection in front of him.

"Better that we didn't," said Abigail, sitting on the other bed, working her way through a stack of reading material she'd picked up from their morning excursion to explore Central Park and shop. "The needle would just scratch your new albums."

"You know what would be cool?" Harold picked up his favorite of the three, the 5th Dimension's *Age of Aquarius*. "A transistor radio that played any song you wanted to hear."

"Like a portable jukebox—yeah, that would be great." She shifted position, ending up on her stomach with her chin in her palms and her knees bent, crossing and uncrossing her ankles in a slow, steady rhythm. "But between the batteries and records you'd need for it to work, the thing would weigh so much you'd have to make straps for it, like a backpack."

"Or add wheels." Harold picked up the Barbra Streisand album he'd selected—the soundtrack from *Funny Girl*, since he'd opted for the 5th Dimension album rather than the original cast production of *Hair*. His third choice, *Perry Como Sings Hits from Broadway Shows*, reminded him of his mother, who he remembered singing along to "Some Enchanted Evening" and "Hello, Young Lovers" when she ironed.

Thinking about his mom didn't hurt so much now. Philip had helped Harold to see nothing he could have done would have made any difference. He missed her, and his brother too. But Philip was right. He wasn't going to let what happened define him.

A loud, continuous knocking interrupted his thoughts. Harold leaped from the bed to open the door. "Terrence!"

"Hey, bud." Terrence nodded at Abigail as he wrapped his arms around Harold, squeezing tight. "I sure am glad to see you." After a moment, he pushed him away and looked him over. "Your hair looks great."

"Thanks!" After he'd left the foster family the state had put him with after his parents died and had come to live with Terrence and Philip, hating the buzz cut he'd been forced to wear his whole life, Harold had sworn he'd never cut his hair again. He hadn't either, letting it grow for more than a year. His hair now resembled a pageboy, but instead of straight across his brow, his bangs fell in a ragged line that blended into the sides, with the back falling just over his collar.

"New clothes too?" Terrence pointed at Harold and drew circles in the air with his finger. "Turn around and let me see."

Harold walked from one end of the room to the other with his hands jammed deep into the pockets of his pleated shorts, imitating the exaggerated movements of a model on the runway. His new outfit was more masculine than he preferred, but in a casual, yet elegant, way that appealed to him. His short-sleeved shirt was made to look like a gold V-neck sweater over a pale yellow crewneck T-shirt that exactly matched the sweater's trim and the stylish shorts. "Very Gatsby, don't you think?"

Terrence nodded. "I've never seen pleated Bermuda shorts before, and that goldenrod color really looks good on you."

Abigail giggled. "They were trousers when he bought them. We cut them off above the knee and added the cuffs."

"You two are so clever." He turned to Abigail. "Wow, that's quite an outfit."

She jumped up from the bed and spun around. "It's a culotte dress." She dug through the pile of shopping bags on the floor and retrieved a box. "And I got these white patent leather go-go boots to wear with it."

Harold had selected the hip pants dress for her. With her above-average height and thin frame, the cut of the culottes suited her well, making her appear feminine and dainty rather than boyish. The large white, yellow, and red flowers on a bright blue background were printed on a lightweight fabric that billowed and flowed as she moved.

"I love it. Very modern," Terrence said, glancing around the room. "Where's Philip?"

"In his room, I think," Harold said, taking in Terrence's striped bell-bottoms and V-neck tunic top. The hippy look was the first Harold had seen that worked with, rather than against, Terrence's curly hair. "We haven't seen much of him since we got to New York."

"Yeah," Abigail said. "We had breakfast with him and Mr. Walker this morning, but otherwise, we've been on our own since yesterday when he gave us the ground rules."

"Ah, yes." Terrence smiled. "The burden of Philip's trust."

"Mom taught him everything she knows," Abigail said as she struggled to get the knee-high boots on her feet.

"He still calls her two or three times a week," Harold said, moving toward the connecting door between their room and Philip's.

Abigail stood up and wiggled her knees and ankles to settle her feet into the boots. "She really looks forward to his calls too, but now they don't talk about us so much." She leaned close to the mirror and inspected her face. "Dad fusses about the time Mom spends on the phone with Philip. Listening to her is his husbandly duty, but I think he's more grateful for the breaks than jealous."

Harold knocked and, after a moment, heard the deadbolt slide on the other side before Philip opened the door, wearing linen pants, penny loafers, and a pale green short-sleeved shirt that made his eyes stand out. Philip's taste in clothing had made a big impression the first time Harold had seen him and had influenced his purchase of the outfit he wore now. Only rather than penny loafers, Harold had opted for a pair of tan and ivory saddle oxfords. He stepped aside as Philip and Terrence exchanged greetings, blocking the connecting door for a moment, trapping Mr. Walker in the living room of the suite. Harold couldn't remember ever seeing Mr. Walker without a coat and had long suspected the man slept in a suit and tie. Seeing him in navy pants with flared legs and a wild print shirt made Harold smile.

He was about to compliment him, but Terrence beat him to it. "George, look at you! Welcome to the sixties."

"Do you like it?" Mr. Walker looked down at his outfit, his expression suggesting he didn't quite believe what he saw.

"You look great," Harold said, and he did. The flared pants accentuated his slender waist. The colorful printed shirt fit him too well to have been bought off the rack, but Harold could detect no alterations, and the print lined up in all the seams. He'd have to find out who his tailor was. "Are those boots?"

Mr. Walker lifted a leg and yanked on the knee of his pants to show his shoes. "No, they look like boots, but they only go up to just above the ankle and they zip on the side."

"Good to see you, George." Terrence and George shook hands. "Philip didn't mention you'd be joining us."

Mr. Walker shot Philip a quick look. "Maxine was supposed to take the train down from Boston to meet me for dinner and a show, but her mother took ill, and Maxine's afraid to leave her."

"Nothing serious," Philip interjected. "George was going to run up to Boston, but Maxine insisted that wasn't necessary."

"And that I not let our tickets go to waste," George added. "Philip has graciously agreed to take her place."

Harold wondered if Mrs. Walker was really in Boston, whether her mother was sick, and if she'd ever had any plans to come to New York. She had a way of backing out of things at the last minute that didn't line up with his impression of her. "What are you going to see?"

Mr. Walker's face turned red, and he stammered for a moment before Philip came to his rescue. "*Oh! Calcutta!*"

"Cool," Abigail said. "Isn't that the one where everybody is naked?"

"Is it?" Philip's eyebrows went up. "I had no idea!"

He was lying. Philip had told Harold about the revolutionary show after reading a review in the *New Yorker*. Terrence was right about Philip and Mr. Walker being a couple. And the first chance Harold got—probably back in Washington—he was going to have a few words with Philip about honesty and trust.

CHAPTER TWENTY-TWO

When Terrence had first met Harold, Harold had envied his long, curly hair. Now the tables had turned. Terrence was admiring the way Harold's coffee-colored tresses rippled as he moved, when Harold's expression changed—making it clear he'd put two and two together and was onto Philip and George. Before the silence became uncomfortable, Terrence directed everyone's attention elsewhere. "Well, if you two are going to the show, we need to get going."

Harold and Abigail moved toward the door leading from their room to the hallway and a set of elevators. Terrence followed Philip and George back through the door to the connecting room, taking in the books, newspapers, and beverage glasses that pointed to the men having had a lazy, leisurely day together in the living room of the suite.

"We'll meet you out in the hall," Philip said to Harold. Then he closed the door and slid the deadbolt into place.

"Geez, that was awkward," George said, his voice low.

"Harold is onto you," Terrence whispered. He noticed the deadlock on the connecting door on the opposite wall from the one he'd just come through was unlocked.

"And you as well, I see," Philip said, as he led them through the living room of the suite toward the door to the hall. "We'll talk later."

Terrence would wait until Philip brought the subject up again to remind him he'd always known about their relationship, that he'd never cared, and was happy they'd found a way to make things work. The three of them reconnected with Harold and Abigail in the hall, and the entourage proceeded to the elevators. Harold's pensive look had disappeared by the time they reached the lobby. Despite his excitement, Terrence knew he was still upset.

Though Harold hadn't believed him at the time, Terrence regretted telling him about the relationship between Philip and George. If they'd wanted Harold to know, they'd have told him. Now they didn't have a choice.

He wished he hadn't given Cameron his card either. Any other weekend, unless he went out to grab a bite to eat or to the library to study, he'd have been home for his call. If he called. Not knowing was driving him crazy.

Inventing an excuse and calling Philip to beg off for tonight had crossed his mind. But Harold had been looking forward to their time together, and he didn't want to disappoint him. Besides, if he was home and the phone never rang… well, that was worse than not knowing.

Abigail tugged on his sleeve. "Are we going to eat dinner at the Stonewall Inn Restaurant?"

Terrence grimaced and shook his head. "No, they don't serve food. I wouldn't eat there if they did. The place is a dive."

"I thought that's where we were going tonight," Harold said, like Terrence had just punched him in the stomach.

"We are," Terrence said, feeling guilty about his forgotten promise to take Harold dancing. "After dinner." Knowing they'd end up at the Stonewall Inn made Terrence feel a bit better. Maybe he'd see Cameron.

George hailed a taxi. His embarrassment had faded, and he seemed anxious not to miss any of the show. Abigail and Harold chattered nonstop the length of Sixth Avenue, debating which popular dances would be the most appropriate for each song they hoped to hear. Terrence wondered if they'd be more disappointed or surprised by the absence of anything so ordinary in the back room.

In no time the five of them were piling out of the cab onto Charles Street in front of Mama's Chick'N'Rib. As George paid the cabbie, Abigail and Harold ran to the door. Philip tugged on Terrence's tunic and said, "Are you okay? You seem a bit distracted."

Terrence sometimes wondered if Philip could read minds. He forced a smile. Philip wouldn't be fooled, but he made the effort anyway. "School. Hoping I did okay on my test today."

Philip studied his face but said nothing as they caught up with everyone else.

They squeezed into a booth by the window. Philip and George sat on one side; Harold sat between Terrence and Abigail on the other. "Interesting choice, Terrence," Philip said, glancing around the little restaurant.

"For guys like us," Terrence said, "this place is like the Empire State Building or the Statue of Liberty. You can't come to New York without stopping at Mama's."

"I feel the same way about Delmonico's," George said, his look not quite concealing his impression that Mama's didn't measure up to his favorite restaurant.

The waiter arrived with menus under his arm and five glasses of water. "Welcome to Mama's." He distributed the water and the menus around the table. "I'm Jack. Can I bring you something else to drink?"

Torn between the soft drinks ordered by his younger companions and the coffee the men had requested, Terrence opted for the coffee. "Extra cream and sugar, please." He waited for Jack to leave. "They call him Joan Crawford. He's a legend around here and the reason Mama's is so popular with the gay crowd."

"Ah, so this is the place," Philip said. "Friends from the Mattachine Society tell wild tales about tampering with the heat to steam up the windows so nobody could see inside. Joan Crawford would lock the doors to keep the police out for several hours of dancing and stolen kisses."

"Still happens, but not that often," Terrence said, closing his menu. "Now everybody dances at the Stonewall Inn." *Not everyone.* Cameron never danced. He just stood in the shadows, watching. Was he there now? Or maybe he was waiting at that very minute for Terrence to answer the phone.

He pushed the thought from his mind as Jack returned to take their orders. Terrence loved Philip, Harold, and George more than anyone he'd ever known. This little group was the closest thing to a family he would have. His miserable attempts to patch things up with his mother had failed too often for him to ever try again.

Philip made sure Terrence sent cards every year for her birthday, Mother's Day, and Christmas, insisting he enclose five or ten dollars in every envelope because she needed the money. He'd resented Philip for forcing him to do something he didn't want to do. But Philip had not relented, insisting Terrence would never be sorry he'd done it.

Being the bigger person was overrated. Sending her cards and money didn't bother Terrence so much as the lack of any response. No telephone call to acknowledge his card, even though he always included his number. No thank you note, no letters, no cards on his birthday or for any holiday. Nothing. Ever.

Suspecting her address had changed and someone was stealing the money he intended for her, Terrence had borrowed George's Thunderbird and driven by the ramshackle house where he'd spent the first fifteen years of his life. She was sitting on the rickety front porch in a dime-store lawn chair, looking twenty years older than she had the last time he'd seen her. Rather than anger, seeing her sad, tired face made him feel sorry for her.

He supposed she loved him, in her way. But without job skills, education, or a husband, she was forced to rely on the kindness of the mean-spirited men who preyed upon castoffs like her—and their children. Philip had helped Terrence understand what had motivated her choices, explaining that few—especially women like his mother—possessed the courage that had enabled Terrence to make a different choice.

His mother was trapped in a life where what she wanted didn't matter. Maybe it never had. Terrence couldn't imagine living without the freedom to come and go as he pleased. Some might look at what he'd been through and call him a victim, but he'd never seen himself as anything but a survivor.

Harold nudged him under the table, and Terrence realized Jack was waiting for his order. "I'm sorry." Jack and everyone at the table stared at him. "I'd like the fried chicken dinner." He handed Jack his menu and noticed Philip watching him.

"Abigail and I ran into a friend of yours yesterday," Harold said.

Abigail nodded. "Yeah. Miss Kreema Dee Kropp, the heiress. Too bad about all that mess with the Internal Revenue Service."

"So I heard," Terrence said, grateful for the bone Harold had thrown his way. "And saw. You really did an amazing job."

CHAPTER TWENTY-THREE

Something was up with Terrence. Philip had never seen him so distracted. Terrence poked at his dinner but hadn't eaten much. He was troubled, and Philip didn't think school was to blame. He wanted to know what was going on but decided to wait until they were alone to ask.

He listened as Harold and Abigail recounted their transformation of the drag queen they'd met in a park in Greenwich Village. Harold never ceased to amaze him. The boy had an ability to hold on to what he believed, no matter the opposition. Harold was always right, and everyone else was wrong. That was all there was to it.

Philip had seen right away that Harold needed an ally—like Abigail—who never judged him or questioned what he wanted to do. Letting Harold experiment with various identities had been a challenge, but Philip felt good about the results. The Harold he saw nibbling on a cheeseburger as Abigail described the thrift shop where they'd found the perfect dress for the makeover knew who he was and what he wanted to do with his life.

Assuming, of course, Philip let him. Allowing Harold to do what he wanted at school had scared the hell out of Philip. Letting Harold fight his own battles was maybe the hardest thing he'd ever done. Every day Harold left for school, Philip had wondered what ill would befall him before he got home. Yet, somehow, no matter what came his way, Harold bounced back, stronger than he'd been before.

As Abigail described the various techniques Harold had used to render the transformation, Philip thought about Harold's dream of dolling up the rich and famous for red-carpet events and celebrity parties. He definitely had the talent, but Philip didn't see how anyone could make a living at something so frivolous. A college education would serve him well, no matter what he wanted to do.

George attacked his ribs with vigor and enthusiasm. His boldness—in and out of the bedroom—had spiked in recent weeks. Philip wasn't sure whether a single event had wrought the change or a more gradual process had occurred. The contrast between the conservative lawyer in his Brooks Brothers suit and wingtip shoes and the modern gay man George became when they traveled together amused Philip. He sometimes teased George about what his clients would think were he to show up for an appointment in such casual attire.

Harold and Abigail claimed too much excitement for dessert. A usually voracious Terrence hadn't eaten more than three bites of his dinner. Philip declined dessert as well, forcing a disappointed George to pass on the chocolate pie he'd been ogling since they came through the door.

"What's your itinerary for the evening?" Philip asked.

Harold and Abigail turned to Terrence, who jumped from Harold's not-so-subtle kick under the table. "Well." He glanced at his watch. "We've got time to stop by my apartment for a few minutes if you want."

Harold and Abigail nodded. Philip remembered the little room being just big enough for the three of them to stand in and predicted the visit would be short. But the apartment was clean, safe, air-conditioned, and rent-controlled. Terrence had been excited about living alone, and Philip had been relieved to find a place cheap enough for Terrence to live without the distraction of a roommate.

"Then we'll head over to the Stonewall Inn," Terrence said.

Talking about the Stonewall Inn seemed to perk Terrence up. Alcohol wasn't the attraction. Terrence enjoyed the occasional cocktail, but Philip had never had reason to worry about how much he drank. Ditto for drugs. As far as Philip knew, Terrence hadn't even tried marijuana. He wasn't the kind to numb himself from a reality he wanted to avoid. No, Terrence would alter his reality.

George settled the tab with Jack and they exited to the sidewalk. "I'll be back in my room as soon as the show is over," Philip said. "Do you still have the hotel matchbook with the telephone number?"

After a quick dig through pockets and purse compartments, Harold and Abigail gave each other sheepish looks. Philip pulled several more from his pocket and handed one to each of them. "Leave a message with the operator if I'm not there."

PHILIP WATCHED Terrence leading Abigail and Harold up Charles Street toward his apartment as the cab pulled away from the curb and entered traffic. "Wonder what's up with Terrence," Philip said, turning to George, sitting behind the driver.

"Right off the top of my head, I'd say his love life."

Philip looked at him, stunned. "Do you really think so?" He hadn't thought of man trouble.

George shrugged. "His grades couldn't be better, and he's never been interested in drugs or alcohol. What else could it be?"

Philip stroked his goatee, wondering what surprised him more—that Terrence hadn't told him or that George had. "You're probably right. I'm ashamed to admit I hadn't even thought of that before you said something."

"He's always been so independent and self-reliant," George said. "Frankly, I'm glad to see he's opened up his heart. I was afraid he'd put up walls nobody would ever be able to break through."

Philip nodded. He'd often thought the same thing but worried more about something happening to the object of Terrence's affection. Losing another close friend, whether they were lovers or not, might prevent him from ever letting anyone get close again. His thoughts turned to the other boy in his care. "I still fear Harold will never get intimate with anyone, man or woman."

George smiled and placed his hand on Philip's knee. "You know, everyone isn't like you. Just because you can't imagine life without a lover doesn't mean others feel the same way. Maybe he's more like Maxine."

"Perhaps." Philip pinched the bridge of his nose. "Speaking of Maxine, what do I tell Harold about us?"

"The truth," George replied, without hesitation. "Would you rather I talked to him? I mean, it's my fault."

"Your fault?" Philip found George's willingness to take the blame endearing, whether warranted or not. "How so?"

"Well, I'm the one who insists on keeping our relationship a secret."

"Yes, and I agreed, so we're in this together. But if blame were to be assigned, I arranged for him to come along with us, even after you pointed out the risk."

George squeezed Philip's knee. "What's done is done."

"I know." Philip sighed. "But we're going to have to be more careful. We can't have it both ways. I'll talk to him, but I'm not looking forward to it."

"I'm sorry," George said, giving Philip's knee a reassuring pat. "He'll understand. He's a good kid."

Philip nodded. "I'm not sure I want the responsibility of fixing any more broken young men."

"Then don't. Harold will be gone soon."

"That's my point." Philip stared out the window, not noticing the cab had come to a stop by the curb. "When he leaves, for the first time in years, I'll be alone."

"Eden Theater," the cabbie said.

George handed him five dollars. "Keep the change." Then he stepped out onto the sidewalk and waited for Philip to slide across the seat. They walked side by side for a moment until George broke the silence. "As long as I'm alive, you don't ever have to be alone, Philip. Call me and I'll come right over."

"I know you would." But not every night—no more than once or twice a month—and unless Harold spent the night at Abigail's, waking up together was even rarer. "We're lucky Maxine is so understanding." And she was, never placing any demands on George, allowing them to come and go as they pleased with her blessing.

George had been open and honest about his situation and the need to maintain the appearance of a happy marriage. Philip couldn't blame George. Life was about trade-offs, and if Philip sometimes wished for something he couldn't have, he had nobody to blame but himself.

CHAPTER TWENTY-FOUR

CAMERON STARED at the ceiling and prayed for sleep. Tired and defeated, he'd hit the bed for a long nap, but sleep had evaded him. The fan was no match for the hot, humid air. Clammy, sweat-soaked sheets added to his discomfort.

He glanced at the clock and saw maybe two minutes had passed since he'd last checked the time. Frankie would expect to hear from him before too much longer. Cameron didn't think the meeting would go well.

Instead of hanging around, he should hit the road, putting as much distance between him and Frankie as he could. But that meant putting the same distance between him and Terrence. Cameron's mind raced in circles that started and ended with Terrence, interspersed with thoughts of escape, where he'd go, and how he'd live. Could he ever stop looking over his shoulder?

The farther he got from New York, the less he'd need to worry about Frankie. But his attraction to Terrence outweighed his fear. So he stayed.

Asking Terrence to run away with him wasn't an option. Nobody would sacrifice his dreams for a life in the shadows with a retired callboy on the run from the mob—especially a guy like Terrence. Cameron had seen him carrying books and knew he was in college, working toward a bright future. Cameron was the worst thing that could happen to him. Destroying his own dreams was one thing. He wouldn't take Terrence down with him.

Whether he stayed or ran away, Frankie stood between Cameron and an acting career. If he managed to escape, appearing on stage or screen would be suicide. He'd need to be as close to invisible as possible to keep Frankie and his goons from finding him.

His dreams had been destroyed. No, not dreams. Fantasies. An imaginary world where anything was possible beat the hell out of his crushing reality. Until they disintegrated, his hopes for the future had kept him going. But his predicament was permanent—a life sentence. Despair filled the void left by his shattered dreams. Killing himself was a commitment he just couldn't make. Doing something that might get him killed, however, was another story, and really, his only option.

Cameron could go anywhere. But where? Frankie's reach extended well beyond New York. Cameron had stashed enough money for a bus ticket to just about anywhere, but that would leave little for anything else. Besides, Frankie kept at least one of his goons around the bus stations to watch for more victims among the hordes of runaways and dreamers who flocked to the city.

Cameron couldn't think of anywhere he wanted to go. What would he do once he got there? He'd need to find a place to stay and a job—fast. Using his real name wouldn't be an option. He tossed around several before deciding on Mark Jones, anonymous like John Smith without being as obvious.

If he managed to escape, Cameron wouldn't leave acting entirely behind him. The persona he assumed would be the most important role of his life. He just wished his performance didn't have to be a one-man show.

FRANKIE DRUMMED his fingers on the desk, pinkie to pointer, in a slow, steady rhythm. He glared at Cameron. Though the expression on his face was blank, he was furious. The quieter he got, the madder he was. Frankie stared at him in silence for a long moment, never varying the tempo of his tapping fingers. "I don't understand how you come to me today with no money."

Cameron studied the stack of receipts impaled on a silver spike on the desk and shrugged without saying anything. The less said, the better.

"This got anything to do with Wednesday night?" Frankie continued tapping the desk. "Tommy told me things got a little rough. That prick didn't hurt you, did he?"

The kind words didn't match the menacing tone. "No, sir." Cameron's injured right hand went to his left cheek. Though still sore, his face hadn't bruised as much as he'd expected.

Frankie ceased the drumming, lifting his hand to stroke his chin as he studied Cameron. "I tell you what I'm gonna do." Frankie leaned forward and laced his fingers together on the desk. "Because I like you, we're going to call this little break payment for all your pain and suffering."

Cameron couldn't believe he was getting off so easy. He looked at Frankie for some sign he was joking, expecting him to call in Tommy and a few of his pals to rough him up.

"Since the little fiasco about that play a few years ago, I ain't never had any trouble outa you," Frankie said. "I owe you that much."

"Thanks." Cameron resisted the urge to sneer.

"Now we're even," Frankie said. "*Capisce?*"

The threat was clear. Frankie expected Cameron to get back to work. He'd been given a pass for Thursday, but taking another night off wouldn't be tolerated. "Yes, sir."

"Get outa here." Frankie waved him away and picked up the *New York Daily News*. "I got a lot to do."

Cameron wasted no time leaving Frankie's office. He glanced at his watch—a little past eleven, too early to head to Midtown. He made for the back bar for a drink to calm his nerves.

Considering the hour, the size of the crowd in the front room surprised him. Patsy Cline faded into Marvin Gaye as he passed into an even more crowded back room. The dim glow from the black lights around the room prevented him from recognizing anyone, but he saw no blond curls among the heads bobbing on the dance floor.

As disappointment washed over him, Cameron realized how much he'd been looking forward to seeing Terrence again. Their brief encounter in the dark alley haunted him. His selfish desires battled with his conscience. He wanted to see Terrence again but feared what would happen—to both of them—if he did.

Frankie's reprieve was a gift from God, affirming Cameron's commitment to keep doing what was right. Going to Midtown to do what Frankie wanted was no longer an option. Cameron couldn't change what he'd done or repair the damage his actions had caused to countless men in the past. He'd pay for his sins one day, and when that day came, Cameron wanted to be able to say he'd left his wicked ways behind him.

He had less than twenty-four hours to find a way out of New York. Making the decision to leave was the easy part. How he'd escape was a bigger challenge. Hitchhiking was his best bet. Frankie and his goons would never know. He'd figure out where to go when he was well out of the city.

Giddy with a mixture of fear and excitement, Cameron scanned the back room again. His eyes had adjusted to the light enough to make out more than dark shapes. Marty and his friends danced near the jukebox, but he saw no sign of Terrence.

Just as well. Running into Terrence would only slow him down and complicate an already-difficult situation. Wanting to see him one more time was a selfish desire from which no good could come. He glanced around once more, just to make sure he hadn't missed that curly blond hair.

He checked his watch again, but the dim light kept him from seeing the hands. The sooner Cameron left, the farther away he could get before Frankie realized he was gone. After another quick glance around the club, he decided to go back to his room, retrieve the money he'd stashed in the mattress, and head for the Lincoln Tunnel and a ride out of town.

CHAPTER TWENTY-FIVE

THANKS TO Harold's transformation, Kreema hadn't looked forward to a Friday night so much in months, maybe even years. The blue dress his pretty friend had picked out for her at the thrift store, though not her favorite at the time, looked stylish and elegant now that she had it on. The silver pumps she'd gone back to buy with her own money that very afternoon matched the sequins adorning the dress and made her feel like a real lady. The shoes were a tiny bit small, so she'd worn them all afternoon to break them in, stretch them out, and to master walking in three-inch heels.

Last night had been the most profitable of her career. Instead of sucking exhaust and chasing taillights, she'd strolled along the sidewalk and picked her clients from the line of cars that slowed to woo her, the drivers smiling and nodding, sometimes making obscene gestures for what they wanted. If she could make that kind of money every night, she could buy new clothes more often, move into a nicer place, and maybe even take a night or two off now and then.

Washing her face had tested her faith. She'd had many a makeover before but had never come close to the desired look on her own. Harold had taken his time, explaining every step to make sure she understood not just what he was doing, but why. Then he'd washed her face and watched as she applied the makeup, pointing out what she was doing wrong and how to fix it as they went.

Recreating Harold's look had been easier than she'd expected. Wanting to get every detail right, she'd taken her time, and without his help, the transformation had taken longer. She'd washed her face and started over twice but knew where she'd gone wrong, and with the last attempt, felt like Harold himself couldn't have done a better job.

She slung her bag over her shoulder and headed out for a night on the town. In a perfect world, she'd have bought that little clutch she'd seen at the thrift store that matched her shoes. In the real world, without her steel-toed boots, she'd rather not part with her hefty bag and its life-saving contents.

Even in heels, the longer stride of the blue dress made walking easier than had been the case with the snug red gown that lay in tatters across her bed. She doubted a needle and thread would be enough to repair the damage caused by her impromptu run through Central Park from the undercover cop who'd solicited her for sex. A younger man might have caught her, but once she'd ripped the seams enough to yank the skirt high up her long legs so she could run full-out, she'd left the fat-assed bastard with his hands on his knees, gasping and red-faced.

She walked up Christopher Street, ignoring the shocked looks on the faces of people she passed. Many were tourists in town for the weekend or a Fourth of July vacation, and judging from the stares and gaping mouths, unused to seeing a beautiful woman like her. Locals who'd seen her every day for as long as she could remember didn't recognize her. When they did, after years of ignoring her or looking the other way if they happened to catch her eye, all of a sudden they wanted to be her friend. Everyone seemed to think her memories had been made over too. Like a fancy dress, pretty hair, and makeup wiped away years of indifference. But nothing on the inside had changed. She was the same person she'd always been. If she weren't having such a fucking good time, the shallow bastards would piss her off.

By the time she reached the Stonewall Inn, her shoes had become instruments of torture. Each new step hurt more than the one before. Her ankles throbbed, she thought maybe the strap had cut into the side of her foot, and she couldn't feel her toes. She regretted the hours she'd worn the damn things around the apartment and couldn't wait to sit down. Instead of paying the cover and finding a seat in the club, she opted to conserve her remaining cash for a taxi uptown. She limped across the street and dropped onto a bench. "Evening, General." She kicked off the shoes and rubbed her feet together. "Damn, that feels good."

She leaned over to rub and squeeze each foot, moaning with pleasure. "My boots may not be pretty, but they's a hell of a lot more comfortable." After the feeling came back in her toes, she sat up, fluffed her hair away from her face, and dug through her bag for cigarettes. "Mm-hmm. I bet you're sweating up a storm under that coat tonight."

With the cigarette dangling from her lips, she returned the pack to her bag and rifled through the contents for her lighter. She lit her Virginia Slim and settled onto the bench, dabbing the sweat from her brow and beneath her eyes with a napkin, being careful not to smudge her mascara. Even with her wig and the long dress, the stifling heat didn't bother her too much—not nearly so much as the cold and windy winters. Maybe this year, she'd make enough money for a bus ticket to Miami.

No, she'd never go to Miami. She shook her head. Might as well accept she'd never go anywhere. She looked around her. Like it or not, this was her home now, and the people she saw every day were her family. In their own way, the kids who lived around here cared for each other.

Kreema smoked her cigarette and watched as the steady stream of patrons trickling into the Stonewall Inn increased to a slow-moving river of flame queens, street hustlers, drag queens, and the occasional lesbian. By midnight the place would be hopping. Depending on how much fun she was having and whether anyone was buying cocktails for her, she'd hang around until twoish—prime time uptown for horny drunks with twenty dollars to spend. God willing, she'd spend most of the early morning hours on her knees.

CHAPTER TWENTY-SIX

THE PLEATED shorts Harold had loved so much a few hours earlier chafed his sweaty thighs as he walked. His sweater-shirt clung to him, feeling more like plastic wrap than the light, soft fabric he'd admired in the store. He eyed Abigail's breezy culotte dress with envy, half listening as she and Terrence discussed the pros and cons of a college education.

"I just don't see how college would make me a better model," Abigail said. "And I don't want to wait four more years to launch my career."

Harold could relate, but in Abigail's case—as he'd told her many times—he disagreed. The difference in her situation and his, which she refused to see, was that making rich people look great would allow him to "live long and prosper," as Spock would say. She had modeling potential, but the odds were against her, and any success would likely be short-lived—a point on which she begged to differ.

"But Abigail," Terrence said, "what will you do if your modeling plans don't work out? And if they do, what happens after you hit thirty and your career ends?"

Abigail had heard the same thing from Philip, her mother, the high school guidance counselor, and most of her teachers. But then, they'd all said pretty much the same thing to Harold too. He could succeed without college, but Abigail really needed a degree. He'd said his piece and dropped the subject, having decided their friendship was more valuable than being right—at least in this particular instance.

Harold had been born into and, until he'd come to live with Philip, grown up in a black-and-white world with unchanging absolutes. Right and wrong, he'd since learned, were entirely a matter of perspective. Rather than set in concrete, distinctions between the two extremes were fluid and evolving. Philip said telling lies and half-truths was wrong. Yet he'd lied to Harold, concealing the truth about his relationship with Mr. Walker with falsehoods and omissions. Harold couldn't decide what made him angrier, that Philip had lied to him or that he'd felt the need to lie. Fooling around with a married man was a distant third.

"Harold," Terrence said, waving his hand in front of Harold's face. "Anybody in there?"

"I'm sorry," Harold said, dabbing the sweat from his face with a tissue. "Guess my mind wandered off."

"To Philip and George?" Terrence asked. They'd reached his apartment building, and Terrence held the door open for them. "After you." He handed Abigail his keys. "Fourth floor, third door on the right—number 4E. We'll be right up."

"Okay," Abigail said, taking the keys from him. She studied Harold's face for a minute, then headed for the stairs.

Harold folded his arms across his chest and waited to see what Terrence wanted as Abigail made her way up the carpeted steps. Terrence pulled him close and wrapped his arms around him. Harold returned his embrace and rested his head on Terrence's shoulder, savoring the faint scent of sandalwood. They held each other for a moment without saying anything.

Abigail and her mother, the contents of a few battered suitcases, and fading memories were Harold's only links to the past. Frequent visits from Terrence and Abigail after that awful night when his father had killed his mother and brother before taking his own life had helped Harold to survive the tragic loss of his family, long months with a pious foster family, and finding out about the private detective and half a dozen male prostitutes his father had killed. Terrence had been the bridge from an existence Harold had hated but still sometimes missed, to a new life he could never have imagined three years ago.

Harold loved Terrence, Philip, and even Mr. Walker, but he was closest to Terrence. Age was a factor, but Harold appreciated Terrence's directness. Philip's fear of doing the wrong thing made him cautious, which prevented Harold from opening up sometimes. But Terrence wasn't afraid—of anything, as far as Harold knew. Terrence had been the only one, other than the psychologist, to ask Harold about that night and the life he had before. He knew things Harold had never told anyone else.

Terrence grasped him by the shoulders and looked into his eyes. "So you've figured out Philip and George are more than business associates."

Harold nodded. He tried to swallow but couldn't because of a lump in his throat and a sudden urge to cry. "He lied to me." He took a deep breath to regain his composure. "After everything he told me about telling the truth and being honest about who I am, to find out he's been lying all along and pretending to be something he's not really makes me mad."

"You can't help how you feel." Terrence looped an arm across Harold's shoulders. "Be angry if you want, but don't be too hard on Philip."

"But why didn't he tell me? Why didn't he want me to know? He's gone to an awful lot of trouble to keep me in the dark. Doesn't he trust me?"

"It's not about you, Harold," Terrence said, his voice soft. "You know Philip. He'd never do anything to hurt us."

"Yeah, I know." Harold shoved his hands deep into his pockets. What really pissed him off was that he should have known. The evidence was all around him—had been since the day Philip Potter had first come into his life. Since Harold had moved in with Philip, Mr. Walker had been a near-constant presence, whether in person, by phone, or just in conversation. How could he have been so stupid?

"So give him a break. It's Friday night, and you're here in New York City with your best friend and me. Don't let your feelings about Philip and George rain on our parade."

Harold wrapped his arm around Terrence's waist and started up the stairs. "You're right. I need to stay in the moment. But I'm not letting Philip off the hook."

"Why not?"

"Because." Harold smiled. "This is my ticket out of college."

WHEN THEY'D first learned they were going to New York, Harold and Abigail had agreed the night out with Terrence would be the highlight of the trip. No point letting his feelings about Philip and Mr. Walker ruin a much-anticipated evening. By the time they reached the Stonewall Inn, Harold had decided to reserve judgment until he'd had a chance to talk with Philip about his adulterous deception. Terrence was right: Philip's reasons for secrecy, whatever they might be, most likely had nothing to do with him.

Abigail squeezed Harold's wrist. "I'm so excited!"

"Me too!" Harold said. They stopped at the brick arch marking the entrance to the Stonewall Inn.

Terrence waved to a large, masculine woman. "Hey, Kelsey, I was hoping you'd be here."

She waved and walked over to join them. "I thought I might run into you. Is this the little brother you talk so much about?"

Harold didn't want to admit how pleased he was to find out Terrence talked about him with his friend. Referring to him as his little brother filled him with pride. Harold stood there, gaping at the woman, unsure what to say.

"Yep," Terrence replied. "This is Harold and his best friend, Abigail, here for the weekend from Washington."

She extended her hand to Harold. "Kelsey Ryan. You're even cuter than Terrence said you were." Then she turned her attention to Abigail. "And you, young lady, are beautiful!" Kelsey bowed and kissed her fingers. "It's a pleasure to meet you."

A red-faced Abigail giggled. "Nice to meet you too!"

Whereas Harold had never really been sexually attracted to anyone, Abigail thought she might be bisexual, though how far she'd gone in either direction remained a mystery. She'd had dates, but his complete and total lack of interest in her sex life kept her from sharing much more than where they'd gone and whether or not she'd had a good time. Thank God. He wasn't at all jealous. He just didn't want to know.

CHAPTER TWENTY-SEVEN

Running into Kelsey was no accident. Terrence had invited her to join them for dinner, but she'd begged off, citing plans to spend the afternoon with Carrie. She'd promised to come to the Stonewall Inn after seeing Carrie off on a northbound train to spend the long holiday weekend on Cape Cod with her family.

An elegant Kreema Dee Kropp limped toward them, her smile twisting into a grimace with each step. Tiny silver straps cut deep into feet that hid dainty shoes several sizes too small. He suspected she'd been watching for him to show up to pay the cover charge for her. He didn't mind. Being queer made finding a job and a place to live hard enough for white guys who didn't wear dresses. Black drag queens didn't stand a chance. For her to have not just survived, but—in her own way—to have thrived was a testament to the strength of her character.

"Care to join us?" Terrence asked as she neared. "I'm treating Harold and Abigail to a night of dancing."

"I'd be honored," she said, dipping in an awkward curtsy with a wince.

"You look fabulous," Terrence said. He wondered what she might have become in a world free of prejudice. "That dress is stunning."

"Why, thank you." She leaned forward and kissed the air an inch from his cheek. "I owe it all to your little friends." She stooped down to offer a cheek for an air kiss from Harold, and then offered the other cheek to Abigail. "So good to see you again!"

Radiating excitement and raccoon-eyed from the sweat that melted the mascara they wore, the guests of honor circled around Kreema, commenting on the great job she'd done with her makeup as they adjusted her dress and fluffed her hair.

A policeman sauntered over. "All right folks, no loitering. Move along."

"Yes, sir," Terrence said as he herded everyone under the arch to the double doors. He was relieved to see nobody in front of them. On busy nights, rather than standing in line outside the door, the prohibition against loitering meant walking up and down Christopher Street and around the park until the entrance was clear.

Kelsey harrumphed and shook her head. "More harassment."

Terrence paid the three-dollar cover for each of them and distributed the free drink tickets as everyone signed the book. Kreema draped an arm across the shoulders of Abigail and Harold and guided them through the corridor and into the front room. Having failed to do so himself, Terrence was glad she explained about the watered-down drinks, the different crowds in each room, and the pitiful plumbing.

"I can't believe how crowded this place is tonight," Kelsey said, falling in beside Terrence behind the chattering trio.

"Me either," Terrence said, scanning the room for Cameron. "Must be the full moon." The moment Cameron had submitted to his unrelenting kisses replayed through his mind in an endless loop. He didn't know what he'd do when he saw him again. The object of his desire was skittish, like a mouse in a room full of cats. He didn't want to scare him off. Again.

Kreema said something to Abigail and Harold, stopping to point at the go-go boys in gold lamé briefs who gyrated in gilded cages on either end of the bar. He couldn't hear over the music coming from the jukebox and the buzz of laughter and conversation in the crowded club. Terrence stepped around her, dragging Kelsey behind him, turning sideways to squeeze between Kreema and several well-dressed older men on his way to the back room where Cameron would be if he were here.

"Hey," Kelsey yelled. "Slow down!"

Terrence glanced back at her. "Sorry." He turned around and slammed into someone coming through the doorway. "I'm so sorry," he said, gasping when he realized he'd run into Cameron. They stared at each other for a long moment. Cameron looked flustered but showed no sign of bolting.

Kreema glanced at Terrence as she steered Abigail and Harold through the doorway. "Come on, Kelsey. Let's show these kids how we dance in the back room at the Stonewall Inn."

The idea of Kelsey showing anyone how to dance made Terrence smile. The girl couldn't find the beat if her life depended on it. Kelsey saw Cameron, rolled her eyes, and then gave Terrence a pointed look before following the trio into the back room.

Terrence resisted the urge to throw his arms around Cameron and kiss him. He leaned in close so he could be heard above the din without shouting. "I was hoping you'd be here. I'm glad to see you."

Cameron met Terrence's gaze but didn't say anything. Indecision danced in his azure eyes as he studied Terrence's face. He was searching for something, but Terrence couldn't tell if he saw what he wanted to see or not.

"Look," Terrence said after another long silence. "I don't know what's up with you, but Kreema says you need a friend."

"What did she tell you?"

"Nothing," Terrence replied, so close to Cameron he could smell the shampoo in his hair. "She said you'd tell me, if I gave you a chance."

Cameron stared at him, taking his measure, still looking for…. Looking for what? Terrence searched Cameron's face for a clue but found none.

Terrence said, "If you need a friend, to talk to or for whatever, I'm here."

After a furtive glance around the room, Cameron seemed to make a decision. "Is there someplace we can go?" He scanned the dark interior. "Someplace private?"

"My apartment is over on Charles Street," Terrence said, not believing the direction the conversation had taken.

"Okay, we'll go there," Cameron said, looking around again, more nervous than before. "Nobody can see us together."

Terrence backed away, unsure how to react.

"I'm leaving." Cameron leaned in close. "Wait five minutes before you follow me. I'll meet you on the corner of Seventh Avenue and Charles Street."

Then he was gone. Terrence went into the back room and saw Harold dancing with Kreema. Beside them, Abigail was trying to keep up with Kelsey's erratic steps. Terrence jostled his way through the dancing mass to join them.

"I wondered what happened to you," Harold said. "Are you okay?"

"Yeah," Terrence replied, surprised his shock was that obvious. "A friend of mine needs… some help. I have to leave for a bit. I'll be back as soon as I can."

"Okay," Harold said.

Terrence was relieved to see he didn't seem upset. He knew how much Harold had looked forward to their night out together. He sidled over to Kelsey.

"Was that who I think it was?" Kelsey asked.

"Yeah. We're going to my apartment. Keep an eye on the kids until I get back, okay?"

"Sure," Kelsey said, with a big wink. "Take your time."

CHAPTER TWENTY-EIGHT

PHILIP AND George stepped out of the air-conditioned Eden Theater into the stifling humidity of a hot summer night. Philip pulled a silk handkerchief from the pocket of his linen pants and wiped his face. "That was an experience I'm not likely to forget for a while."

George nodded. "Not at all what I expected."

"Me either," Philip agreed, folding the handkerchief and returning it to his pocket. "More like skits you'd see at summer camp, or maybe a fraternity party."

"Only naked," George added.

"I gather you haven't done much camping or fraternizing with college boys." Philip smiled. "What time is it?"

George checked his watch. "Coming up on eleven thirty. Should we check the hotel for messages?"

Philip nodded, not mentioning the calls he'd made from the pay phone in the theater lobby. "I'm really not worried, but better to check just the same." He fished a dime out of his pocket and stepped into the phone booth.

"Superman must be a lot smaller than he looks to change clothes in one of these things," George said as he held open the accordion-pleated glass door.

The tiny space reeked of stale cigarette smoke. Numbers labeled "for a good time, call" and similar phrases along with a variety of graffiti had been inked or scratched onto every available surface. "They say television adds ten pounds, so he must be downright petite." Philip cleared his throat. "Yes, ma'am, this is Philip Potter. Do I have any messages?"

"Still nothing, sir," the operator said.

Philip thought she sounded annoyed. "Thank you so much."

"You're welcome, sir. Will there be anything else?"

"No, thank you. That's all."

"Have a nice evening, sir." The line went dead.

"You too," Philip said. "I'm forever in your debt." He returned the handset to the cradle and stepped onto the sidewalk, allowing the door to slam shut behind him. "No messages."

"Good," George replied. "Should we head back to the hotel?"

Philip shook his head. "Not yet. After sitting all that time, a walk would do me good. Which way should we go?"

George glanced around, then pointed down Second Avenue. "This way looks interesting."

They walked side by side for a time, chatting about the show until they ran out of things to say. Philip appreciated the comfortable silence between them—something he'd enjoyed only in solitude before George came into his life. They were good for each other and quite happy together.

Their situation wasn't perfect. Sometimes, especially when he'd been around his sister and her husband, Philip wished they could fall asleep in each other's arms every night and wake up together every morning. But wishing for something that could never be was a waste of time. Knowing from the start they'd never live together, Philip had learned to stay in the moment. Rather than pining for George when they were apart, he threw himself into his work at the Smithsonian. Evenings and weekends, if he wasn't visiting his nephew in Maryland, then Harold, Terrence, and helping out at the shelter for the teenaged gay runaways who'd otherwise roam the streets all night had kept him busy.

George tapped his shoulder and pointed over the Manhattan skyline. "Can you believe that moon?"

Philip stopped and retrieved his handkerchief to wipe his brow. "Beautiful, and a little surreal with all the skyscrapers in the foreground. The Algonquin called it a Strawberry Moon because the June full moon coincides with harvesting season."

"See any strawberry patches for us to raid?" George pointed to a grassy area behind a spiked iron fence. "Maybe they have a garden."

Philip shook his head. "No, I don't think so. That's Saint Mark's Church in-the-Bowery, one of the oldest churches in Manhattan."

"I could never steal strawberries from a church, no matter how old it was," George said with a smile.

"I'm not so sure about that," Philip said. "Your criminal nature is what first caught my eye." He dabbed his forehead and slipped the folded handkerchief back into his pocket. "Good guys are so boring."

"You must have me confused with my brother."

"No." Philip shook his head. "And don't get me started on Roland."

George laughed. "Okay. Care to elaborate?"

Philip nudged him with his elbow and winked. "If you weren't willing to break the law, we wouldn't be sharing a suite at the Hilton this weekend."

George frowned. "Breaking the law troubles me, if only for the possible damage to my career. But in this case, I happen to believe the law is wrong."

Philip didn't say anything. He didn't have to. They'd spent many hours discussing the legal status of homosexuals, melding Philip's knowledge of history with George's understanding of the law. Different paths had brought them to the same conclusion. The winds of change were blowing. Women and Negroes had made huge strides toward equal rights in the sixties. Gays couldn't be far behind.

They debated the differences as they walked. Being colored or female wasn't a sin, against the law, or considered to be a mental illness. Colored children had colored parents to teach them the way things worked. Mothers taught little girls how to be good wives. Gay children of either gender and any race got no help or support from Mom or Dad. By the time he and George reached Greenwich Village, Philip had resigned himself to a slower path to equal rights for homosexuals.

"This area is rich with history," Philip said, wishing he could take George's hand as they walked.

"Oh?" George said. He sounded distracted.

"There I go boring you with historical trivia again." He smiled. "I'm sorry. It's a professional curse."

"Not at all," George said. "I like traveling with you. You're better than a tour guide. What were you going to say?"

"Even the streets reflect the area's history."

"What do you mean?"

"Greenwich Village is the only part of Manhattan not on the grid system established early in the nineteenth century. The narrow, curvy roads in this part of town with names instead of numbers give the area its unique charm." At Tenth Street Philip stopped. "Care for a nightcap?"

George nodded. "I thought you'd never ask."

"Julius's is right up the street. How does that sound?"

"Perfect," George replied.

PHILIP FOLLOWED George as he worked his way past the men standing along the bar in a hopeless search for a place to sit. Barstools that opened up were claimed before the vinyl-covered padding on the seat could attain its unoccupied height. He was about to suggest they try someplace else when four opened up right beside them, the prior occupants proclaiming a desire to dance at the Stonewall Inn as they pushed their way toward the door.

Demonstrating an impressive combination of strength and grace, George maneuvered the two of them onto the empty stools. The move earned him glares from nearby patrons who weren't quite as quick and an admiring glance from Philip.

"What'll ya have?"

George looked at Philip, waiting for him to order. "I'd like a rusty nail, please—on the rocks."

"Same for me," George said. "With the good stuff—not that rot-gut Scotch in your well."

"You got it." The bartender grabbed two glasses, filled them with ice, and dumped a shot of Johnny Walker Black and splash of Drambuie into each one.

Philip paid for the drinks only because George's interest in what the men sitting next to him were saying had allowed him to win the draw for wallets. His insistence on paying for everything had irked Philip at first. Still did, maybe a little. His salary didn't come close to what George made, and he'd never been the primary beneficiary of anyone's estate. But he made good money—more than enough to pay his fair share—if only George would let him.

"The natives are restless," George said. "The mayor is running for reelection. In the last few weeks, the police have raided just about every gay bar in town."

"They cut down all the trees in Kew Gardens a month or so ago," the guy next to Philip interjected. "All of them more than two hundred years old, just to run off the queers."

"But the courts ruled homosexuals have the right to peaceful assembly," George said. "The suit was filed against Julius's for refusing to serve alcohol to homosexuals in 1966."

"Yeah, yeah, yeah. Lily Law pays more attention to some laws than others," said the longhaired, bearded man beside George. He pounded his fist on the bar. "Enough is enough. Until we fight back, they're not going to stop harassing us."

Philip listened as George decried violence, citing a need for patience as cases worked their way through the system. But here the courts had decided in their favor, and still the harassment hadn't stopped. They'd been more than patient, but if violence was the answer, they were in trouble. The guys around him looked more likely to run from a fight than to join one.

He thought about Terrence as he sipped his cocktail. Now there was a fighter. Surprise was his most dangerous weapon. Nobody expected a skinny, soft-looking waif to throw the first punch. Since Terrence's first blow was likely to be a kick to the groin, as far as Philip knew, he'd never lost a fight.

Though never violent, Harold was a fighter too. Persistence was his weapon of choice. Instead of kicking someone in the balls, Harold stuck to his guns. No matter how much the odds were stacked against him, Harold fought off attempts to change his mind with the style and finesse of a fencing master.

Philip took another swallow of his drink and glanced around the busy bar. The men chatting and laughing in his vicinity were from a different era than Harold and Terrence. They'd come here—most of them, anyway—to escape the overwhelming loneliness of homosexual life in a small town. They were runners, not fighters, fleeing to New York for the relative safety of the herd.

George had his back to Philip and was engaged in an animated discussion with several men beside him. He envied George's ability to strike up conversations with strangers. Philip couldn't hear what they were saying. Whatever it was, all the head-nodding suggested they were in agreement.

As if sensing Philip was watching him, George turned around. "I'm sorry, I got caught up in the conversation." He glanced at his watch. "It's late. Should we head back to the hotel?"

CHAPTER TWENTY-NINE

CAMERON WALKED up Seventh Avenue, hoping he wasn't making a big mistake. He glanced over his shoulder, nearly tripping over a pile of bricks spilling from a construction site into the sidewalk, but saw no sign of Terrence. Risking his own life was one thing. Putting someone else's life in danger was different. If anything happened to Terrence, Cameron would never forgive himself.

Running into Terrence as he was leaving the Stonewall Inn for what he hoped would be the last time seemed too providential to ignore. Perhaps his dreams of Terrence showing him the way out had been prophecy—a psychic vision of a brighter future. Taking the time to talk to him now, however long it took, would keep Cameron from spending the rest of his days regretting he hadn't and wondering how different his life might be if he had.

Going to Terrence's apartment was dangerous. The risk of being seen was low, but Cameron knew better than to underestimate Frankie's reach. After Cameron disappeared, he hated to think what Frankie and his men would do to Terrence if even one of Frankie's informants had seen them together or noticed Cameron coming or going from his apartment.

He'd taken precautions to avoid endangering Terrence's life. With Frankie watching the door, leaving with Terrence would have been like waving a red flag in front of an angry bull. He hoped none of the bartenders or other employees had noticed them talking.

Who was he kidding? He wasn't acting in Terrence's best interest. If he were serious about protecting Terrence, he'd be on his way to the Holland Tunnel instead of wasting valuable time chasing a fantasy. The truth, he had to admit, was he wanted to see Terrence again.

The unknown lurking in Terrence's apartment scared him almost as much as the thought of Frankie finding out he'd been there. Resisting Terrence in the alley had been hard enough. Away from prying eyes, behind the closed apartment door, Cameron doubted the strength of his resolve. But if he wanted to survive, he couldn't dally all night with Terrence—no matter how much he wanted to. He needed every minute to get as far away from New York as he could get.

The irony of his situation hadn't escaped him. Leaving the mob and the life he hated required walking away from the best chance for a loving relationship he'd had since losing his grandmother. Nothing worth having came cheap.

As he approached Charles Street, Cameron searched ahead for a vantage point where he could watch for Terrence without attracting too much attention. Traffic on the sidewalks and streets had slowed to a trickle. He stopped outside a coffee shop with a Closed sign hanging from the door. The hands pointed straight up on an illuminated clock centered on the back wall of the little restaurant.

Midnight.

Cameron's gaze roved between Seventh Avenue and the back wall of the coffee shop. He thought the clock might be broken until he noticed the longer hand had crept forward a tiny fraction of an inch. Each minute seemed like an hour. If he hadn't run into Terrence at the Stonewall Inn, he could have picked up what he wanted from his room by now and been well on his way out of town.

The sight of Terrence coming up the sidewalk was all Cameron needed to know he'd made the right decision. Whatever happened in the next hour, at least he wouldn't have to wonder "what if?" for the rest of his life. He retreated into the shadows and waited, falling in a few steps behind Terrence after he passed.

"Keep walking," Cameron said, his voice low. "I'm here."

He dropped back a safe distance, wishing Terrence had worn that sexy vest or a shirt that didn't hide his slim waist. They walked for a couple of blocks until Terrence stopped, looking back to make sure Cameron saw the building he was about to enter.

He picked up his pace and, when he opened the door, saw Terrence waiting for him at the foot of a carpeted staircase. He closed the door behind him, and they stood, an arm's length apart, looking at each other for a long moment under the bright hallway light. Until then, Cameron hadn't known how tan Terrence was or that his eyes were hazel.

"You're so damn pretty." Cameron's face grew hot. He could have kicked himself for saying something so stupid.

"Thank you," Terrence replied, holding his gaze. "You're the finest-looking man I've ever seen." He smiled. "And that's saying something." He took Cameron by the hand and led him toward the stairs. "Come on. My apartment is on the fourth floor."

When they reached number 4E, Terrence let go of Cameron's hand to fish the key from his pocket. His fingers trembled as he slid the key into the lock. Seeing Terrence was as nervous as he was helped Cameron relax a bit.

Before the door had closed all the way, Cameron wrapped his arms around Terrence and kissed him. A flood of sensations overwhelmed him as Terrence's tongue slipped into his mouth. He closed his eyes, sliding his hands down to Terrence's narrow hips and pulling him close. He ran a hand through Terrence's hair, relishing the softness of the silky, sandalwood-scented curls between his fingers as they kissed.

They stood by the door, their mouths glued together as they reached for buttons and zippers. Cameron pulled Terrence's tunic over his head, tossed it on the floor, and traced with his fingertips the happy trail he'd admired from afar and seen in his dreams.

Terrence slid his hands over Cameron's shoulders and across his chest, stopping for a minute to undo another button before slipping a hand inside to play with the hair on his chest. He unbuttoned the shirt and allowed it to fall to the floor as he reached for Cameron's belt.

Cameron grabbed Terrence's wrists and stopped him. "There's nothing I'd rather do than get naked and fall into that bed with you, but I don't have a lot of time, and there's something I need to tell you."

CHAPTER THIRTY

Saturday, June 28, 1969

LIANA SALVATORE loved her job, even if the crazy hours prevented her from having much of a life. Tonight was a perfect example. While normal people were out celebrating the end of the workweek, she was dressed like a lesbian, meeting with the rest of the team that would raid the vile and disgusting Stonewall Inn.

Not that homosexuals bothered her… too much. Her revulsion was directed at the mob. As the youngest child in a big Italian family, everyone she'd ever known for as long as she could remember had believed all of her relatives were in the Mafia. Not that they weren't, some of them anyway, maybe even most. But *her* father made a comfortable living running a concrete company.

For the mob to be operating queer bars was beyond ironic. Italian men valued machismo even more than *omertà*—the strictly enforced code of silence that made busting up the mob so difficult. But the State Liquor Authority, under section 106.6, had determined the mere presence of homosexuals made an establishment disorderly. Given the hordes of homos in New York, this interpretation of the law created an opportunity for the Mafia to cash in on an unmet need. Moving into queer bars had also enabled their expansion into male prostitution and, for the hustler's more affluent clients, blackmail.

The *Cosa Nostra* was the reason she was here. The Mafioso cloud hanging over her head her whole life had motivated her to pursue a career in law enforcement. Since joining the force, she'd run into at least a dozen men of Italian descent, her age or younger, possessed of the same motivation. She assumed at least a few of the older Italians on the force were good cops, but most were just thugs in uniform, more loyal to the mob than any sense of law and order.

Volunteering for undercover assignments early in her career had caught the attention of her superiors. Over time, she'd gained their respect, and now she worked undercover full-time. Removing muggers, prostitutes, and drug dealers from the streets, even if they weren't tied to the mob, made New York a better place. Shutting down another mob-owned establishment, however, was better than sex.

Not that she'd know about any kind of sex, really, good or bad. An early fling she'd fast come to regret kept her from dating her coworkers. Sure, they were a well-intentioned bunch, but if she was ever going to have a family, somebody had to be home at night instead of working another case. Never mind that mixing business and pleasure was a recipe for disaster.

She looked forward to carrying out tonight's assignment. Raiding the Stonewall Inn after midnight on one of the busiest nights of the week would hit the owners in the pocketbook. Not that the mob was hurting for money. They threw so much cash around the police department that putting a team together for a raid without any informants on board was a challenge.

Hawk-nosed Lester Hanks, Deputy Inspector with the First Division of Public Morals, was leading tonight's operation. She'd heard rumors that the mayor, who was running for reelection, had ordered him to clean up Greenwich Village by going after the mob-owned establishments. His handpicked team included an inspector from the Department of Consumer Affairs to document alcohol violations, an agent from the Bureau of Alcohol, Tobacco, and Firearms, two male undercover officers she'd worked with a few times before, a gum-popping female Liana didn't know, four plainclothes Public Morals officers in dark suits, and two uniformed police.

"Unlike Tuesday night," Hanks said, "this time they're not going to reopen an hour after the raid." He smiled, holding up a piece of paper. "I got a warrant signed yesterday enabling us to seize any alcohol we find."

The man is smart, Liana thought. The Mafia's lawyers looked for procedural things, like failure to obtain a warrant, to get cases thrown out of court. But keeping the place closed would take a lot more than removing all the liquor. The mob had more booze—lots more—and could restock the place in a matter of hours.

"This piece of paper...." He waved the warrant in the air. "Also gives us the authority to remove the bars, seating, and anything else on the premises connected with the sale of alcohol, including the jukeboxes."

Now we're talking! Taking out the bars was an unexpected twist that would make reopening tonight impossible. Opening the doors Saturday night would be unlikely, depriving them of revenue from the two busiest nights of the week. Removing the jukeboxes—the reason for the joint's popularity—would be a deathblow.

"Liana, Christie, slip inside the club with Melvin and Carl as soon as we're done here. Blend in. See who's who so we can round up all the employees before they sneak out."

Liana bit back a snort. Between her enormous boobs and platinum-blonde hair, Christie would have a hard time blending in anywhere. Still, sending spotters in ahead of time was a smart move. Employees were trained to hide cash and contraband before disappearing into the crowd. Hanks knew what he was doing and seemed to have it in for the mob as much as she did. Maybe tonight's raid would be more than just an exercise.

"We'll watch the door from the park across the street," Hanks continued. "After you've scoped things out and identified the employees, come outside. Once you four are out, we'll execute the raid."

He scanned the room, making eye contact with each member of the team. "We have three objectives." He held up one finger. "Remove the alcohol and anything connected with selling the stuff from the premises." He raised a second finger. "Arrest the employees. And number three, check IDs. Arrest anyone under eighteen or without identification and release the rest."

Hanks went over each person's assignment. "Liana, I'll need you and Christie to check all the drag queens." He smiled. "Don't worry. You won't have to feel them up. They'll come clean rather than face the embarrassment of a search."

The men in the smoke-filled room snickered.

"If there are no questions, let's get this show on the road."

Metal chairs screeched across the floor as everyone pushed away from the table and stood. With any luck, the cross-dressers would be wearing the mandatory three items of gender-appropriate attire. She sure hoped so. Being in a room full of homos was bad enough. Just the idea of checking out men in dresses turned her stomach.

CHAPTER THIRTY-ONE

No MATTER what song played on the jukebox, Kreema's aching tootsies kept her from dancing. Just standing hurt enough, and sitting on a barstool for a spell hadn't eased the pain as much as she'd hoped. But when she heard the opening bars of "Put a Little Love in Your Heart," she could sit no longer. She kicked off the dainty shoes, dropped them into her bag, and dragged a startled Harold behind her onto the dance floor.

The line-dancing crowd, shoulder to shoulder and reeking of Tabu perfume, slowed her progress to the center of the floor where she preferred to dance. Motivated by the three-dollar cover charge, the doorman would keep admitting anyone with even the flimsiest proof they were at least eighteen years old no matter how crowded the place got.

As she made her way to the center of the dance floor, the blue dress she wore and the makeover Harold had given her earned compliments and wolf whistles from her sisters in drag and the flame queens—the ultrafeminine boys with teased hair who liked to wear makeup and a ladies' garment or two, usually "borrowed" from an unsuspecting relative or stolen from laundry hung out to dry. Thanks to Harold and Abigail, tonight Kreema was the belle of the ball.

Abigail followed behind Harold and Kreema, a reluctant Kelsey in tow. Kreema couldn't believe how little effort was needed to make a sturdy woman like Kelsey look like a man. A short haircut and some menswear completed the transformation. But Kreema could conceal her generous endowment. They didn't make an elastic bandage with the oomph to flatten Kelsey's big breasts.

Kreema shoved a dancing couple off her spot and stopped. "Mm-hmm." She released Harold's hand and addressed the boys line-dancing around them. "Let's show these DC folks how we dance here in the Big Apple." She watched the line for a moment, then joined their steps. "Come on, Harold. Ain't nothing to it."

Harold caught on fast, and before long was adding his own twist to the routine. Abigail struggled at first, but mastered the more complicated moves soon enough. The stocky lesbian, however, could sooner fly. Kreema smiled and put a hand on Kelsey's shoulder. "That's right, girl. Dance to your own drummer."

Kelsey shrugged. "Terrence says I dance like a straight boy at his first sock hop."

Kreema slapped her thighs and laughed but thought she looked more like a shoeless football player crossing hot pavement. And she'd have said so too, but Kelsey was Terrence's friend. "Don't you worry about what nobody else thinks, honey. You having fun?"

"A blast," Kelsey replied, lurching and rocking to a beat nobody else could hear.

"Mm-hmm, that's what counts."

Jackie DeShannon gave way to the Rolling Stones. "Satisfaction" wasn't one of Kreema's songs, but she didn't want to give up the spot she'd staked out. Her feet didn't hurt as much, perhaps numbed by the spilled alcohol covering the dance floor. Harold had drifted off and danced amid the flame queens. Kreema couldn't tell if he didn't notice or just ignored their fawning looks. However, the way he danced made her think he was well aware of his admirers.

An angry, intimidating man in a dark three-piece suit shoved his way through the dancers to the jukebox. He reached behind the machine, yanked the cord, and the music slowed to a stop. Bright fluorescent lights came on and a chorus of boos erupted from around the crowded club.

"Again?" Kelsey said. "The police just raided the place Tuesday night."

Kreema nodded. "I can't ever remember them coming on a Friday or Saturday night." Everybody knew the police came during the week at a prearranged time—early enough to reopen by midnight, if not before. Bartenders stuffing cash into cigar boxes and pouring liquor down floor drains made Kreema think that unlike most raids, this one had been a surprise.

Anxious men dashed around the club, searching for a way out. The nervous group around her stood where they'd danced seconds earlier. Kreema suspected the most frightened men had wives and kids at home and hoped to avoid the humiliation of an arrest.

"What's going on?" Harold asked, looking around the room.

"A police raid," Kelsey replied.

Abigail's eyes grew wide. "Are we in trouble?"

Kreema put a protective arm over her shoulders. "Don't you worry, baby. They'll check our IDs and then shoo us all out the door."

The employees were rounded up and herded to the other side of the back room, where two men in dark suits waited. A couple of uniformed officers ushered patrons into the front room. "You," one of them pointed to Kreema. "Get your identification out and line up over there." He nodded toward the women's restroom, where a lesbian and a flashy blonde waited—undercover officers, she assumed.

"Are you talking to me?" Kreema asked, batting her long lashes.

"Yes," he replied. "Now move it."

She put her hands on her hips and glared at him. "Where are your manners? Didn't your momma teach you to say please?"

"I ain't asking you, I'm telling you." He took a step toward her.

Though the police often harassed her, thanks to a combination of wisdom and speed, they hadn't roughed her up in months. She knew better than to provoke Patty Pig in such close quarters. But he was ruining her night out, and his tone rubbed her the wrong way. She'd never let anyone push her around, and she wasn't about to start now. "And I'm telling you, if you want sumpin' from me, you're going to have to ask nice-like." She smiled and fluffed her hair back from her face.

Anger transformed him. "Come on." He grabbed her elbow and yanked her toward the bathrooms.

She knocked his hand away and took a step back. "Motherfucker, get your damn hands off of me!"

"That's right, Miss Kreema. You tell him!"

The encouragement came from a young cross-dresser at the front of the line, and was echoed by a dozen more waiting behind her for the lady cops to check their IDs. Every one of them, Kreema noted, could benefit from a few hours with Harold and Abigail—especially the lady cops.

"I need to see some identification," he said, glaring at her, his hand hovering near his nightstick.

Emboldened by her audience, she gave him her sweetest smile. "What's the magic word?"

Her fans laughed and taunted the angry cop. "Come on, say it!"

He drew his nightstick and stepped toward her. "I'm not telling you again."

Everyone in the room watched to see what she would do. Running wasn't an option, and resisting further was asking for a beating she preferred to avoid. "Mm-hmm, you don't know any better 'cause you ain't nothing but trash." She turned her back on him and sashayed to the front of the line of queens waiting to be checked. "Can I cut in front of you, honey? I've got places to go and people to see."

The little queen in a blonde wig at the front of the line smiled and took a step back. "Yes, ma'am."

The lesbian cop scowled at Kreema. "I need to see some identification."

"You wanna know who I am? Just ask anyone here." She looked back at the line behind her. "Tell Betty Badge here who I am."

"Kreema Dee Kropp!"

The chorus of responses made her smile. "Anything else you wanna know?"

"So everybody knows you," the phony lesbian said, crossing her arms and giving Kreema a stern look. "I still need to see some ID."

Kreema adopted her most regal pose and peered down her nose at the woman. "Mm-hmm, and people in hell want ice water."

CHAPTER THIRTY-TWO

HAROLD AND Abigail followed Kelsey into the front room where they joined a long line snaking through the club waiting to present identification to the police. Bursts of laughter from the back room in response to Kreema's ongoing performance punctuated the buzz of nervous conversations. Although everyone steered clear of the police, nobody seemed very concerned.

Dancing amid guys with teased hair and makeup, wearing blouses and high-heel shoes, had been life-changing. Sitting alone in the school lunchroom all those years had left Harold believing he was a freak of nature. He'd seen the admiring looks his one-of-a-kind outfit had garnered as he danced. Although none of the flamboyant young men in the club possessed Harold's panache, he applauded the effort and thought a few showed real promise.

Abigail grabbed Harold's hand and whispered, "Isn't this exciting?"

"Yes!" Harold replied. "Do you think we'll get arrested?" He didn't mean to sound hopeful, but spending time in jail would add another highlight to a night he knew he'd talk about for the rest of his life.

"Unlikely," Kelsey said, shifting back and forth from one foot to the other and glancing around the room. "They'll arrest a drag queen or two to establish the place as disorderly. Until the Mafia pays their bail, the employees will spend a few hours in jail. For everyone else, the cops will check our IDs and send us on our merry way. Do what they say, and we'll be out of here in no time."

Kelsey wiggled in between Harold and Abigail and draped an arm across their shoulders. Since they'd come to the front room, the line hadn't moved. With so many people inside and the cops' preoccupation with the liquor, the employees, and the drag queens, the process of checking IDs had created a logjam.

Crowbar-wielding policemen entered the room and ripped apart the wooden benches built around the perimeter. The squeal of nails pulling loose and the clatter of falling lumber cast a pall over the building.

"Shit!" Kelsey watched the destruction around her unfold. "This joint may be a dump, but it's practically home for a lot of these kids." She folded her arms across her chest and glared at the cops tearing the place up. "Raiding our hangout is one thing. Destroying it…." She shook her head. "Just more harassment by the establishment."

A pair of plainclothes officers escorted a handcuffed line of employees from the back room to the door. The derisive comments coming from the crowd surprised Harold. The workers had no fans among the patrons. Four cops dragged an embattled Kreema Dee Kropp, kicking and screaming, through the front room. The anger of the onlookers was palpable. Her flailing legs enabled her to break free for a moment, igniting the rage of her captors. The thud of batons against flesh sickened Harold. Abigail grabbed his arm and put a hand to her mouth in horror as the police whisked their friend outside. The upsetting violence had turned his excitement to fear.

"You said nobody would get hurt."

Kelsey folded her arms across her chest and stroked her chin for a moment. "That's the way these things usually play out." She surveyed the faces of the people waiting in line, glanced around the club, and nodded. "Something about tonight feels different."

Cheers replaced the anger over Kreema's rough treatment when the police escorted the last of the employees out in handcuffs. Harold, Kelsey, and Abigail joined the cheering, laughing along with everyone else as the drag queens filed out, cutting up and flirting with the police every step of the way.

When at last the line inched forward, Harold watched the front of the queue. Patrons who presented IDs were pushed out the double doors to the street. Police escorted the few without identification beyond the exit to the coatroom.

A tall, dark-haired young man in line in front of Harold and a blond boy with a really bad haircut had seen the same thing. The taller kid handed something from his wallet to his friend. "Here, Dwayne. Go to the back of the line and use my library card for your ID. I'll wait for you outside. They'll never notice two of us have the same name."

After his blond-haired friend with the ragged bowl cut left, the dark-haired guy turned and gave Harold a shy smile. "Hi. I'm Marty." He glanced toward the end of the line and then to Harold. "Don't think I've seen you around here before." Raven bangs fell across his forehead, almost concealing the mascaraed eyes Harold believed to be his best feature. An unruly dark mop of ratted hair fell over his ears and the back of his neck. Something shorter with less fluff would accentuate his wide-set eyes and work better with his high cheekbones and narrow chin.

"I'm Harold, and these are my friends, Abigail and Kelsey. We're visiting from Washington, DC, and Kelsey is our guide."

Marty nodded at Kelsey and Abigail and focused his attention on Harold. "I love your outfit." He reached over and pinched the sleeve of Harold's shirt, rubbing the garment between his fingers. "What kind of fabric is that?"

"Ban-Lon," Harold replied. "It's pretty but doesn't breathe. I'd be cooler wrapped in plastic."

Marty laughed. "I noticed as soon as you came in tonight. Very Gatsby, only more now."

Harold's face grew hot. "Thank you." He didn't know why a compliment from someone he'd only just met would make him blush. At a loss for words, he studied the grimy, wet floor.

"I'm sorry if I embarrassed you," Marty said. "I really like it— especially those shorts. Don't think I've ever seen a pair like them before."

Harold tried to think of something to say but drew a blank. The intensity of Marty's gaze unnerved him. Nobody had ever stared at him quite like that before. So much attention from a boy his age had never ended well. Having been beaten and bullied at school, interacting with other guys put him on guard.

"We made them," Abigail said.

He sighed with relief, grateful his friend broke the uncomfortable silence. He had no reason to fear. Marty wasn't like the boys at school. He had no interest in hurting Harold with words or blows. The experience was so unfamiliar, he didn't know how to act.

"You made them?" Marty asked, admiration in his voice.

"Not exactly," Harold replied. "More like… altered."

"Yeah," Abigail interjected. "They were trousers when we bought them."

"Neato." Marty dropped his gaze to the cuff of Harold's shorts. "I never would have thought to cut off a pair of brand-new pants."

They'd reached the front of the line. A plainclothes officer asked Kelsey for identification. He glanced at the driver's license in her hand and waved her on. "Hit the street."

"Why?" Kelsey asked, returning her license to her pocket. "I have a right to be here. This is a peaceful assembly. You can't make me leave."

Harold, Abigail, and Marty stepped back in surprise.

The officer folded his arms across his chest and looked at her. "I can, and if you don't leave now, I will." He lowered his hands to his sides, like a wrestler preparing to grapple.

Kelsey stood firm. "I'm not going anywhere."

CHAPTER THIRTY-THREE

CAMERON STUDIED Terrence's face for some kind of reaction, but saw none. Just the same reassuring and unquestioning hazel eyes that had held his gaze from the minute Cameron had launched into his story until the end. Terrence had listened, never once interrupting to ask questions or to comment on something Cameron had said.

Telling another person made him feel better. Whether he'd scared Terrence away or not, at least the truth was out. Cameron had held nothing back—unless the way he felt about Terrence counted. He didn't think it should. After all, they'd only just met. Proclaiming his undying love seemed a bit premature, even if it were true.

They sat cross-legged across from each other on Terrence's bed. Terrence had reached over and taken Cameron's hands, stroking the hair on the back of each one with his thumbs as Cameron bared his soul. The strength of his grip again surprised him, and he tried to ignore the sensuous touch as Terrence continued massaging the backs of Cameron's hands.

"You must think I'm one sorry excuse for a man," Cameron said, dropping his head. He tried to put himself in Terrence's shoes but couldn't decide which part of being a homeless prostitute on the run from the mob would most offend him. Coming here and involving Terrence in his troubles was a mistake. No matter how much he might change, nobody could ever accept the things he'd done and what he had become.

"Look at me," Terrence commanded, his voice soft.

Cameron met his gaze. At least now he'd know, sparing him a lifetime of "if only" and "what if" conversations with himself. Terrence tightened his grip on Cameron's hands.

"I'm glad you told me." He paused, and Cameron felt like his hazel eyes peered directly into his soul. "Except for the part about coming from Kentucky and being ready to break free, I already knew the rest of your story, more or less."

"Kreema—"

"No." Terrence shook his head. "She didn't tell me anything except that you needed a friend. Putting the rest together was easy. I knew the signs."

"And you still…?"

"I won't bore you with the details, but a couple of years ago, I was a hustler too." Terrence held his gaze.

Cameron couldn't conceal his surprise. "You turned tricks?"

Terrence nodded. "But I was an independent operator. Even without your… connections, I didn't think I'd ever escape the life."

He stared at Terrence in amazement. Never in a million years would Cameron have ever guessed they had so much in common. "How did you do it?"

"I didn't escape on my own," Terrence said. "That's for damn sure." He jumped off the bed, pulling Cameron to his feet. "Come on. If you're serious about running away tonight, we need to get moving."

"We…?"

"Yeah," Terrence said, digging the packet of matches from his pocket. "We." He dialed the number and, after a moment, said, "Philip Potter's room, please."

"Philip Potter?"

Terrence covered the mouthpiece with his hand. "If he can't help you, nobody can. And he just happens to be in town this weekend." He took his hand away. "Yes, ma'am, I would like to leave a message."

As his words echoed in Cameron's head, he remembered what Kreema had said.

You gotta know the right people and be one lucky son of a bitch.

Whether the result of prayer or blind luck, Cameron didn't know, but his prospects for the future had taken an unexpected, positive turn. Had his dreams been premonitions? Was this Philip Potter the secret way out the Terrence of his dreams had promised to show him?

Terrence hung up the phone and wrapped his arms around Cameron, squeezing him tight. "Your hairy chest feels great against mine."

Cameron returned his hug, caressing his lower back and burying his face in Terrence's neck. He wanted the moment to last forever almost as much as he wanted to throw Terrence back onto the bed to finish what they'd started before Cameron had proclaimed he needed to talk.

Terrence pushed him away and picked his shirt up off the floor. "Get dressed." A mass of blond curls came through the neck of the shirt, followed by the hazel eyes Cameron had stared into for most of the last hour. "If tonight's the night, there's no time to waste."

A quick glance around the room turned up Cameron's shirt, on the floor midway between the bed and the door. He slid it on, and Terrence pushed his hands away to button it for him. After fastening the last one, he grabbed the collar, pulled him close, and gave Cameron a kiss he felt all the way down to his toes. "We have to stop while we still can," Terrence said, breathing hard. "But I couldn't walk out of here without kissing you again."

Cameron hugged him tight and kissed the tip of his nose. "I'm glad you did. I'd like to do a lot more than kiss you."

"Yeah, me too. But I see that taking more time than we've got tonight." He winked at Cameron. "Now, slide into those boots of yours, cowboy. Time to hit the trail."

As THEY walked past the coffee shop, Cameron checked the clock and saw it was after one o'clock in the morning. "Where are we going?"

"The Hilton uptown, where Philip Potter is staying."

Cameron stopped. "I can't go there."

Terrence stopped and put his hands on his hips. "Why not?" He sounded annoyed.

"I'm sorry," Cameron said. "But half that hotel is on Frankie's payroll."

"Oh." Terrence's face fell. "I had no idea."

"It's okay," Cameron said. "You had no way of knowing."

"Shit!" Terrence palmed his forehead. "I forgot all about Harold and Abigail!"

"Who?"

"Friends of mine from DC and the reason Philip is in town." Terrence pushed the curls off his face. "I'm supposed to be showing them a good time, but I went off and left them at the Stonewall Inn."

"My fault," Cameron said. True enough. If they hadn't run into each other, Terrence would still be dancing with his friends.

"We've got to go back for them," Terrence said, a pained expression on his pretty face.

"No, you go. I need to run back to my room to get my stuff."

"Okay." Terrence nodded. "Get what you need and meet me back at the Stonewall Inn."

Cameron shook his head. "I can't. *Everyone* who works there is on Frankie's payroll."

Terrence laughed. "Oh yeah, I guess so."

"Go find your friends," Cameron said. "There's a park across the street from the Stonewall Inn. After you find them, wait for me in front of the general's statue. I'll be there as soon as I can."

CHAPTER THIRTY-FOUR

Despite Lester Hanks's impressive advanced planning and obsessive attention to detail, Liana Salvatore didn't think the raid was going well. They'd gotten off to a late start. She and the other undercover cops had identified all the employees and were about to leave when the shift had changed, forcing them to stay long enough to see who did what among the new arrivals.

A steady stream of people coming through the entrance had doubled the crowd inside during the half-hour delay. The handful of officers on hand weren't nearly enough to process everyone inside the club. More than two hundred people, if she had to guess.

Once the raiding team got inside, she and the other undercover officers pointed out the employees from both shifts who had served alcohol. They were herded into the back room for questioning by a pair of plainclothes officers. The other two men in suits collected cases of beer and bottles of liquor, labeling each with the location where it had been found under the watchful eyes of everyone in the club.

Getting organized to process the hapless patrons milling about took a while. The longer the homos stood around waiting, the more agitated they became. Tearing the joint apart in front of its loyal customers might not have been the best plan either. Waiting until they'd cleared out the place would have freed up more cops to check IDs and avoided the crowd's visceral reaction to the destruction.

Processing more than a dozen cross-dressers who hadn't worn three articles of men's clothing wasn't going as planned either. The drag queens were supposed to come clean, admitting they were men and submitting to arrest, sparing her the embarrassment of groping their man-parts. This one, apparently, never got the memo. Not that there'd actually been a memo.

The belligerent drag queen's refusal to cooperate was getting old. Liana stared at the barefoot cross-dresser in the blue dress. Support from the crowd had bolstered his defiance. Swapping insults with a drag queen would get her nowhere. Liana folded her arms across her chest and gave him a stern look. "Very well, then."

The bewigged man towering over her met her gaze. "I'm free to leave?" He nodded at the other drag queens and smiled. "My public awaits."

She shook her head. "Not until you prove you're a woman." She glanced at Christie, who, except for the movement of her jaw and the noise she made popping her gum, may as well have been a cardboard cutout.

He glared. "Are you fucking blind or sumpin'?" Then, much to the amusement of his admiring onlookers, he spun around several times, posing every half turn or so and flipping the hair from his wig off his shoulders.

Liana tried to maintain the upper hand. "Your choice. Show me some identification or come with me to the ladies' room." Not that she really wanted to go into the bathroom with him. But if push came to shove, she would.

He folded his arms across his chest and studied her, taking her measure, trying to decide how far he could push her. Drag queen or not, that's always what it came down to with a man. Power and control. "Mm-hmm. I know you want some of this, honey, but Kreema don't swing that way."

The onlookers erupted into laughter and egged him on with lewd comments. Liana knew if she didn't get control, things could get bad, fast. Her partner's value in a pinch remained to be seen, but Liana saw no reason for optimism in her blank, gum-chomping face. She glared at the drag queen. "The ladies' room is for your privacy. We can do it right here if you'd rather." Liana held his gaze, waiting for a reaction.

His rebellious attitude had infected everyone in the room. Taunts came at her from every direction. "Whatsa matta honey? Afraid you'll find a dick down there?"

Us against them. The weight of the revolver in an inside pocket of her vest gave her some comfort, but more "us" and fewer "them" would have given her more. She wondered if Hanks had called for backup. At least they weren't dealing with those campus radicals. Queers were a peaceful bunch, more likely to cry about a ruined career or whine about embarrassing the family than to put up a fight or resist arrest.

"What's it going to be?" She fought to keep from blinking. "Easy or hard?"

Bawdy gibes favored hard over easy by at least three to one. Her face grew hot, and she knew she was blushing. After seven years undercover, part of her was surprised she still could.

"Now that's a difficult choice," he said, a red-nailed finger on his chin as he pondered. "I like it both ways."

The son of a bitch was making her look bad now, and that pissed her off. She wanted to knee him in the nuts but thought the fabric of his dress—already stretched to the breaking point—would repel her knee every bit as well as the cups her brothers had worn back when they played football. She took a step forward and reached for his elbow, determined to drag the queen into the ladies' room.

He raised his hand up to stop her. "Don't touch me."

She hesitated for half a second, then grabbed his arm. He shook free, grabbed the strap of the big bag he carried, and swung. The impact of the heavy bag surprised her, knocking her back a few steps and making her see stars.

Christie came to life and rushed to her defense. The drag queen seemed just as shocked, which gave her gum-chewing partner the advantage. Liana joined the struggle, but the two of them were no match for the athletic devil in the blue dress.

The bastard must have kicked her fifteen times, and when he freed an arm, gave her head a resounding whack that made her see more stars. He was gaining the upper hand when two of the uniformed boys entered the fray. The crowd hurled insults at the cops as the four of them wrestled the enraged queen out the door.

The mood of the crowd turned dark. Their taunts took on a malicious tone she didn't like. She hoped backup would arrive soon. Now would be a good time for the cavalry to show up, waving nightsticks with badges gleaming.

CHAPTER THIRTY-FIVE

WANTING TO help Cameron flee New York and being able to help him are two different things, Terrence thought as he hurried down Waverly Place toward Christopher Street. On his own, there really wasn't anything he could do. Enlisting the support of Philip and George would make him feel better, assuming they were willing, but he wasn't sure how much help they could be either. Even the police didn't mess with the mob.

Concentrating on Cameron's words had been a challenge that had tested Terrence's will. Like a force of gravity, the man's full lips, fur-covered chest, and the rest of his beautiful, semidressed form kept drawing his attention from the sky-blue eyes. Sitting across from Cameron, in the privacy of his apartment, in the bed he slept in every night, was almost more than he could stand. How many nights had he dreamed of Cameron in that very bed? Desire washing over him in waves had further challenged his ability to listen. Holding Cameron's hands had at least given Terrence something to do that had freed up the part of his brain obsessed with touching Cameron enough to focus on his words.

The lilt of Cameron's husky voice had been a siren's song from which Terrence couldn't escape, drawing him in with each uttered word. His head kept telling him to slow down until he got to know Cameron better. His heart wanted more time—time they didn't have—to figure out if lust, love, or something else drove his desire.

His doleful confession had touched Terrence. Seeing his expression change from hopeless to unbelieving and then to elated had sealed the deal. He'd do whatever he could to help him. At least they'd have a little time together, but how Cameron would escape and what form Terrence's help might take remained a mystery.

The obvious solution was for Cameron to leave New York. He'd need money, a new name with appropriate identification, and maybe a couple of letters of reference to help him get a job. Nothing the foundation couldn't handle.

But where could he go? Cameron had no particular place in mind and had said he was willing to go anywhere he'd be safe. That narrowed things down a lot. Close by would be convenient—someplace between New York and DC—so Terrence could visit now and then. But a nearby town was unlikely. Cameron wanted as much distance as possible from Frankie and his band of not-so-merry men.

Terrence wasn't sure if the reach of the Mafia extended outside Chicago and New York, or whether the different factions cooperated or competed with each other. He'd heard tales of power struggles and, judging from the level of violence involved, suspected minimal cooperation between the families.

Wherever Cameron went, going with him was out of the question. Graduating from an Ivy League college was Terrence's number-one priority. He couldn't let anything or anyone knock him off course, not even Cameron. Besides, they'd only just met. They needed more time to get to know each other for a decision like running off together.

How long did they have before anyone noticed Cameron was gone? Hours? Maybe days? He knew they didn't have a week.

Two paddy wagons sped by, turning onto Christopher Street. Everyone was heading in the same direction. Some even ran. Terrence quickened his pace and when he reached the corner, joined everyone else running toward the domed red lights spinning atop three squad cars parked in front of the Stonewall Inn.

More than a hundred bystanders stood in the street, blocking traffic. His first thought was a fight—a big fight, judging from the chaotic scene before him. Petty squabbles sometimes turned violent, but this looked to be more than a tiff over a cheating boyfriend or a snatched wig.

The paddy wagons crept toward the Stonewall Inn behind baton-wielding police who shoved onlookers out of the way. Terrence searched for Harold and Abigail but saw no sign of them as he worked his way through the throng toward the club's entrance.

Despite anger at the police presence, the atmosphere was more in line with a block party or street fair. Half a dozen drag queens marched down the sidewalk, arm in arm, singing, "We just wanna cum" to the tune of the popular protest song. Bystanders yelled encouragement and roared with laughter.

Terrence stopped a few feet from the front edge of the crowd. Rather than a fight, a raid explained the police presence. Several police blocked the door and kept the onlookers at bay. Getting inside to look for Harold and Abigail wasn't an option. They would be fine. No need to worry. Kreema and Kelsey would look out for them until the cops let them go.

The crowd roared its approval as the police escorted the handcuffed employees to the paddy wagon. Terrence wondered how long they'd stay in jail. Having Cameron's boss locked up was an unexpected stroke of good luck that might give them more time.

The double doors opened again, expelling a handful of flame queens onto the sidewalk. They took advantage of their moment in the spotlight to wave and blow kisses, eliciting roars of approving laughter, before fading into the crowd. Terrence was glad to see they'd been released. Abigail and Harold wouldn't be far behind them.

Every few minutes a few more people came out of the club. Each new wave of freed patrons camped it up to the delight of an ever-growing crowd of curious residents and tourists. The noise of the boisterous revelers was enough to wake all but the soundest of sleepers. Apartment-dwellers leaned from windows and fire escapes to see what was happening below. Futile requests for quiet went unheard or were met with invitations to join the party.

A group who'd been inside the club joined their friends a few feet from Terrence. He edged closer to eavesdrop on their conversation.

"Betty Badge tore down the bar and ripped out all the benches."

"Looks like Patty Pig is confiscating the jukeboxes along with all the booze. They're even taking the cigarette machine."

The news disturbed him as much as everyone else who'd heard. This didn't appear to be the standard, run-of-the-mill raid. Sending cops into a place on a Saturday was unusual enough. Tearing things up was unprecedented, as far as he knew. Terrence tapped a thin blond boy who'd come out of the club on the shoulder. "Excuse me. Did you see a guy about your size in mustard-colored shorts with a tall blonde girl inside?"

"Yeah, I think so," he replied. "They were dancing with Kreema before the raid, but I haven't seen them since the cops rounded up all the drag queens."

News of the destruction and rough treatment by police spread through the street like wildfire. Terrence couldn't imagine Harold or Abigail attracting the attention of the police, but anything was possible. The thought of something happening to either of his charges filled Terrence with dread.

The doors opened again, and Terrence heard a familiar voice cry out. "Police brutality!"

CHAPTER THIRTY-SIX

BESIDES THE cash Cameron had managed to stuff into the mattress over the years and the clothes on his back, he thought about what else he might take with him. His electric fan? No—too hard to carry. The few clothes Cameron had worth taking and a pair of tennis shoes left plenty of room in the brown paper shopping bag for his wind-up alarm clock. Even after wrapping the timepiece in a pair of blue jeans, he could still hear the monotonous but comforting tick.

The life savings he'd invested in Seedy Mattress & Trust amounted to a little less than three hundred dollars. He divvied up the money, putting some in his wallet, more in the secret compartment in his belt, and the rest in the bottom of each of the boots he wore. He looked around his shabby room one last time, closed the door behind him, and descended the steps toward the street.

Exhilaration replaced the fear he'd felt earlier. He didn't know which excited him more, his freedom—however long it might last—or seeing Terrence again. He'd sat on Terrence's bed and stared into those hazel eyes, fearing what might happen with even a glance at his pouty lips, the happy trail that beckoned from his flat belly, or the halo of abundant curls framing his beautiful face.

Terrence's success since he'd left the street gave Cameron hope. Maybe he could go to college too. Or attend a trade school, perhaps become a carpenter or a stonemason. After tearing so many lives apart, the idea of building things he could stand back and admire when he'd finished appealed to him.

He owed a tremendous debt of gratitude to Kreema Dee Kropp. Since making her acquaintance, his life had changed in unexpected ways. She'd been his salvation. Cameron wasn't sure how, but she'd also brought him and Terrence together. He would never wear a wig, a dress, and high-heel shoes, but wherever he ended up, he'd never look down on drag queens again.

When he rounded the corner onto Christopher Street, flashing red lights in front of the Stonewall Inn stopped him in his tracks. The jeering crowd spilling out into the street and into the nearby park made the hairs on the back of his neck stand up. Aside from the annual Thanksgiving

Parade, he'd never seen so many people in one place, especially in Greenwich Village. He broke into a run, his eyes seeking the blond curls that would indicate Terrence's location.

Cameron trotted through the park but saw no sign of him. After stashing the paper sack containing all his worldly possessions under a shrub, he scanned the crowd again and saw Terrence's curls moving through the mob toward the epicenter of the action—the brick arch marking the entrance to the Stonewall Inn. He hesitated. Coming so close to the club, even during a raid, was risky business. He was supposed to be working the Hilton and knew Frankie would not be happy to find him here.

The doors opened and cheers erupted as several police officers steered the club's employees into the waiting patrol wagon. Frankie and his goons went first, followed by the rest of the staff who, like Cameron, were employed by the mob, but were not Mafioso. Seeing his employer in handcuffs made his day. He knew Frankie wouldn't stay behind bars long, but his arrest and the raid were a welcome diversion, buying him at least a couple of extra hours.

With the blond curls for his beacon, Cameron moved through the restless sea of people who had gathered to behold the spectacle. As he maneuvered through the throng, he overheard bits and pieces of angry conversation. Yes, the police had raided the Stonewall Inn, but this time, they'd taken things too far and were dismantling the shabby interior. Aside from the structure itself, everything in the building but the jukeboxes and the toilets had been constructed of cheap plywood, painted black.

Four street kids came out the door and, after taking in the sizeable audience gathered on the streets, launched into a cancan that made Cameron think of the Rockettes. They linked arms and kicked their legs high in the air, to the delight of the cheering crowd, before taking a bow and disappearing into the mass on the street.

The door opened again, and Cameron heard Kreema's unmistakable voice. "Police brutality! Let go of me, motherfucker!"

His heart caught in his throat. He stared at the entrance and gasped when Kreema came through the door, surrounded by cops. She broke loose from her captors and, when one of them lunged for her, swung her bag in a wide arc, knocking him to the ground.

Three officers who'd been guarding the door rushed her, beating her across the head and shoulders with nightsticks. Cameron heard thuds as they pummeled her with their batons. A lady cop managed to secure Kreema's flailing arms with handcuffs. They surrounded her, carrying her between them like pallbearers at a funeral toward the open door of the patrol wagon.

"Police brutality!" she screamed, writhing and kicking as her captors edged closer to the waiting paddy wagon. "Help!"

Cameron tried to move faster, but the press of the crowd slowed him down. He watched in horror as Terrence jumped onto the back of one of men holding her. Two of the uniformed officers leaped on him, pounding him with their batons until he fell onto the sidewalk.

The rough treatment from the cops elicited boos and catcalls from the onlookers. The cops dumped Kreema in the paddy wagon and retreated back through the entrance to the club, leaving Terrence's crumpled form on the sidewalk and the taunting crowd to the uniformed officers who stood guard.

People near the paddy wagon pounded and pushed on the sides, shouting, "Turn it over!" Everyone close by pushed, causing the paddy wagon to rock back and forth. The police shoved half a dozen more drag queens into the back of the truck and slammed the doors shut. The driver, fear evident on his face, crept the vehicle forward as police used batons to clear the way to let it pass.

Another cry rang out. "Coppers for the cops!" Pennies bounced off the side as the paddy wagon moved forward. A beer can slid across the windshield, spewing its contents down the front of the truck. Someone yelled, "Gay power!" A few echoed the phrase, until a loud "Slap them silly, girls!" from the back of the mob caused everyone to laugh.

Cameron surged forward, shoving people out of his way as he made for the sidewalk where Terrence had gone down. As he neared, coins and pieces of trash that fell short of their intended target struck those standing in the front of the crowd. He put his hands up to protect his head and pushed on, earning nasty looks and a few ugly comments from the boys who stood between him and where he believed Terrence to be.

He reached the edge of the crowd and saw Terrence, sitting up on the sidewalk in the no-man's-land between the crowd and the baton-wielding cops. Cameron ran the last few steps, kneeled down beside him, and put his hand on Terrence's arm. "Hey, I'm here. Are you okay?"

CHAPTER THIRTY-SEVEN

HAROLD HELD Abigail's hand as a defiant Kelsey continued her standoff with the plainclothes cop who'd ordered her to leave. They stood glaring at each other for a long moment before the officer grabbed her elbow and shoved her hard. "Put your hands on the wall and spread your legs," he barked.

She scowled but did as he'd asked. He patted her down, starting with her ankles. Kelsey stared straight ahead, passive and compliant, as he worked his way up her body, even enduring his inappropriate touching on her legs and rear end. But when he groped her breasts, she whipped around and punched him in the face, bloodying his nose.

Abigail screamed when several officers swarmed Kelsey, striking her about the head with batons. Harold watched the assault, thinking he should do something, feeling like he might throw up. Terrence would never just stand by. Harold thought about kicking somebody in the groin, but before he could act, four of the thuggish police dragged her, writhing and kicking, out the door.

Hitting a woman—even if she was more masculine than most of the guys in the room would ever be—had enraged those who still waited to have their identification checked. A hawk-nosed man who seemed to be in charge came inside, said something to the cops still checking identification, and the three of them ran out the door. Harold looked around the front room but saw no police—in uniforms or plainclothes—anywhere in sight.

He was scared. Except for Marty, he didn't know anyone still inside the club. Abigail grabbed his hand, and Harold realized she expected him to take charge. If only he had some idea of what they should do.

Kreema and Kelsey had promised everyone would be fine. Seeing the brutality they'd suffered at the hands of the police that Philip had always said to trust frightened Harold. He put his arm around a sobbing Abigail, trying to reassure her despite his own fear and uncertainty about what was going to happen to them.

A harried officer came back inside and addressed the thirty or so people still waiting in line to have their identification checked. "Okay, you're free to go."

Cheers rang out as the last patrons moved toward the entryway. Cases of beer had been stacked near the door along with several boxes filled with bottles of booze. Even the jukeboxes had been pushed closer to the exit, an act that had further riled those still waiting inside. The front room bar and built-in seating around the perimeter had been reduced to scrap lumber, and Harold suspected the same was true for the back room.

"Come on," Marty said, taking Harold by the hand and leading him and a still-sobbing Abigail to the club's entrance.

The scene outside was unlike anything Harold had ever seen before. He stopped to take in the chaos. Hundreds of people filled the street. The sound of their shouting mixed with breaking glass from bottles and rocks hurled at the building. An alarm clock hit the sidewalk a few feet from where he stood and shattered into pieces. The police kept the angry crowd away from the entrance with batons. The mob yelled obscenities at the police, calling them pigs and pelting them with rocks, bricks, and pieces of trash.

"Follow me," Marty said. He guided them along the front of the building, away from the beleaguered police and the belligerent mass filling the streets.

Harold hurried along behind him, half dragging a hiccupping Abigail in his wake. He looked around for Terrence but didn't see him. Marty led the way past the crowded street, skirted the back edge of the mob, and stopped in the park where Harold and Abigail had first encountered Kreema Dee Kropp. Harold looked back and saw a handful of police fighting a sea of waving arms pushing them even closer to the club's entrance.

"Can you believe it? The tables are turned." Marty laughed. "Tonight the fags are roughing up the cops."

Harold didn't know what to think. The crowd's anger frightened him, but the inability of the police to maintain law and order scared him even more. The few officers still fighting outside the Stonewall Inn couldn't hold out much longer. What would happen in a world where the cops lose?

A couple of guys picked up a big metal garbage can and ran with it toward the Stonewall Inn. They stopped a few feet from the building and heaved the metal container into the window, shattering the glass. The trash can, somehow, remained suspended in the window. Bystanders picked through the contents strewn on the ground, flinging the heavier pieces at the police.

The police continued to retreat, backing up a few steps at a time as the crowd pressed forward. A roar of approval accompanied the departing squad cars and paddy wagons. The police who'd cleared the way for the vehicles joined the handful of cops left guarding the entrance, giving up more ground until they defended only the double doors of the entrance. A brick sailed through the air, striking one of the officers in the shoulder. The hawk-nosed man yelled something Harold couldn't hear, and the officers backed up into the club and closed the double doors behind them.

The crowd in the streets went wild. Those close enough surged forward, recycling the bricks and stones on the sidewalk to beat on doors and the plywood-covered windows. He couldn't imagine what the din must sound like to the cops trapped inside.

Harold wanted to cry but knew if he did, Abigail would fall apart. He jammed his hands into his pockets so she and Marty wouldn't see how much they were shaking and gaped at the scene before him.

"Come on," Marty said, tugging his elbow. "Follow me."

CHAPTER THIRTY-EIGHT

TERRENCE'S HEAD hurt from the licks the police had given him, but otherwise, as far as he could tell, he was okay. He allowed Cameron to help him up, and they headed back to the relative safety of the angry crowd. "Did you see the way they were beating her?" Terrence rubbed the back of his head. "I just reacted." The hand he wiped across his mouth came back bloody. "One of these days I'll learn that mixing up with the cops never ends well."

Cameron pulled a wadded-up handkerchief from his pocket and dabbed Terrence's lip. "Figures. I finally meet a guy I want to kiss and he gets a fat lip."

The double doors opened again, and a quartet of men manhandled another fighter toward the open back doors of a squad car.

"Kelsey!" He took a step toward her, but Cameron grabbed his arm to keep him from running to her aid. "Let me go!"

Cameron didn't let go. "Remember what you said about taking on the cops."

Kelsey fought the police every step of the way. They wrestled her into the squad car, but she slid across the seat and jumped out the other side before they could close the door. She ran a few steps, but the police fell on her and the battle was on again.

Cries of "Let her go!" and "Leave her alone!" erupted from the spectators. Kelsey fought for all she was worth, punching, kicking, and head-butting until one of the cops clubbed her with a nightstick. Terrence felt Cameron's grip tighten on his arm. Before she could recover from the glancing blow, the brute shoved her hard toward the open door of the squad car.

As the police struggled to get her into the car, she broke free from her captors again. She scanned the crowd, and Terrence could see she was scared. She saw him standing with Cameron and said, "Do something!"

The officers renewed their attack, clobbering her with nightsticks. Between the fear he'd seen on her face and her desperate plea, Terrence couldn't stand by another minute. He wasn't going to watch his friend get her ass kicked. He disengaged from Cameron's grasp and joined the fray, kicking one of her assailants in the groin, causing him to double over in pain. He leapt onto the back of another, wrapping an arm around his adversary's neck and fighting for control of the baton he wielded with the other.

The crowd surged forward, yelling "Pigs!" and "Police brutality!" A deluge of coins rained down on them as they fought. Terrence grunted from the force of a blow to his back. He glanced back and saw Cameron, fists raised like a prizefighter, as he took on Terrence's attacker.

Hands on his shoulders and in the waistband of his pants wrested him from the cop's back and tossed him to the sidewalk with a thud that knocked the breath out of him. Batons and boots struck him several times. Fighting for air, Terrence raised his arms to his head and curled into a fetal position to minimize the damage.

When the beating ceased, he opened his eyes as the police shoved a bloodied Kelsey into the backseat of the squad car. They slammed the door closed, and as the car drove off, the two men turned their attention to the cop struggling with Cameron.

Nightsticks in hand, they moved toward Cameron, who still wrestled with the cop who had jumped Terrence. Cameron held him from behind in a bear hug, rendering his baton useless. Terrence rose to his knees to help, grimacing from the stab of pain that shot through his ribcage, and a few seconds later tried to stand.

Onlookers tossed more coins, empty cans, and anything else they could find at the exiting car with Kelsey inside. A large cobblestone bounced off the trunk of the last remaining squad car with a booming thud and the screech of stone against metal. The noise drew the attention of all the police gathered around the entrance. The vehicle moved forward on flattened tires beneath a barrage of debris flung by the mob.

Having been freed from Cameron's grasp, Terrence's attacker had joined forces with his rescuers to pummel Cameron with batons. A man in a suit issued an order Terrence couldn't hear. Cameron's foes released him, shoving him into the crowd, and then backed up closer to the entrance of the club as the crowd roared its approval.

Cameron knelt beside Terrence. "Are you okay?"

Terrence nodded, wincing as Cameron helped him to his feet. "I think so." Moving slowly, Cameron put his arm around Terrence to help him up. He cried out in pain. "My ribs hurt like hell."

The deluge of flying objects continued to rain on the handful of cops waving batons at anyone who got too close to the double doors. A brick bounced off one of the cop's shoulders, and another right behind it narrowly missed his head.

The man in the suit yelled, "Get inside!" The handful of police still on the street retreated into the club and closed the double doors behind them.

LESS THAN a block from the front doors of the Stonewall Inn, Terrence and Cameron waited to use the pay phone. Nobody wanted to miss any of the excitement, so the line moved fast as friends who'd stayed home or retired early for the evening were called and summoned to the scene on Christopher Street.

Cameron waited outside the booth while Terrence called Philip at the hotel for the fourth time in the last ninety minutes. The glass wall between Terrence and the street did little to dampen the sound of the mob chanting "gay power!" as they hurled whatever they could find at the twin brick arches. While Terrence waited for the hotel operator to put his call through, a bunch of kids rocked a parking meter back and forth until the device broke free from the concrete.

He didn't have to wait for the operator to come back on the line for another message. Philip answered on the second ring.

CHAPTER THIRTY-NINE

A FLASHING red glow illuminated the dark hotel room. Philip flipped on the light and saw the blinking dome on the telephone indicating a message waiting for him. He dialed the hotel switchboard.

"Yes, Mr. Potter, I have three messages for you."

Phillip's knees went weak and he sat on the edge of the bed. Something was wrong. He reached for the notepad and pen beside the telephone. "Go ahead."

"Clarence called at twelve forty-five. He said to stay at the hotel, and he'd be there as soon as he could."

Clarence? She must mean Terrence. "And the second?"

"Lawrence called at one fifteen and said for you to meet him at his apartment."

Philip detected a note of disapproval in her voice. Now he was sure she meant Terrence. He took a deep breath and tried to keep the irritation from creeping into his voice. "And the last?"

"Terrence called at one thirty and said to meet him outside the Stonewall Inn." She snickered. "Said it was urgent."

He thought about asking for her name so he could speak to the management about the errors in her messages and her condescending tone, but he didn't have time. Terrence had left his last message more than an hour earlier. "Thank you, you've been more than kind."

A lot more, he thought as he slammed the handset into the cradle. The telephone rang right away. Until it rang again, he thought his slam had jangled the ringer. If the operator was calling him back to fuss about his forceful hang up…. "Hello?"

"Where the hell have you been? I've been calling all night."

"I'm sorry, Terrence. We stopped and had a drink after the show. What's going on?"

George stood behind him, massaging his shoulders. Philip held the phone away from his ear so George could hear.

"The police raided the Stonewall Inn tonight, all hell's broke loose around here, and Harold and Abigail are still inside."

Philip heard chanting in the background but couldn't make out the words. "How did you get out without them?"

"I wasn't inside when the police came. I'll tell you about that part when you get here." The sound of breaking glass came through the phone, followed by the angry roar of a crowd.

"What's going on, Terrence?"

"The cops have retreated inside the Stonewall. A bunch of kids are pounding the entrance with a parking meter they ripped out of the ground."

Philip looked at George, who was already putting his shoes on. "We'll be there as fast as we can."

HEADS TURNED as Philip and George ran through the lobby, sliding a bit on the terrazzo flooring as they rounded the corner and bolted through the glass doors of the hotel entrance. Seeing no taxis waiting for fares, they hurried toward the curb, waving at the yellow vehicles speeding by. Dozens passed without even slowing down before one pulled up to the curb in front of them.

"The Stonewall Inn on Christopher Street," Philip said as he slid across the seat. George followed, slamming the door shut behind him.

"No can do," the driver said. "Dispatch just issued a warning to stay clear of the area." He reached down and set the meter. "They haven't warned us away from an area that size since the commie students fought with police at Columbia University."

Philip and George exchanged glances. George leaned forward. "Well, get us as close as you can," he said. "And hurry!"

"The homos must really be up to something big," the driver said, pulling away from the curb into traffic. "That's all that lives around there, ya know." He nodded. "Hippies and homos."

Commies, hippies, and homos? Indeed. Philip wanted to slap the bumbling idiot on the back of his head, but fighting with a cab driver served no purpose, particularly in light of how long hailing one had taken. Besides, Philip was angry with Terrence for leaving Abigail and Harold. The poor driver was just a convenient target.

"I'm sure they'll be fine," George said, placing a hand on Philip's knee and squeezing.

"I hope you're right," Philip said, pulling a handkerchief from his pocket to dry his sweaty palms. "If anything happens to them...."

"Nothing will happen to them," George said. "Terrence can take care of himself, and Harold is tougher than he looks."

But Philip could tell George was every bit as anxious as he was. They rode in silence, somehow managing to hit every red light on Seventh Avenue. At West Tenth Street, the driver pulled the cab over to the curb. "This is as close as I can get," he said. "Sorry."

Philip threw open the door and stepped onto the street as George paid the fare. He was about to ask the driver for directions when he heard the clamor coming from south of where they stood. They hurried down Seventh Avenue toward the frightening sounds of violence that echoed through the narrow streets.

The closer they got, the more alarmed Philip became. Breaking glass punctuated the loud, angry cries of a large and unruly mob. Panting, with sweat pouring from his face, Philip rounded the corner onto Christopher Street and came to such an abrupt stop that George crashed into him.

A blazing bottle sailed through the air, shattering against the exterior of the besieged Stonewall Inn before bursting into flames. Bricks, more flaming bottles, and other projectiles fell like fiery hail. Most struck the club and had been lobbed by someone in the street, but many of the nonflaming variety came from open windows in nearby buildings and were directed at the crowd.

Philip searched the terrifying panorama for Terrence, Harold, and Abigail but saw no sign of them. "What should we do?"

George studied the scene before them. "I don't see any police at all, do you?"

"Not one." Philip scanned the crowd again. "Just a bunch of angry kids."

"A bunch?" George gazed out over the rampaging mass. "Hundreds is more like it—maybe even a thousand."

Philip nodded, his eyes still searching the crowd for familiar faces. "I never thought I'd see the day…."

George nodded. "From what the guys at Julius's said, the pressure has been building for weeks."

"We can't just stand here and watch," Philip said, wringing his hands.

"No, we can't." George surveyed the scene before them again. "Let's stick to the back of the crowd and see if we can find our kids."

CHAPTER FORTY

HANKS AND several very rattled officers came back into the club, closed the heavy wooden doors behind them, and threw the bolt.

"Grab what you can and barricade the doors and windows," Hanks said.

Liana pushed a table toward the entrance. She didn't know what to think. Breaking glass and the sound of heavy objects striking the boards covering the shattered windows echoed through the nearly empty club. In addition to her and Hanks, inside were the three members of the team from federal and state agencies, Christie, four plainclothes cops, and a man she didn't know who she'd heard was a reporter. The din from outside was deafening.

"This is Hanks." He spoke into a portable radio. "We need backup at the Stonewall Inn, yesterday!"

Instead of confirming the order, through the static, a voice said, "Disregard that call."

"Disregard?" Hanks glared at the device. "Officers are under attack. Send every available officer to the Stonewall Inn!"

"Disregard that call."

Hanks tossed the radio across the room—an act of frustration that frightened Liana. They were trapped inside a seamy Mafia-owned club for fairies with nothing but thin sheets of cheap lumber separating them from the raging homos outside.

He picked up the office telephone, raised it to his ear, and pounded on the base to get a dial tone. "Dammit. The lines have been cut."

The intermittent roaring of the crowd and the constant thud of heavy objects striking the plywood propelled Liana and the others into action. The team members trapped inside hurried around the club, adding anything they could find to the growing pile of tables, chairs, and pieces of wood separating them from the angry mob.

Christie edged toward the window and leaned over to peer through a crack between two boards. "Jesus Christ! How many are out there?"

"Hundreds," Hanks replied. "Maybe even a thousand, with more coming all the time like swarming hornets."

A loud boom echoed through the club. A moment later, another followed, louder than the first, causing the double doors to rattle on their hinges.

"Can you see what's going on out there?" Hanks asked.

Christie peered through the crack, jumping back as a bottle smashed against the plywood. "They're using something as a battering ram." She peered through the gap. "Shit! Looks like a parking meter."

The plainclothes officers ran to the entrance and leaned their shoulders into the door to keep the marauders from gaining entry. Every time the force of the assault caused the double doors to swing open, through a shower of bricks, bottles, and cobblestones, the men guarding the entrance pushed back, somehow managing to slam them shut again.

The lumber covering the window frames shook with the impact of projectiles flung from the street and began to splinter in places. Although she was terrified, Liana maintained her composure. Sweat from the heat and the adrenaline coursing through her veins covered her skin and soaked the clothing she wore.

A bottle crashed against the plywood and flames licked through the splintered lumber. The double doors burst open again, and another fiery bottle sailed inside, exploding into yellow-tipped blue flames.

Liana ran for a firebox she remembered seeing on the wall in the back room. Fearing that adding water to the fuel would just make things worse, she opted for the fire extinguisher rather than the coiled hose. She pulled the pin, aimed the device at the burning plywood, and squeezed the handle, launching a cloud of white powder to smother the flames.

As the protestors continued lobbing Molotov cocktails, Liana blasted the flames, but soon the fire extinguisher was empty. Hanks dragged the hose to the front of the building and doused the smoking plywood. Liana was relieved to see the flames die down.

The next time the doors opened, Hanks stood waiting with the hose. He leveled the stream at the combatants, but the flow, while sufficient to put out the fires, had no effect on those who tried to enter the club. The men shouldered the doors closed again, and the relentless pounding resumed.

The incessant cacophony wore on the nerves of everyone inside. Liana had never been in such a tense situation and wondered how much longer they could hold out. She pulled the pistol from her vest pocket, but the weight of the weapon in her hand did little to calm her nerves. She glanced around and saw the reporter holding a red fire axe. Everyone else aimed pistols at the thundering plywood.

"Don't shoot!" Hanks yelled, pistol in hand. "Fire without my order and you're in big trouble." He walked over to Liana and touched her shoulder. "You doing okay, Liana?"

"Yes, sir," she replied.

Hanks moved around the room, putting a hand on Christie and each of the men, calling them by name to calm them. His words and reassuring touch made a difference.

Everyone kept their weapons out, but the tension in the room eased a bit.

Shooting someone wouldn't help and would likely make things worse. They were so outnumbered, sooner or later—no matter how many they managed to stop with gunfire—they'd be overwhelmed.

"You." Hanks pointed at the men shouldering the double doors. "Keep doing what you're doing. The rest of you, fan out and see if you can find another way out of this place."

Liana knew the double doors were the only way in or out of the club, but she followed orders, returning to the back room to look around. The axe-wielding stranger pointed to a vent in the ceiling. "Where do you think that goes?"

"Salvatore," Hanks barked. "Think you can squeeze through?"

"I'll give it a try, sir."

Two men hoisted her onto their shoulders. She pushed, and after a moment of resistance, the grid covering the vent moved. She slid the cover to the side and peered inside. "Looks like I can get out onto the roof, sir."

"Good," Hanks said. "There's a firehouse a block away where you can call for reinforcements. Go across the roof and see if you can find a way down. Stay the hell away from Christopher Street!"

"Yes, sir." The opening was almost too small, but she managed to wiggle her way into the shaft and began crawling through the dust and grime. The rusty screen covering the opening gave way, and she scrabbled onto the roof.

Hanks's caution to avoid Christopher Street was unnecessary. The enraged mob was deterrent enough. She stared, mesmerized for a moment by the crush of people. The scope of the situation hadn't been apparent from inside. She'd never seen anything like the seething, bottle-tossing mob. Moving toward the back of the building, she stayed low to avoid detection and scanned the alley for a way down.

CHAPTER FORTY-ONE

Marty's hand in his was reassuring, offering more comfort than Harold would have expected possible from a near-stranger's touch. The hair-raising scene around the club frightened him and changed his mind about getting arrested. Were it not for Marty, Harold didn't know where he and Abigail might be or what they would have done.

Pale, with rivulets of mascara trailing down her cheeks, Abigail had stopped crying and, despite the heat, stood shivering, clutching Harold's hand. "Do you think Kreema and Kelsey are okay?"

Harold hoped so but didn't know how to answer. The brutality of the New York cops had shocked him. He'd always thought of the police as allies—someone to turn to for protection. He'd never forget the way they had treated his new friends, who, as far as he could tell, had done nothing wrong. Not until they were provoked, anyway.

"They're both pretty tough," Marty replied. "I don't think they were hurt too bad."

Harold wasn't so sure. The sickening thud of nightsticks against flesh had left an indelible impression. The violence horrified him, and he knew the images would haunt his dreams for years to come.

A stream of water arching from the Stonewall Inn's double doors caught the crowd's attention. People close to the front got soaked and, for a time, splashed around like children playing in a sprinkler. As hot as it was, Harold wished he were close enough to join the guys frolicking in the water.

A gang of boys using a parking meter as a battering ram, having failed to breach the doors, refocused their assault on the wood covering the window on the west side of the club. The crowd had grown so large that those in the front fell victim to flying projectiles tossed from behind. People left the scene holding bloody shirts to wounds to stem the bleeding as still more protesters arrived and joined the fray. Residents leaned out apartment windows to watch. Many threw bottles and other objects at the crowd, their demands for a little peace and quiet unheard by the raging mass.

The absence of police in the area was striking and unsettling. The mob had the upper hand now. The guys wielding the parking meter broke through the plywood-covered window as another group pushed through the double doors. They scooped up the trash that had been flung at the club, tossing the refuse through the breaches, while others doused the garbage with lighter fluid. When the volatile debris ignited, flames leapt up the front of the building and clouds of smoke billowed skyward.

Above the roar of the rioters, Harold heard a distant wail. "Do you hear that?"

"Hear what?" Marty asked.

Harold cupped his hand to his ear and tried to tune out the crowd. "Sirens."

"Yeah, I hear them," Abigail replied.

"Every cop in New York will be here soon," Marty said. "Come on, we need to scram before they show up and really bust some heads."

THE SIRENS originated from a pair of fire engines circling the block, seeking a way to the burning club through the uncooperative crowd packing the streets. By the time Harold, Marty, and Abigail reached the park, more police had arrived on Christopher Street and were clearing the way for the firefighters to get close enough to the Stonewall Inn to battle the blaze.

The three of them stood with Harold in the middle, holding hands and staring at the scene before them. Dark smoke billowed from the flame-filled windows as onlookers chanted, "Gay power!" Bricks and other flying objects pelted the building.

"There you are!"

Harold turned toward the voice and saw the young blond man with the bad haircut who Marty had provided with identification. Marty dropped Harold's hand and addressed his friend. "I've been looking for you, Dwayne."

"Can you believe it?" The blond-haired boy pulled a dozen or so wallets out of his shirt. "Great night for picking pockets."

Marty and his friend must be homeless. Terrence had told him stories about the things he'd done to survive on the streets. Stealing had kept him from starving, with well-heeled tourists being a favored target. Until Terrence handed it back to him, grinning from ear to ear, Harold had never noticed his own wallet was gone in the more than fifty times Terrence had demonstrated his skill.

"Who's this?" Dwayne gave Harold a quick once-over and a pointed look.

"Harold and his friend," Marty said, shoving his hands deep into the pockets of his shorts. He studied the ground and kicked a scuffed-up shoe against the sidewalk. "They're visiting from Washington, DC."

"Hi, I'm Abigail." She let go of Harold and offered the blond boy her hand, keeping a firm grip on her purse with the other.

Ignoring her proffered hand, Dwayne looked her up and down. Then he grabbed Marty by the hand. "Come on, before the crowd breaks up."

Marty gave Harold an embarrassed look. "I gotta go."

"Nice to meet you," Harold said through the lump in his throat. "Thanks for looking out for us."

"Yeah," Abigail said. "Thanks."

Dwayne scolded Marty as they rejoined the crowd. Harold had no idea why he felt sick to his stomach, and he didn't want to admit how upset he was that Marty had abandoned them for the blond pickpocket.

Abigail took his hand and squeezed. "Dwayne isn't half as cute as you are."

Harold wasn't sure he agreed but didn't say so.

She squeezed his hand again. "Now what do we do?"

"I don't know," Harold replied, shaking his head. He hadn't been afraid to explore the city with Abigail before, but now he feared for their safety. He scanned the area again for any sign of Terrence but didn't see him. "I guess we either find Terrence or return to the hotel."

"We could see if he's at his apartment," Abigail said, looking around.

"I don't know if I could find it again," Harold said. Other than the general vicinity of the Stonewall Inn, he had no idea where he was.

Abigail pulled a map from her purse and unfolded it. "We're on Grove Street." She studied the map for a moment, then looked up and pointed. "Terrence's apartment is that way."

"We have to go back through that crowd?"

Abigail nodded. "We could keep going this way and detour back around, but if Terrence was on his way back here, we'd miss him."

Harold preferred escaping the madness and returning to the hotel. But if he did, Terrence might spend the rest of the night wandering the streets in search of him. "Okay. Let's go to Terrence's apartment."

Abigail took his hand and headed back toward the melee. "We can stay on Grove Street to miss the worst of it."

The closer they got to the Stonewall Inn, the more certain Harold was they'd made a mistake. The smell of smoke, lighter fluid, and stale beer filled the air. A roiling sea of angry people filled the streets and sidewalks between where he and Abigail stood and the Stonewall Inn. That the anger was directed at the police holed up inside the club did little to lessen his anxiety about pressing forward. Every cell in his body screamed for him to flee, to run as fast as he could away from the noise and the flames and all the shouting.

Abigail grabbed his hand. "Come on. We'll stick to the back edge of the crowd as much as we can."

Harold followed behind her, still searching for Terrence. A bottle thrown from an upper floor shattered on the sidewalk, missing them by inches. More than anything, he wanted to cry, but crying wouldn't solve anything. He remembered Terrence's advice. *Put some starch in that wrist and act tough. If you're lucky, nobody will ever know you're faking.* He crossed his fingers, held his head up high, and tried not to think about what could happen.

CHAPTER FORTY-TWO

THE ROAR of the mob ebbed and flowed, punctuated by shattering glass and loud crashes as flying objects struck the Stonewall Inn and fell onto the sidewalk. Whenever someone jostled or bumped him, Terrence cried out from the searing pain in his chest. Cameron steered them through the burgeoning throng, protecting him as best he could, but with so many people crowded together, contact was hard to avoid.

Keeping a hand over the top of his head to fend off bricks, bottles, and other projectiles that fell short of their target, Terrence grabbed a belt loop on the back of Cameron's pants and followed as close as he could behind him. Thirty or forty kids—mostly flame queens and street hustlers—antagonized the police, getting close enough to lob rocks, bottles, and insults before disappearing into the crowd.

Fans cheered the marauding queens as detractors cursed them from windows and fire escapes overlooking the action. Concern about friends who'd been carted off by the police or who still remained inside the club motivated many to stick around. Others who'd been inside also lingered, joined by passersby who stopped to see what was going on and the friends who'd been called from one of the many pay phones in the area.

Terrence searched for Philip and George but wasn't tall enough to see over the surging sea of people gathered in front of the Stonewall Inn. He didn't look forward to facing Philip. He'd be disappointed Terrence had abandoned Harold and Abigail. Terrence's anger with the police for the raid and their rough treatment of Kreema and Kelsey was surpassed only by his anger at himself for having let Philip down. Whatever happened to Harold or Abigail was on Terrence.

And what about Cameron and his predicament? Since leaving a mother nobody could save, Terrence had devoted a considerable amount of time to rescuing—and falling for—men who needed him.

He winced as a blond-haired street urchin brushed up against him. The risk of falling victim to friendly fire had diminished as they moved farther away from the club. Terrence lowered his left arm to brace his chest and held on to the belt loop with his right hand as Cameron pressed forward, reaching out now and then to shield Terrence from anyone coming too close.

Of course, of the men Terrence had loved, only Danny Bradbury from his time at the shelter had fallen in love with him. He sighed. No matter what Philip said, if Terrence had gone along the night Danny was murdered instead of staying in to watch television, Danny would still be alive today. And if Danny had lived, Anthony Vincent wouldn't have been investigating his death, and he'd be alive too. Terrence had known Anthony was straight and, in light of the friendship they enjoyed in pursuit of Danny's killer, hadn't been too wounded by his persistent rejection of Terrence's advances.

If Danny and Anthony had lived, Terrence would never have met Philip Potter. Who wouldn't fall in love with the most kind-hearted and gentle man on the planet? Handsome and elegant George had been in love with Philip for as long as Terrence had known him. Seeing the two of them together now made Terrence happy.

Would Cameron be next?

Terrence sure hoped so. Never mind the complications life with him would entail. Could Terrence throw away everything he'd worked so hard to achieve, this close to reaching his goal? Philip's resounding "no!" echoed through his head, almost drowning out George's admonition to "follow your heart."

The crowd had thinned enough for Terrence to walk alongside Cameron. He glanced back, wincing in pain. Flames licked the front of the building and black plumes of smoke billowed skyward.

"Hang on a second," Cameron said, stopping. Terrence let go of his belt loop and Cameron stepped off the sidewalk. He reached under a shrub and pulled out an empty brown shopping bag. "Dammit! Somebody stole my clock."

A STOOP on Grove Street gave Terrence his first chance to gauge the size of the crowd. Between the Stonewall Inn and where he stood, hundreds of angry queers from all walks of life had united to take a stand. Unwilling to tolerate another minute of police harassment and brutality, queens of every variety, lesbians, and street hustlers fought alongside leathermen, bikers, and truckers from the docks. Seeing homosexuals standing up for themselves instead of running away filled his heart with pride.

The pain from his tender ribs wasn't the only thing preventing him from joining the fight. More important tasks demanded his attention, like finding Harold and Abigail safe and sound, preferably before running into Philip and George. He scanned the sea of heads filling the streets, sidewalks, and any open spaces but saw no sign of them.

"May as well stay here," Cameron said. "You're up high enough." He smiled. "Anyone you know should be able to spot that hair of yours now."

Between them, Terrence had taken the bigger beating. The searing pain in his chest suggested a few cracked or broken ribs. He had a fat lip, angry red welts across his arms and shoulders, and a raging headache from several small lumps on his head. By comparison Cameron had come through almost unscathed, complaining about bruised and bleeding knuckles, a dozen or so tender spots scattered about his body that would likely turn to ugly bruises, and a grape-sized knot on the back of his head.

Directly across from Terrence, a dozen baton-wielding police beat bystanders back from the burning club. Behind them, firemen carrying hoses connected to hydrants and pumper trucks doused the burning building. When the flames had been extinguished, they turned their hoses on the protestors, washing them away like leaves with a garden hose. To his left, busloads of police in riot gear formed a wedge that crept up Christopher Street toward Seventh Avenue.

A splash of color to his right caught Terrence's eye. He jerked his head around and saw Abigail in her loud culotte dress, waving at him. Beside her was the unmistakable mustard-clad form of Harold, who had also seen Terrence and was pointing him out to someone he couldn't see. Terrence looked closer and saw Philip and George hovering behind them. Terrence grabbed Cameron's shoulder and pointed. "There they are!" He jumped from the stoop, earning a sharp, instantaneous reminder of his damaged ribs.

Cameron again led the way and, in minutes, the six of them were standing together down from Sheridan Park on West Fourth Street, far from the ensuing clash with the riot squad.

Terrence, still bracing his rib cage, raised an arm as Harold and Philip approached to hug him, shaking his head.

Philip stopped and looked Terrence over. "Are you okay?"

Harold, Abigail, and George studied him too as they waited for his answer.

"Just a few bruises. Nothing serious. I'll live." Terrence ran a hand through Harold's hair and nodded at Cameron. "This is Cameron McKenzie. He needs our help."

CHAPTER FORTY-THREE

THE WARM embraces Cameron received from Mr. Potter and Mr. Walker, and, after Terrence had brought everyone up to speed on his situation, their assurance that everything would work out fine had surprised him. After believing nobody cared what happened to him for so long, to have stumbled across such a caring group when he most needed the support had to be a miraculous response to his fervent prayers.

Compared with Cameron's room at the boarding house, Terrence's apartment was spacious and luxurious, but six people crowded inside was at least three too many. Looking like the street kids who frequented the Stonewall Inn would look if they had the money, stylish Harold and his skinny girlfriend sat on the floor as Mr. Walker paced the few feet between them, from what Terrence called "the kitchen unit" to the side of the bed where Cameron sat with Terrence and Mr. Potter.

"Creating a new identity for you isn't a huge problem," Mr. Walker said, pausing to clear his throat. "Some trusted friends owe me a favor. Just tell me who you want to be and I'll arrange everything."

"Mark Jones," Cameron replied with no hesitation.

"Mark Jones?" Terrence scowled. "Are you kidding?" He shook his head. "You get a do-over with your name and you pick Mark Fucking Jones?"

"Terrence Bottom!" Mr. Potter thumped him on the head. "Watch your language!"

"I hadn't really planned on having a middle name," Cameron said, feeling his face grow hot when everybody laughed.

"When do you need to know?" Harold asked. "Give us an hour and we'll brainstorm some options."

Mr. Walker nodded. "We'll need that long to come up with a plan."

Terrence leaned over and pulled a spiral notebook from under the mattress. "I'll help. Harold, see if there's a pen in that top drawer." He slid off the bed, and the three of them put their heads together, whispering suggestions Cameron couldn't quite hear.

His head reeled as he thought about the decisions he needed to make. Just little stuff, like who he'd be for the rest of his life, where he would live, and what he'd do with himself. "Things are happening so fast."

"So far, the only thing that has happened is that you didn't go to work last night." Mr. Potter wrapped an arm around Cameron and gave him a reassuring hug. "Anything else is just talk of options and possibilities."

"Yes, first things first." Mr. Walker nodded. "We need to get you out of New York. Then you can worry about a new name and where you want to go." He massaged his temples. "Making all the arrangements will take several days." He looked at Cameron. "We'll find a place for you to stay in Washington while we work out all the details."

Mr. Potter turned to Cameron. "You can stay with Harold and me until everything gets sorted out. Your former employer will never look for you there."

"I...." Cameron's voice caught in his throat. "Gosh, I don't know what to say."

Terrence popped his head up. "Say yes, Mr. Denver Collins."

"Denver Collins?" Cameron laughed. "Are you serious? Sounds like a cocktail."

"Beats the hell out of Mark Jones," Terrence smirked.

Mr. Potter stroked his chin and stared at the ceiling. "Renting a car is the easiest way to get back to Washington."

"I'll call the place I use when I need a car in New York," Mr. Walker said, reaching for his wallet. He patted both hips, checked his front pockets, and the pocket on his shirt. "My wallet is gone!"

"Gone?" Mr. Potter asked. "Are you sure you haven't misplaced it?"

"I'm sure." He scratched his head. "Unless maybe it fell out of my pocket when I paid our tab at Julius's."

"Here, you can use my credit card," Mr. Potter said, reaching for his back pocket. He jumped up, patted all four pockets, and then looked to see if it had fallen on the bed.

Cameron stood up, but the wallet hadn't wiggled its way under him.

"Oh dear," Mr. Potter said. "Seems my wallet has also gone missing."

Terrence jumped up and patted his pockets. "Dammit! Mine's gone too."

"I bet Marty's friend, Dwayne, took them," Abigail said.

Harold nodded. "I bet he did too."

Harold and Abigail scrounged up almost twenty dollars between them, including a few coins Mr. Walker, Mr. Potter, and Terrence had found in their pockets. Cameron still had his wallet, probably thanks to Terrence holding on to his belt loop. He cleared his throat. "My wallet is still in my pocket." He patted his hip pocket. "I have about three hundred dollars."

"No." Mr. Potter shook his head. "Keep your money. The foundation will cover your moving and relocation expenses."

"The foundation?"

"Yeah," Terrence answered. "That's how I can afford to go to Columbia and live in my own apartment."

"We started the foundation several years ago," Mr. Walker said. "To help young men whose families abandoned them because of who they love."

"Oh." Cameron hung his head. "Then I wouldn't qualify. My family didn't abandon me. They died."

"I'm certain the board would approve an amendment to the rules," Mr. Potter said. He turned to Mr. Walker. "Aren't you?"

"That's mighty nice of you, Mr. Potter, but I couldn't ask you to go to all that trouble on my account." He shook his head. "Besides, we don't have that kind of time."

"Perhaps we should convene an emergency meeting of the board," Mr. Walker said.

"Yes," Mr. Potter agreed, nodding his head. "Do we have a quorum?"

Mr. Walker scanned the room. "Yes, two-thirds of the board is in attendance."

"Well, then," Mr. Potter said, clearing his throat. "I move the foundation add 'and those on the run from the Mafia' to our purpose statement. Is there a second?"

Mr. Walker raised his hand. "I second the motion."

"Excellent," Mr. Potter said. "All in favor?"

"Aye!"

"Any opposed?" He waited for a moment. "Very well, then, the motion carries. There being no further business on the agenda, this meeting is adjourned."

Cameron looked from Mr. Potter to Mr. Walker and then to Terrence. "What just happened here?"

"The board is comprised of myself, Philip, and my wife, Maxine."

"Wait." Cameron looked at Mr. Potter, and then back to Mr. Walker. "You're married?"

Mr. Walker glanced at Mr. Potter, who eyeballed the trio on the floor. "Yes. It's all rather complicated, really."

"What just happened," Mr. Potter said, turning to Cameron, "is that you now have the full support of the foundation." He extended his hand. "Congratulations."

Mr. Walker started pacing again. "Since Cameron can't be seen at the hotel—or anywhere, really—we'll make this our base of operations."

"Cozy," Terrence said, returning to his spot on the bed beside Cameron.

"Philip, I'll meet you back at the hotel as soon as I can. But first, I want to see what I can find out about your friends, Kreema Dee Kropp and Kelsey Ryan."

Cameron and Terrence stood by the door as everyone filed out. Mr. Potter brought up the rear. He started to hug Terrence but stopped. "I don't expect we'll be back much before eleven." Then he turned to Cameron. "Take good care of him."

"Yes, sir, Mr. Potter. I will."

CHAPTER FORTY-FOUR

GETTING DOWN from the roof wasn't as easy as Liana had expected. She wasted valuable time walking back and forth across the building, surveying her options. Shimmying down a rainspout seemed like a good idea—until she tried. But lowering herself over the edge of the roof, even if her legs had been long enough to reach the wall, would mean letting go of the roof to grab the spout. And if she missed, she'd fall and break her neck.

Dropping onto a cluster of trash receptacles looked to be the safest way down. Here again, coming up with the idea was a lot easier than carrying it out. She got down on her belly, swung her legs over the edge, and eased herself lower and lower until gravity took over and she fell into the large bin. The trash inside did buffer her fall, and the smell would wash off.

She darted down the alley, stopping to peer around the corner. Seeing the coast was clear, she ventured onto the sidewalk and hurried up the street in search of the fire station. Several firefighters sat on the sidewalk in front of the station in heavy wooden chairs that belonged under somebody's dining room table.

"Excuse me, gentlemen," Liana said as she approached.

"Evening," said a mustachioed older man, exhaling a cloud of smoke as he looked her over. His compatriots nodded greetings and added to the cloud. "If you're hungry, go around to the kitchen." He pointed to a door on the side of the station. "There's a big pot of chili on the stove. Help yourself."

"No, I'm not looking for a handout." Not that she wasn't hungry or had ever met a pot of chili she didn't like. She pulled her badge from her vest pocket and flipped open the case. "Liana Salvatore, Division of Public Morals." Skeptical looks returned her gaze as she put her badge back in her pocket. "Things kind of got out of hand during a raid tonight."

They puffed on their cigarettes, waiting for her to continue.

"I need to use your phone. We got our own little version of the Alamo going on at the Stonewall Inn, only instead of Mexicans overwhelming Davy Crockett, a bunch of homos have some New York police trapped inside."

The mustachioed man snorted. "Are you shitting me?"

"No, I'm not." She turned back toward the riots and pointed. "See all that smoke?"

"Smoke! Why didn't you say so?" They jumped out of their chairs like they'd been shot from cannons and ran for the trucks.

Convincing the firemen to send trucks to a burning Stonewall Inn had been easy, once they had seen the smoke. Getting the desk sergeant to believe fags were rioting and had pinned the good guys inside the seedy place, however, was an uphill battle.

"No way." She heard him snicker through the phone. "You girls couldn't handle the fairies? Geez."

"With all due respect, sir." Liana fought to keep the anger out of her voice. "If backup doesn't get here fast, somebody is going to start shooting."

"Come on, Salvatore. You gotta be pulling my leg."

"No, sir, I am not kidding."

"You expect me to believe a bunch of fags have pinned back the ears of New York's finest?"

"Worse than that, sir." She paused. "The fags have them cornered and, while we've been enjoying this little chat, have lofted a couple of dozen Molotovs at the place." Not that she could actually see, but the last time she'd checked, somebody had been throwing the flaming bottles.

"Molotov cocktails?"

"Yes, sir. I can see the smoke from here."

"Sounds like a job for the Tactical Police Force."

"I think you're right, sir."

LIANA LEFT the fire station and headed back to the Stonewall Inn. A sense of accomplishment and the reassuring weight of the pistol in her vest pocket calmed her nerves. She caught a glimpse of her reflection in a storefront window and understood why the firemen had offered her food. Wiggling through the filthy vent, belly crawling on the roof, and rolling around in trash had made her look like she lived under a bridge somewhere.

The fire trucks had reached the burning building, aided by a handful of uniformed cops waving batons to keep the protesters at bay. The police presence outside the club surprised her and further riled up an already-angry crowd. The uproar must have attracted the attention of beat cops patrolling in the vicinity.

Hanks and the others she'd left inside were nowhere in sight. She surveyed the scene around her and thought about what she should do. On the one hand, most of her team remained inside the Stonewall Inn. Though few in number, the police outside had reclaimed the entrance and appeared to have the upper hand. Instead of pressing forward, the crowd backed away. A couple of good whacks with a baton had made them wary.

The raid was over. The employees had been arrested, and the alcohol was ready to be removed from the premises. She'd carried out her orders to call for backup. Dealing with the chaos outside the club required specially trained officers and wasn't her job.

The mob hurled projectiles and derogatory remarks at the police from a distance just beyond the reach of their batons. Getting whipped never sat well with the men on the force, and tonight they had been thoroughly spanked. To add insult to injury, their asses had been handed to them by a bunch of pansies, dykes, and drag queens.

Christie and the reporter came out of the club arm in arm. The rest of the team followed, with Hanks bringing up the rear. He looked around, taking in the chaotic scene for a moment, then slid with the agency guys into the back of an unmarked car and left. With the team leader gone, Liana could think of no reason to stay.

The arrival of the Tactical Police Force in three buses confirmed her decision. Let the uniformed cops and riot police deal with the crowd. Her job here was done.

CHAPTER FORTY-FIVE

PHILIP CLOSED and bolted the connecting door to the room where Harold and Abigail slept and glanced at the clock on the bedside table. Going on four in the morning. No wonder the kids were so tired.

He didn't think he'd missed George getting back, but to be sure, Philip walked across the room, slid open the bolt, and rapped his knuckles against the door to George's room. No answer. He decided to leave his side open so he wouldn't have to get up again when George got back. Or in case he fell asleep. Philip stifled a yawn. He kicked off his shoes, stepped out of his clothes, and slid into the delightful coolness of his maroon silk pajamas. Though they were in need of dry cleaning, he put his shirt and linen pants on hangers and hung them up, sliding them across the closet, away from outfits he hadn't yet worn.

An exhausted Harold and Abigail had shared a cab with him back to the hotel. Had he not stayed after them, the fatigued pair would have gone to bed without washing their faces or brushing their teeth. He draped the washcloth he'd used on his own face across the tap, refolded the hand towel he'd patted his face dry with, and picked up his toothbrush.

Though she'd been frightened half to death, Abigail would be fine. The brutality she'd witnessed had shaken her. Seeing friends beaten with nightsticks left a lasting impression and had a way of altering views about law and order. Her outrage at the injustice was a good sign.

He rinsed the sink, dried his hands, and turned out the bathroom light. The comfy bed called to him, but he settled into the armchair, too anxious for sleep. He had plenty to occupy his mind until George returned.

As he often did, Harold had withdrawn into himself. Early in their relationship, the way Harold shut him out had concerned Philip. But rather than running away or escaping from reality, Harold was just taking a break from attending to the world around him to process new information. Philip had no idea what occupied him tonight. A lot had happened since midnight. Whether Harold was just tired, was licking his wounds, or had something else going on, Philip couldn't say, and he knew better than to pry. Harold didn't seem upset—quite the contrary. His smug demeanor suggested he was rather pleased with himself about something.

Hearing the bolt slide, Philip looked up to see George coming through the door carrying a bottle of Scotch and two ice-filled glasses. "One finger or two?" He set the glasses on the table and twisted the top from the bottle.

"One, thank you." Philip waited as George poured the drinks and handed Philip his before settling onto the loveseat.

"I found Miss Kropp and Miss Ryan," George said, then tossed back the rest of his drink and poured another. "In a holding tank at the Sixth Precinct station a few blocks from the Stonewall Inn."

"Are they okay?"

George downed the contents of his glass. He reached for the bottle to pour another but changed his mind. "They're black-and-blue with cuts that need stitches and bones that should be X-rayed." He rattled the ice in his glass and turned it up. "But they'll be okay." He shook his head and plunked the glass down beside the bottle. "They're the two strongest women I've ever met."

"Where are they now? Still in jail?" Being out of town and without any identification, Philip suspected George had been unable to do much.

"They're out, thanks to our friend Shirley White, and resting as comfortably as I could make them at Kelsey's apartment."

"You called Shirley?"

George shook his head and smiled. "I would have, but the guy in charge had worked with her in DC years ago and had no interest in finding himself on her bad side, which I assured him would be the case were I to wake her so early on a Saturday morning to vouch for my clients."

Philip smiled. He'd wound up on the wrong side of Lieutenant White a few times and hoped he never had occasion to be there again. "So you got them out of jail with nothing but your pretty face?"

"Well, that and my devilish charm." He winked. "And a most serendipitous call from Miss Harris, the most capable secretary in the world, seeking information about the whereabouts of two important clients of her employers, the lawyers at Walker, Cochran, and Lowe." He laughed. "She also arranged several wire transfers for me and has started the ball rolling on the paperwork to replace the contents of our wallets."

"Secretary?" Philip shook his head. "Miss Harris deserves a more fitting title." He stroked his chin and studied the ceiling for a moment. "Something like Executive Assistant, or maybe Supreme Goddess."

"She's a remarkable woman, with an uncanny ability to get things done and to find out what she wants to know," George said.

Philip walked over, settled in beside him on the loveseat, and hugged him. "You never cease to amaze me."

George returned the hug and kissed him on the forehead. "Behind every great man is a woman like Joan Harris and a lover like Philip Potter." He loosened the top button on Philip's pajamas and started on the next, but Philip stopped him.

"We should have made Terrence go to the hospital."

"Like anyone could make Terrence do anything he didn't already want to do."

"Of course you're right." Philip would sooner pry into Harold's business than argue with Terrence about something. He shook his head. "That boy has a stubborn streak a mile wide."

"He'll pay tomorrow," George said.

"Yes," Philip agreed. "With so much pain tonight, he'll be miserable." Philip added aspirin to his mental shopping list and wondered about some kind of brace for Terrence's rib cage. "And what about Cameron?"

George shrugged. "Despite the mess he's in, he seems like a nice-enough guy. Terrence sure likes him a lot."

"Yes, the torches they carry for each other burn bright." Phillip stroked his goatee for a moment. "I worry about the impact he might have on Terrence's ambitions. He's worked too hard and come too far to walk away from his degree now."

George looked at him for a long moment without saying anything. Philip couldn't read his expression. Never could when he put on his lawyer face.

George placed his hand on Philip's knee. "You've done everything you can for Terrence. He's a fine young man with a good head on his shoulders. The path he chooses now is up to him."

"But what if he makes a decision I don't like?" Philip sighed.

"You support him and whatever decision he makes—even if he's wrong."

"What if he wants to disappear with Cameron?" Philip pulled a handkerchief from George's pocket and wiped his eyes.

"We give him our blessing and do whatever we can to help him."

"Even if it means never seeing him again?"

"Yes," George said. "But I don't think it will come to that."

"But the Mafia… if they find him…."

"Once Cameron gets out of New York, he's footloose and fancy free."

"What makes you say that?"

"Cameron has no ties to anyone, anywhere. As long as he avoids the spotlight and, just to be safe, Mafia strongholds, they have no idea where to look for him." George patted Philip's knee. "We have no prior relationship with Cameron, so they have no reason to connect us to his disappearance."

"What are you saying?"

"If Terrence decides to go with him, they have no reason to hide from us."

Philip stroked his chin. "So we could visit?"

"If they'd have us."

"Why on earth wouldn't they want us to come?"

"No reason." He kissed Philip on the forehead. "Until we give them one."

Philip sighed. "Yes, of course you're right."

"Besides, even before you knew him, Terrence has always made good decisions. He escaped a bad home situation, stayed in school, and avoided alcohol and drugs."

Knowing George was right didn't keep Philip from worrying, but standing in the way of what Terrence wanted would do more harm than good. He pinched the bridge of his nose and sighed. "No matter what he decides, I'll support his decision."

George laughed. "If you hadn't lost your wallet today, I'd ask you to put some money on that one."

"Lucky for you," Philip said. "Because I'd be happy to take that bet and your money."

CHAPTER FORTY-SIX

Terrence clung to a panting Cameron, both men slick with sweat. Cameron's urgent kisses on already-bruised lips had caused the occasional whimper, and every shift in position made him yelp from the pressure to his ribs. Even so, Terrence didn't think he'd ever been so happy.

"Did I hurt you?" Cameron kissed the tip of Terrence's nose and traced the edge of his bruised lips with a finger.

He shook his head. "No." Setting aside the beard burn over most of his face, nipples too sensitive to touch, and a tender sphincter. "No more than I hurt you." Terrence stroked Cameron's bruised back, causing him to wince.

"I didn't really notice the pain." He ran a hand through Terrence's curls and kissed his eyebrow.

"Me either." Terrence smiled. "Well, maybe a couple of times."

"I'm sorry." Cameron knotted his fingers into Terrence's hair and turned his head to kiss the other eyebrow.

"No need to apologize." Terrence kissed him, ignoring the pain from his bruised lips. "Good thing we had a reason to be gentle or somebody might have really gotten hurt." Terrence rose up on his elbow, drawing a sharp breath as the pain shot through his chest. He squeezed his eyes shut for a moment, and when the pain subsided, took in Cameron's unflinching gaze. Cameron's blue eyes and sober expression gave no indication of his thoughts. His slow, absentminded strokes up and down Terrence's belly sent shivers up his spine. He'd recycled Cameron's breaths long enough to wonder if he was maybe a little oxygen deprived.

"Thank you," Cameron said.

Terrence looked at him, puzzled. "For what?"

"For a first time I will never forget."

"Your first time?" Terrence laughed. "Don't forget, I know all about your shady past." He regretted his words and their sarcastic tone the moment he said them.

Cameron slipped a hand into Terrence's hair and peered into his eyes. "Yeah, so you should understand that was work. But other than work…."

Terrence stared at him, stunned.

"I'm not saying I never enjoyed what I did before." Cameron paused and swallowed. "But being with you was different."

"How so?"

"You're the first guy I've been with since Kreema made me see I was queer." He shrugged. "That makes you the first person I've ever kissed who didn't have to force me, and the only one I've ever slept with for free."

"Ever?" Terrence tried not to show his surprise. "Not even when you were in high school?"

Cameron shook his head. "Never."

"Wow." Terrence didn't know what else to say. His stepfather had been his first, and he had enjoyed none of the experience.

"I know I shouldn't tell you." He cupped the nape of Terrence's neck with his hand. "But if I don't say what's on my mind now, while I have the chance, I'll spend the rest of my life wondering what you would have said."

"Then tell me." Terrence wondered what could be so important.

Cameron studied Terrence's face for a long moment. "You being my first makes this sound even more foolish." He ran a hand through his hair.

Terrence shook his head. "I doubt that. What do you want to tell me? Out with it."

Cameron paused and took a couple of deep breaths. "I didn't understand what was going on at the time, but now I see I fell in love with you the first time I saw you."

Terrence snorted. "Well, you sure had a funny way of showing it."

"I'm sorry." Cameron kissed his nose. "My attraction to you scared me. I thought I was straight and didn't know what to do with my feelings." He brushed the hair off Terrence's face with his fingers. "Still don't, really. We don't even know each other, but I can't stand the thought of leaving here and never seeing you again, and I have to know if you feel the same way."

Terrence took a deep breath and let it out slowly as he collected his thoughts. He'd expected a deep, dark secret from the past, not concern about a future together. He shrugged. "I don't know."

"You don't know?" Cameron sat up. "What do you mean, you don't know?"

There was no time for games. No matter how much telling the truth pained him, Terrence had to fess up. Unable to look him in the eyes, Terrence stared at the bedding. "I'm afraid." He picked at the hem of sheet. "For the first time in my life, I'm fucking afraid, and I don't know what to do."

"Afraid of what?"

The concern in Cameron's voice surprised him. Grunting from the pain, Terrence sat up and faced him. "Making the wrong decision."

"About what?"

"Do I have to spell it out for you?" Terrence hadn't meant to sound so angry. He'd banished fear from his life when he'd chosen to run away from home. The unexpected return of the exiled emotion pissed him off.

Cameron furrowed his brow. "I'm not the fastest horse out of the starting gate. Maybe you'd better."

Terrence pushed his hair out of his face. "Thanks to Philip, I'm going to an Ivy League college with normal kids who know nothing about my past, building a résumé George guarantees will land me a slot in a prestigious law school."

"Sorry for being so dense, but I still don't understand why you're afraid."

Terrence studied Cameron's handsome face. Until a few hours ago, only Terrence's head and heart had been involved in the debate about what he should do. Now his whole body had weighed in, and the close race had turned into a landslide. When the votes were tallied, his head had been defeated by a wide margin. "I'd throw it all away to go with you." He paused for a moment, waiting for Cameron to say something before continuing. "It's crazy, I know. I mean, sure, we've seen each other around, but we only met yesterday." He paused, giving Cameron a chance to speak that he again failed to take. Terrence willed himself to shut up, but the words kept coming out. "I mean, if you want me to go with you...."

As he'd done when he'd bared his soul such a short time ago, Cameron sat on the bed facing him. Terrence couldn't believe fewer than twelve hours had passed since they'd first come to his apartment. He studied Cameron's face and waited for him to say something.

Cameron reached out and grasped his shoulders. "I want to be with you more than I've ever wanted anything." He shook his head. "But not if going with me means giving up your dreams and everything you've worked for. I couldn't live with myself."

"Well, the decision is mine to make." He placed his palm against Cameron's scruffy cheek. "Should I decide to go, you have no reason to feel guilty about my abandoned dreams." He smiled. "Besides, I've dreamed about you a hell of a lot more these last few weeks than I've ever dreamed about law school."

CHAPTER FORTY-SEVEN

CAMERON TURNED off the lights and tried not to jostle Terrence as he climbed into the bed. The twin-sized mattress left little room for error and required them to lie almost on top of each other. Terrence sucked in air and grimaced as Cameron slid in beside him.

"You really should let a doctor take a look at you," Cameron said. "At least they could give you something for the pain."

"It only hurts when I move." Terrence slid his head across the pillow and rubbed noses with Cameron. "Besides, pain pills make me pass out." Terrence grinned. "I'd rather have the pain than miss anything that's happened here since Philip and them left." Terrence wrapped his arms around Cameron's neck and draped a leg over his hip.

Cameron nestled in closer, until they were chest to chest. He nuzzled into Terrence's neck, running his palm up and down Terrence's thigh as he wondered where he'd be come August. The almost unlimited number of options was more than Cameron could wrap his head around. "Where would you go?"

"I don't know." Terrence shrugged. "Anyplace in the world?"

"Mr. Walker didn't say, but I don't think I'd want to leave the United States." He furrowed his brow. "I've never lived anywhere but here and little Paris, Kentucky." He shook his head. "How do I decide where to go when I've never been anywhere?"

"Criteria." Terrence nodded. "If you could dream up a place to live, what would it look like?"

"A tropical island, in the middle of nowhere, with just the two of us and everything we'd need to survive."

Terrence snorted. "You do not want to be responsible for giving me all the attention I need." He shook his head. "I'd want to live in a city where guys like us can go out for drinks or dinner without fear of harassment by police or anyone else."

Cameron nodded slowly as he considered what Terrence had said. "Never thought about the city."

"Why not?"

He shrugged. "If I wanted to disappear, I'd head up into the mountains or to some tiny little town in the middle of nowhere."

"Where everyone within walking distance would wonder who you were and what you were running from every time they saw you?" Terrence shook his head. "No, if you really want to disappear, the city is the place to be."

He stroked Terrence's cheek with his knuckle. "Starting over in a big city would give me more options."

"And rule out most of the country." Terrence kissed the back of Cameron's hand. "Now you're down to just big cities. What about the climate?"

"Heat doesn't bother me too bad, but I hate cold weather."

Terrence nodded. "That knocks a bunch more off the list."

"And as far away from New York and Frankie as I can get."

"You're down to Atlanta, Miami, maybe New Orleans, a couple of cities in Texas, and California."

"I've always wanted to see the Pacific Ocean," Cameron said.

"That means California." Terrence's hand dropped from Cameron's ear to trace little circles in the hair on his chest with his fingertips. "San Diego, Los Angeles, maybe as far north as San Francisco."

Cameron had heard of San Diego but knew squat about the place. Los Angeles was close to Hollywood, but with an acting career now out of the question, he had no interest in living there. San Francisco had Alcatraz, the Golden Gate Bridge, Chinatown, and, if the song was true, people wearing flowers in their hair. "San Francisco."

Terrence nodded. "I could live in San Francisco." He groaned.

"What is it?"

"The sun is up, and we still haven't slept." He snuggled into Cameron and kissed his neck. "See? That wasn't so hard."

Cameron growled. "No, but keep up what you're doing and it will get that way."

"Again?" Terrence purred.

"I'm a professional, remember?" He smiled. "Satisfaction guaranteed, or your money back."

"Oh, I'm very satisfied." Terrence trailed wet kisses between Cameron's ear and collarbone.

"Wait." He leaned away from Terrence. "Just one more thing."

"What's so important that you'd keep a customer waiting?"

"Now that I know where I'm going, I need to decide on my new name."

"Denver Collins still gets my vote."

Cameron laughed. "Sorry, I'm not spending the rest of my life sharing my last name with a cocktail." He shrugged. "A name should mean something—say something about a person's place in the world. That's why naming a baby is such a big deal."

"You've got a point," Terrence said. "I withdraw my vote."

"My parents both had grandfathers named Cameron." He pinched his chin. "I thought about using my father's first name, Ervil, with Starnes, my mother's maiden name."

"Ervil Starnes?" Terrence winced.

"Yeah, nice idea, but a bad fit. I don't believe I could ever get used to the sound of it." He wiggled his elbow. "My arm's going to sleep."

Terrence lifted his head and Cameron sat up, sliding far enough to rest his back against the headboard. Cameron looped an arm over Terrence's shoulder and Terrence snuggled into the crook of Cameron's elbow.

"If they were alive, my parents would disown me for bringing nothing but dishonor and shame to the family name. I'm glad they didn't live long enough to see the person I've become."

Terrence turned and looked Cameron in the eye. "You don't know what they'd think—"

"I'm not talking about the queer thing." Cameron shook his head. "They'd never understand and would probably just look the other way. People have a way of seeing what they want to see." He shrugged. "I'm glad they never knew." Terrence started to say something, but Cameron continued. "They might eventually have forgiven me for selling my ass, but the rest, the lives I ruined…."

They sat in silence for a long moment, with foreheads and noses touching. Terrence kissed him. "You're being way too hard on yourself."

Cameron shrugged. "What's done is done. Nothing I can do about the past except to leave it behind. I've got a second chance. When I leave here, the guy who did all those terrible things is dead to me. I don't want some dashing or clever stage name. Since I get to pick the one I want, it should mean something to me."

"Sounds like you've decided on something," Terrence said.

Cameron nodded. "My life changed the day I met Kreema Dee Kropp. If she gives me her blessing, I'd like to go with Harold's suggestion: Clayton Taylor."

Terrence nodded his approval. "She'll be thrilled."

Cameron kissed him, wishing he didn't have that bruised lip. "Sorry to keep you waiting, sir." He smiled. "Now where were we?"

CHAPTER FORTY-EIGHT

PHILIP AND George, their arms loaded with shopping bags, waited on the sidewalk outside the building where Terrence lived. After telling him they wouldn't arrive before eleven, Philip wasn't about to show up even one minute early. Unlike Harold, who sometimes got distracted and lost track of time, Terrence was always on time or early for his appointments. Still, Philip would rather give him a few extra minutes than run the risk of embarrassing anyone, himself included.

"Think they slept much?" George chuckled. "I'll never forget our first night together."

"Me either," Philip said. "So many surprises! I'd planned to lead you into the world of homosexual love a little at a time, over weeks or even months. I never imagined you'd master things so quickly."

"Well, I'd thought about it a lot." His brow furrowed. "And as I recall, showed you a thing or two you hadn't seen before."

"I still say you picked them up from a dirty movie or something. What time do you have?"

George shifted the bags in his arms to look at his watch. "A few minutes after eleven."

"Let's see how the little lovebirds are doing this morning."

CAMERON OPENED the door right away. Philip swept past him and saw Terrence comfortably ensconced on the bed with pillows tucked around him. The apartment had been tidied, and the boys—judging from their still-damp hair—hadn't long been out of the shower. He stepped over to the kitchen unit and set his bags on the counter, pointing for George to do the same with his.

Philip reached into a sack and pulled out a green bottle. "I brought you some over-the-counter pain medicine and an elastic bandage to wrap around your chest." He poured a glass of water from the tap and handed it to Terrence with two pills. "You can have two more around five or six this evening." He filled another glass for Cameron. "How about you?"

"Thank you, Mr. Potter," Cameron said, then swallowed the pills with a swig of water and a quick tilt of his head.

"Please, call me Philip."

"Yes, sir, Mr. Philip."

Whether by accident or design, Cameron was scoring points right and left. Philip wouldn't put it past Terrence to have coached him. "Are you boys hungry?" They nodded in unison. "I picked up bacon, eggs, and stuff to make pancakes." The stove only had two burners, but he figured he could broil the bacon in the oven.

"That sounds great," Terrence said. "I'd like—"

"Yes, Terrence, I know. Over easy eggs and little pancakes—so the egg yolks won't run into the syrup. What about you, Cameron?"

"Whatever Terrence is having is fine with me. Can I help?"

Philip shook his head. "No. I've got breakfast under control." He arranged all the ingredients on the small countertop and was glad he'd left nothing to chance. Terrence's cupboards were beyond bare. "George, fill them in while I fix breakfast."

"Fill us in on what?" Terrence asked.

"Factors we need to consider." George paused for a moment, collecting his thoughts. "I asked my secretary to see what she could find out about your former employer." He cleared his throat. "According to her executive summary, Frankie Caldarone is, and I quote, 'one bad-ass motherfucker.'"

Philip gasped. "Miss Harris used those words?"

George nodded. "She says he's very well connected. If the fortune he pays out in bribes is any indication, his revenue puts him in the upper echelon of the Mafia power structure. And like that's not enough, he squeezes favors out of a number of closeted homosexuals with government and military positions that he's netted with his little extortion scheme."

"Frankie keeps files with photos and detailed notes," Cameron said. "He says information is the source of money and power. I've seen some of the pictures in J. Edgar Hoover's file." He shook his head and shuddered. "Even with Harold's help and all the makeup in the world, he wouldn't be a very pretty woman."

"I've heard rumors," Philip said, shaking his head.

"Okay," Terrence said. "We get the picture. The head of the FBI is a cross-dresser and Frankie is a scumbag. Now what?"

"Have you thought about where you'd like to go?"

"Yes, sir, Mr. Walker." Cameron glanced at Terrence. "Do you want to tell them or shall I?"

Philip turned around. "Tell us what?"

Terrence looked at him and Philip saw the familiar stubborn tilt to his jaw. "I haven't made up my mind for sure." He paused. "I know what all's at stake, and I don't want to rush into anything."

"Rush into what?" Philip asked, exasperated.

Terrence glanced at Cameron and took a deep breath. "I'm thinking about going with Cameron… to San Francisco."

"Absolutely not!" Philip's fears had come true. "I will not allow you—"

"Now hold on, Philip," George said. "You heard what he said. He's not rushing into anything."

Philip glared at him. "Whose side are you on?"

George put a hand on Philip's shoulder. "We talked about this, remember?" He sniffed and looked back at the kitchen unit. "I think something is burning."

"Oh dear!" Philip yanked the over door open. "I've scorched the bacon."

George leaned against the wall and stroked his chin. "Why San Francisco?"

"Process of elimination," Terrence replied. "He wants to live in a big city, with a mild climate, as far away from New York as possible."

George nodded. "Makes sense."

Philip wanted to punch him. He handed Cameron and Terrence each a plate. "Well if you ask me—"

"Nobody asked you, Philip," George said with a pointed look. "Didn't have to. You've made your position quite clear." He smiled. "You didn't ask, but I'd like mine scrambled. If it's not too much trouble…."

Philip harrumphed and turned back to the kitchen unit. He broke two eggs into a bowl and beat them with a fork until they were frothy. He dumped the contents of the bowl into a skillet sizzling with butter and stirred them with a wooden spoon every now and then as he loaded a plate with several ill-formed pancakes and the most scorched pieces of bacon in the pan. He thought about serving him undercooked eggs but didn't. That would have been deliberate. He hadn't meant to burn the bacon or mangle the pancakes. Somebody had to eat them.

"So," George said, addressing the boys as they wolfed down their food. "The two of you are in love and want to spend the rest of your lives together."

Philip's mouth fell open, and the plate with George's breakfast fell with a crash to the floor. "I'm sorry." He bent over to clean up the mess he'd made, watching Terrence and Cameron out of the corner of his eye.

"Well," Terrence said with a quick glance at Cameron. "I don't know about that. I mean, we barely know each other."

George shook his head. "It's not that complicated. You're either in love with each other, or you're not."

Philip gasped, and the pieces of plate he'd picked up fell back to the floor.

"I fell in love with Philip the first time I saw him." George smiled. "He was madder than a wet hen."

"And naked," Terrence said, smiling too.

"You both exaggerate," Philip said as he dropped the pieces of plate into the trash. "I was a little perturbed, and I had on my bathrobe."

"Yes." George nodded. "He had on a bathrobe, but he was naked underneath, and the robe kept falling open." He chuckled. "I'll never forget."

"So for you and Mr. Potter, er, I mean Mr. Philip, it was love at first sight?"

George nodded. "Yes, Cameron, that's how it happens. There's no other way, and anyone who says otherwise isn't being honest. You know right away. Figuring out whether or not it will last is what takes time."

Had Philip fallen in love with George the first time he'd seen him? The day stood out in his memory too. He'd attributed his vivid recollection to his anger at George's brother. But more than two years later, what he remembered was George's kind face and his shock at hearing what his brother had done to keep his son's death a secret.

"In different circumstances," George continued, "you'd keep your feelings to yourself until enough time had passed to know for sure." He turned to Terrence. "You're a smart guy with a good head on your shoulders. Setting all else aside, are you in love with this man?"

Terrence turned to Cameron, and Philip knew what Terrence would say. "Yes, I am."

"Cameron, what about you? Are you in love with Terrence?"

Cameron held Terrence's gaze and both his hands. "Yes, sir, Mr. Walker."

"Good," George said. "Then it's settled. Whatever you decide, Philip and I are behind you 100 percent. Right, Philip?"

"Yes." Philip nodded, pulling a handkerchief from his pocket. "One hundred percent." He sniffed and then wiped away his tears. Whether caused by the sweet scene George had orchestrated between Terrence and Cameron or his sense of loss for the time Terrence had spent pursuing his dreams, he couldn't say.

CHAPTER FORTY-NINE

An envelope with Harold's name across the front in Philip's familiar, ornate script had been slid under the connecting-room door while they slept. Inside, Harold found forty dollars and a note to call Philip at Terrence's apartment after they got up.

Abigail sat up, stretched, and rubbed the sleep from her eyes. "What time is it?"

"Almost noon." Harold sat on the bed and dialed the number. Terrence answered after two rings. "How are you and Cameron feeling this morning?"

"Much better," Terrence replied. "Philip and George stopped by about an hour ago with drugs, bandages, and the usual tender loving care. Philip even made pancakes for us."

Harold heard Philip talking in the background and then Terrence came back on the line.

"Philip said for you and Abigail to get something to eat and then come by my apartment. Do you remember how to get here?"

"No. You know me and my sense of direction," Harold replied. "Abigail has a map. We'll find it. See you in a bit." Harold hung up the phone and fell back onto his pillow.

"Are we going to Terrence's apartment?"

"Yeah, after we eat."

"Oh good!" Abigail put her feet on the floor and stretched again. "We'll get to see that dreamy Cameron again." She fanned her face with both hands. "He's the best-looking man I've ever seen."

Harold nodded. "I bet he looks great even when he rolls out of bed in the morning." He ran a hand through his disarranged hair and shrugged. "But I've never really been attracted to supermasculine men."

Abigail laughed. "As far as I know, you've never been attracted to anyone." She studied his face for a moment. "You're not jealous, are you?" She glanced at the floor and back to his face. "I mean… I know you love Terrence, but I always thought…."

"That he's like a brother to me?" Harold nodded. "He is."

She palmed her forehead. "Of course! I'm sorry. I wasn't thinking." She climbed onto his bed, snuggled up close, and rested her head on his shoulder. "You're not losing Terrence. You're gaining another big brother."

Harold put his arm around her and shook his head. "No, I'm not worried about losing him. I'll always love Terrence, and I know he feels the same way about me."

She kissed his cheek. "I know you've missed him."

He twirled a strand of her hair with his fingers and stared at the ceiling. "The months I shared a bedroom with Terrence were the happiest days of my life." He paused, not wanting to cry, and swallowed. "He said knowing everything about each other would make us family." He smiled. "We talked as much as we ever slept—sometimes until the sun came up."

Abigail slid her hand into his. "And then he moved to New York."

Harold nodded and squeezed her hand. "The first few weeks were hard."

"I remember." She shook her head. "Poor Philip was worried sick."

"It was like losing my family all over again. When he left...." He sighed. "I shut down."

"That was more than two years ago." Abigail brushed her fingertips over his brow to push the hair from his eyes. "You're a lot better about talking things out now."

"I locked myself in my bedroom, refused to let Philip in, and wouldn't come out."

"I came by a few times. You wouldn't let me in either, but I knew you'd open the door sooner or later."

Harold smiled. "Philip's patience ran out on the third day. He said he missed Terrence just as much as I did and, thanks to my childish behavior, had nobody to talk to about his feelings."

"Did you let him in?"

Harold shook his head. "It's the only time I've ever heard him raise his voice."

Abigail sat up. "What did he say?"

"He said if I didn't open the goddamn door by the time he counted to ten, he'd break it down."

She gasped. "Philip said that?"

Harold nodded. "Shocked me too. Before he got to four, I opened the door."

Abigail looked at Harold, eyes wide, and after a moment said, "My dad would beat my butt with a belt if I ever pushed him that far. What did he do?"

"He hugged me and we both cried." Harold wiped the tears from his face with the edge of the sheet. "Philip sat on the side of the bed, pulled me into his lap, and held me until we'd cried ourselves out."

"My dad would rather die than cry." She snapped her fingers. "That's what I'll make him for Christmas! Would Rather Die Than Cry in big letters across the front of a manly sweatshirt."

Harold swung his feet to the floor and sat on the side of the bed. "Terrence moving on doesn't bother me. People come and go, things change...." He shrugged. "I'll be moving on soon, to California, with or without Philip's blessing and the support of the foundation."

Abigail frowned. "Then what's wrong?"

Harold looked at her. "What's wrong with what?"

"Something is bothering you. I can tell."

He put his head in his hands and knotted his fingers in his hair. "I just think getting tangled up with the Mafia is a bad idea."

Abigail sat beside him. "You'd rather Philip and Mr. Walker turned their backs on him?" She didn't give him a chance to answer. "They can't help who they are. They'd help Cameron whether Terrence asked them to or not. And don't forget, Cameron didn't ask. Terrence did."

He shrugged. "I don't have anything against Cameron. But I would if something were to happen to Terrence, Mr. Walker, or Philip."

"Mr. Walker is a lawyer. He knows what he's doing."

"I sure hope you're right." Harold looked at the clock on the bedside table. "We need to get moving. You know Philip doesn't like to be kept waiting."

"What time are we supposed to be at Terrence's?"

Harold shook his head. "He didn't say."

CHAPTER FIFTY

KREEMA WOKE up unsure of where she was. The plush pillows, comfortable mattress, and luxurious bedding suggested a fancy hotel. But when she opened her eyes, the baseball memorabilia everywhere made her think she'd fallen asleep in a shrine to the New York Yankees. She remembered where she was when she turned and saw shelves filled with trophies and framed photographs of Kelsey at different ages posed for action in various uniforms.

She stood up and stretched, enjoying the softness of the frilly, transparent nightgown Kelsey had loaned her against her bruised skin. She slid tender feet into pink chenille house slippers, poked her arms through the sleeves of a matching chenille robe, and then snatched her wig from the bedpost and tugged it on, flipping the hair back off her face and forward on her shoulders just a little.

She caught a whiff of coffee and, following her nose, found Kelsey sitting at the kitchen table wearing boxer shorts, a tank-style T-shirt, and brown leather slippers. She had a mug in one hand and held a bag of frozen peas against the left side of her face with the other. She looked up when Kreema came in and nodded. "Good morning." She gestured with her mug to a stainless-steel electric percolator on the kitchen counter. "Help yourself. Did you sleep well?"

"Mm-hmm, like a little baby." Kreema poured coffee into the mug Kelsey had left out for her. "How about you? Feeling any better this morning?"

Kelsey shrugged and took a swig of coffee. "No worse." She turned the mug up, set it down on the table with a clunk, and wiped the back of her hand across her mouth. "Didn't sleep much." She shook her head. "Couldn't get comfortable."

"Another cup?"

"Thanks." Kelsey held out her mug.

Kreema filled the mug and slid onto the chair across the table from Kelsey. "Girl." She shook her head. "What the hell were we thinking? We're old enough to know better than to fuck with the cops."

Kelsey shook her head and smiled. "You started it." She repositioned the bag of peas against her face.

"Mm-hmm. Couldn't help myself. You know they always gotta bust a drag queen." She took a sip of her coffee and wished for a cigarette. "I figured it might as well be me. Besides, the motherfucker rubbed me the wrong way. Got me all riled up, and everybody knows that show ain't over until the black lady sings." She laughed and slapped her thigh. "What about you, honey?" She looked across the table at her. "What made you decide to fight?"

Kelsey gulped her coffee. "Police raids twice in one week—and on a Friday night when the place was packed—pissed me off. Watching them tear everything apart just made me madder. By the time they carried you out, I was furious." She tossed back the rest of her coffee and slammed the mug on the table. "That asshole groping my tits was the last straw. I slugged him, just like I would any man who touched me like that."

"Are you gonna sue? Mr. Walker said he'd represent you."

She shook her head. "No. I just want to put it behind me. Carrie, this girl I've been seeing, called this morning. She wants me to come to Cape Cod. Her family is renting a cabin there for the summer." She shrugged. "Might as well. School doesn't start back until August."

Kreema nodded. "Go. Time away from the city would be good for you—especially if a lady friend is involved."

"She didn't have to ask me twice," Kelsey said, with a chuckle. "That robe looks nice on you." She smiled. "Fits pretty good too."

"I just love the sexy negligee!" Kreema looked at her. "But I'm a little surprised you have garments like these." She pointed to her robe and the negligee. "No offense, but these ain't the kind of clothes I picture you wearing."

"No offense taken." She pointed over her shoulder toward the back of the two-bedroom apartment. "I've got closets full of them. My mother, all my aunts, and both grandmothers send me girly clothes for birthdays and Christmas every year." She shook her head. "They send 'something appropriate' for weddings, funerals, and other family get-togethers too. They've done the same thing since I was a little girl."

Kreema ran her hand over the thick chenille. "Ever wear any of them?"

"Nope. Never even try them on. I wouldn't be caught dead wearing that stuff. Every so often I donate everything to Goodwill."

"Mind if I take a look?"

Kreema sat in her customary spot, chatting with the general and smoking a cigarette. Her legs were crossed, and she bounced her foot so the pink chenille slipper flapped against her heel. The general declined to comment on her outfit, the events of the early morning hours, or, considering it was going on two in the afternoon, the unusual level of activity around the park. Even for a Saturday, there were a lot of people around.

Marty waved and ran across the street when he saw her. "Are you okay?"

She looked up, lifting the floppy brim of her white straw hat so she could see his face. "I'm fine, thank you, honey. Just a little bruising—no permanent damage."

A loud crash drew their attention to the Stonewall Inn. The windows had been covered with boards that several of the employees were busy painting black. Passersby stopped to see what was going on, chatting in small groups until the police made them move on.

"After last night, with the fire and all the damage inside and out," Marty said, "I thought that place was done for good."

"Up from the ashes." She exhaled a big plume of smoke. "All that hammering and sawing and carrying-on makes me think they'll reopen today."

"Do you think your friends from Washington will come out to dance tonight?"

She tilted her head back to see him better. "Harold and Abigail?"

"Yeah." Marty nodded. "Harold."

She pressed her knees together and slid her feet under her, arranging the hem of the long flowered skirt around her knees. "I'm not sure. Before we could discuss our plans for this evening, we were rudely interrupted."

"Oh, okay." Marty glanced around. "I was just wondering." He patted her on the shoulder. "I'm glad you're okay. Dwayne is waiting for me. He wants to go to the docks. I gotta run."

She watched him run over to join Dwayne and his friends. Marty was a good kid who deserved better treatment than he got. She'd often thought about bending Dwayne over her knee and giving him the spanking he deserved. "Mm-hmm, 'spare the rod and spoil the chile.' That's what my momma always said."

Over the next hour, people she barely knew stopped to say how glad they were to see she was okay and how proud of her they were for standing up to the man. She really didn't understand the big to-do. Last night wasn't the first time she'd mixed it up with the cops. Drag queens resisted arrest every night.

When she saw her Washington friends coming down the sidewalk, she stood, holding the wide brim back out of her face with her forearm. "Yoo-hoo! Harold! Abigail!" She waved her free arm in wide arcs.

"Kreema!" They ran to her and wrapped their arms around her.

"We were afraid they'd really hurt you," Harold said.

"I'm tougher than I look, honey." She hugged them, then took a step back and posed. "How do I look?"

CHAPTER FIFTY-ONE

Whether from the blows he'd received from the police or Philip's incessant, nervous chatter, Terrence couldn't say, but the pain relievers had had no effect on his headache. He glanced at his watch and saw he still had hours to wait before he could take another dose. He'd tough it out until then. If the pain worsened, he could always go to the hospital.

Philip, quiet at last, sat on the end of the bed, thumbing through the pages of Terrence's sociology textbook. Cameron and George were stretched out side by side on the floor, talking about thoroughbred racehorses.

"I wouldn't know a mare from a stallion," Terrence declared.

"Oh, I'm pretty sure you would." Cameron smirked. "Ever heard the expression 'hung like a horse'?"

Terrence shook his head. "No. But now the story I heard about a sex show with an animal act makes a lot more sense." He'd never seen Cameron so animated and was glad he got along with George and Philip and seemed to like them.

Philip glanced at Terrence, shook his head, and returned his attention to the textbook.

"Unless another Man o' War comes along, a horse's racing career lasts only a few years, and less than half ever win a race," Cameron said. "But a stallion with a good track record can make more money in stud fees than he ever won racing."

"I had no idea so much money was involved," George said as he stroked his chin.

"The sport of kings," Philip said. "The central Kentucky area where Cameron grew up is the horse-racing capital of the world." A knock on the door launched Philip from the bed. He stepped over Cameron and George to let Harold and Abigail into the already-crowded apartment. The men on the floor sat up and made room for the newcomers.

"Sorry it took us so long to get here," Harold said. "We detoured by the Stonewall Inn on the way and ran into Kreema."

"I called Kelsey to check on them," Terrence said. "She told me Kreema had just left, after raiding her closet." He grinned. "She's creative, even if she sometimes pushes the boundaries of good taste, but I can't imagine her finding much to wear in Kelsey's apartment."

"She's getting better about putting things together," Abigail said. "She had on an enormous wide-brimmed hat, a peasant blouse with big poufy sleeves, a frilly, floral-print skirt, and pink chenille house shoes."

Harold nodded. "Except for the house shoes—which matched a long ribbon on her hat—she looked pretty good."

"She found that getup at Kelsey's?" Terrence shook his head. "I'll have to ask Kelsey where she got clothes like that next time I talk to her." He turned to Harold. "How did the club look in the light of day?"

"Almost like last night never happened," Harold replied. "The streets have been swept clean, the trash picked up, and a crew was hammering away getting the Stonewall Inn ready to reopen."

"That should keep Mr. Caldarone busy," George said. "At least until we get Cameron out of New York." He stood and looked around the room like he was addressing a jury. "Because of Mr. Caldarone's connections and an abundance of caution, getting Cameron out of New York poses a number of challenges. Given the stakes…." He glanced at Cameron. "I'd prefer overestimating rather than underestimating his reach."

"Good idea," Terrence said. "Better safe than sorry."

"We have four train tickets for Washington back at the hotel," Philip said. "Why don't we just use them?"

Cameron scratched his head and frowned. "Frankie keeps an eye on Penn Station and Grand Central Station."

Philip scowled and wiped his forehead with a handkerchief. "Yes, I suppose a creep like him would be on the lookout for promising new runaways to prey upon."

George nodded. "Let's assume he has the resources and the wherewithal to keep an eye on airports and car rental companies too. The Mafia's involvement in trucking and shipping even make hitchhiking a risky option."

"I still say we take the train," Philip said.

"The guys who work for Frankie know me." Cameron shook his head. "Sorry, Mr. Philip. I just don't see me getting on a train without somebody spotting me."

"But what if nobody recognized you?" Philip stroked his goatee.

"You mean, like dye my hair and grow a beard?" Cameron shook his head. "My beard grows fast, but I'd need at least three days."

Harold shook his head. "Too obvious."

"I agree with Harold," George said. "A disguise would never work, and we don't have that kind of time."

"What do you think?" Philip mussed Harold's hair. "Could you render another transformation?"

"Hmm." Harold and Abigail exchanged glances, then stood and approached Cameron.

"Stand up," Abigail ordered. He complied. Harold and Abigail moved in for a closer inspection. Abigail pressed a finger to her lips as she looked him up and down. "He's short enough for heels."

Harold nodded. "If it wasn't for his big shoulders, we could show off that tiny little waist."

"We'll want something matronly." Abigail circled around Cameron. "The more we can cover up, the better. How about a nun?"

"Remember," Philip said. "Our goal is for him to blend in—not to stand out in the crowd. A lone nun traveling with three male companions would raise eyebrows."

Terrence nodded in agreement. "Yeah, nuns always travel in threes."

Cameron squirmed under their scrutiny.

Terrence tried not to laugh—more to avoid the pain than to spare Cameron's feelings.

Harold held Cameron's chin between his thumb and forefinger and turned his head from side to side. Then he looked at his arms and unbuttoned the top two buttons of his shirt. "Great bone structure, but getting rid of all that hair is going to take some work."

"Get rid of all his hair?" Terrence said.

"Don't worry," Harold said, shrugging. "It will grow back."

Terrence glanced around the room. "With only four tickets, who's going with him?"

Everyone looked at Philip. He cleared his throat. "We could buy more tickets so everyone could go, but I believe, rather than trying to watch to see who boards all the departing trains and buses, if he's looking for you, your former boss will focus his resources on the ticket counters."

Cameron nodded. "Makes sense to me."

"If Mrs. Dombroski approves, I thought perhaps Harold and Abigail could stay in New York for a few more days." He ran his hand over his head, smoothing the hair back. "The events of last night, however, make me wonder if that's such a good idea."

"I'm sorry," Terrence said. "I never would have gone off and left—"

"If I hadn't asked him to," Cameron said. "It's my fault."

"Water under the bridge now," George said. "Besides, Terrence didn't abandon Harold and Abigail. He left them with Kreema and Kelsey."

"For a good cause," Philip added, patting Cameron on the knee.

"You can keep your room at the Hilton," George said, turning to Harold. "And we'll give you spending money for food and maybe another show."

"Or you could stay here if you'd rather." Terrence shrugged. "It's not the Hilton, but the neighborhood is nice."

After a quick glance at Abigail, Harold said, "Until the police came last night, we hadn't had any trouble being on our own in New York. The raid was scary, but nothing happened to us."

"If Mom says it's okay, I'd like to stay," Abigail said.

Harold nodded. "Yeah, we haven't had time to do half the things on our list. We haven't even seen the Statue of Liberty." He sat on the bed next to Terrence. "No offense, but with beds of our own, maid service, and chairs to sit in, we'll stay at the Hilton."

"Good." George got up off the floor and stood. "Then everything is settled."

Philip rose from the bed and stood beside him. "We're going back to the hotel. If Mrs. Dee approves, I'll make arrangements with the front desk for the extra nights for Harold and Abigail. Do you kids want to share a cab with us?"

Harold shook his head. "No, I'd like to hang out with Terrence for a while." He looked from Philip to Terrence. "If that's okay."

Terrence glanced at Cameron and then nodded. "Okay? My feelings would be hurt if you didn't. I've missed my old roommate."

CHAPTER FIFTY-TWO

CAMERON CLOSED the door behind Mr. Philip and Mr. Walker and tried to remember when he'd last received such warm and affectionate hugs. His grandmother had been a thumper, whacking him on the back hard enough to knock the breath out of him. His father hadn't been the affectionate type either. He couldn't say for sure, but suspected his mother had most likely been responsible for his last loving hug.

Harold had taken his place on the bed beside Terrence, so Cameron sat on the floor with his back against the wall and his legs crossed at the ankles.

Abigail reached out and ran her hand over his shin. "You sure are hairy."

"All over, except for his back," Terrence said. "Like a big teddy bear."

Cameron's face grew hot. He didn't know what to say and, having said more since midnight than he'd said in months, was about talked out. "Uh, thanks."

He was thrilled to be with Terrence and appreciated the warm welcome he'd received from his friends. But until yesterday, solitude had been his only companion, and he hadn't had a moment with his old friend since the night before. Were it not for Mr. Philip's orders to stay inside the apartment, he would have gone for a long walk.

"Kreema said some guy asked about me," Harold said. "He wanted to know if I'd be at the Stonewall Inn tonight."

Terrence's jaw dropped. "Some guy?"

"Not just any guy," Abigail said. "Harold has a crush on him!"

Harold's face turned red. "I don't even know him."

Abigail shrugged. "He's definitely interested in you." She turned to Terrence. "After the police arrested Kreema and Kelsey, Marty took us under his wing."

"Marty?" Cameron sat up and folded his arms across his knees. "Teased black hair?"

Harold nodded.

"Nice kid," Cameron said. "Not sure I'd say the same about some of his friends."

"I think I know who you're talking about," Terrence said. "Do you want to see him again?"

Harold studied his hands, clasped together in his lap. "I think so."

"He does," Abigail said. "First time I've seen anyone turn Harold's head."

Terrence mussed Harold's hair. "Then you should go."

CAMERON CLOSED the door behind Harold and Abigail, ripped off his shirt, stepped out of his shorts, and slid onto the bed. He helped Terrence out of his shirt, grimacing each time he winced, and then looped his arm across Terrence's shoulder.

"Alone at last," Terrence said, resting his head on Cameron's chest.

Cameron tickled the edge of Terrence's ear with his fingertip. "Everyone is so nice."

"They're like family to me," Terrence said. "Only better, because we picked each other." He kissed Cameron's chest. "And now, you're part of the family too."

"I never knew people like Mr. Philip and Mr. Walker existed." He rested his chin on Terrence's head.

"Enough with the mister already. Philip and George."

"I don't know if I can do that." Cameron shook his head. "It's a matter of respect. First names are just so casual—like we're equals."

"George doesn't care one way or the other because he hears it around the office every day, but Philip cringes whenever someone calls him mister."

Cameron pressed his lips against Terrence's forehead. "They're really going to a lot of trouble to help me. I don't know how I'll ever repay them."

"All they ask is that you make them proud." Terrence combed his fingers through Cameron's chest hair. "I wouldn't blame you for being skeptical, but they're sincere."

"I'm sure they are." Until Terrence had planted the seed, Cameron had had no reason to doubt them. But if something sounded too good to be true, it usually was.

"I know. You're trying to figure out their angle—what they're in it for." Terrence raised his head up and looked Cameron in the eye. "They're in it because they care, about all kinds of people, but especially about young homosexuals with no place to go who turn tricks on the streets to survive."

For a fraction of a second, Cameron wondered if Terrence was part of the scam—softening him up and earning his trust, but nothing he'd seen contradicted anything Terrence said. Mr. Walker and Mr. Philip couldn't have been any nicer. Cameron hadn't been around people he could trust for so long he'd forgotten how.

"They support a shelter in DC and sometimes take on special cases." Terrence brushed his fingers through Cameron's hair. "You're the fourth beneficiary of their largesse, along with me, Harold, and George's deceased nephew."

"Why me?" He met Terrence's gaze. "They could find a hundred kids out there who need help more than I do."

"Because I asked." Terrence shrugged. "They'd help everyone if they could, but they can't. And don't think that means you owe me something." Terrence returned his head to Cameron's chest. "I put you in touch with them. The rest was up to you. Once they met you and heard about your situation, they wanted to help."

"I'm grateful." He combed his fingers through Terrence's hair.

"Don't think you're getting something for nothing, because that's not the case at all."

"I'll repay every dime," Cameron said. "I promise."

Terrence shook his head. "That's not what I meant."

Cameron wiggled his way down in the bed so he was nose to nose with Terrence. "What do you mean?"

"Guys like us have been on our own since we were kids. We're used to doing whatever the hell we want without worrying about anyone else." Terrence stroked Cameron's brow. "Having someone care about you is a responsibility. You have to think about their wishes and desires, and sometimes, you have to put their needs before yours."

Cameron nodded. Back in Kentucky, once he'd done his chores—whether for his parents, his grandmother, or when he worked on farms—he'd done whatever he wanted. Working for Frankie had been more or less the same, with different chores and later hours. Beyond that, he hadn't had to answer to anyone else for a long time because nobody really cared what he did.

Terrence cared, and Cameron believed his benefactors did too. "Disappointing Philip or George—or you—is the last thing I'd ever want to do."

"Which brings us to my Gordian knot," Terrence said.

Cameron furrowed his brow. "Your what?"

"My dilemma. If I go with you to San Francisco, Philip will be disappointed that I've abandoned my goal of an Ivy League education. And if I don't—"

Cameron put his finger to Terrence's lips. "Whether you decide to come with me or not, I'm really glad we've had this time together."

"Me too." Terrence stroked the hair over Cameron's ear. "I don't need to decide right away—school doesn't start back until the middle of August. Until then, I'm going to take things one day at a time."

Cameron nodded. His situation had changed so much and so fast, his head was reeling. A day at a time sounded like a good strategy. He sat quiet for a moment and closed his eyes. He may have even fallen asleep. Terrence shook his shoulder.

"Have you thought about what you want to do?"

Cameron blinked his eyes open and nodded. "Mr. Walker… er, I mean George, suggested I think about going back to school to finish my degree in agriculture."

Terrence nodded. "College is a good idea, and agriculture would be a good choice for you. Lots of farms in California."

"I started out in agriculture back home." Cameron shrugged. "Never could pick from all the different majors—too many options." He smiled. "I'd still have a hard time." He turned so they were nose to nose and looped his arm over Terrence's shoulder. "What about you? What comes after law school?"

"I want to make a difference."

Cameron kissed his nose. "If you ask me, you can check that one off your list."

"That's sweet." Terrence kissed him, ignoring the pain from his busted lip. "But I want to change the world. That's why an Ivy League education matters so much to me."

"Hmmm. That's a mighty tall order."

"Reach for the stars." Terrence's face grew serious. "If you want it bad enough, with hard work, anything is possible."

Cameron nodded. "And a little luck."

Terrence smiled. "Yeah, luck helps." He rested his head on Cameron's shoulder. "Last night will stand out in my memory for as long as I live."

"I'm flattered," Cameron said. "I'll never forget either."

Terrence kissed his cheek. "That too, but I was talking about the big clash with the police." He stroked his chin and stared into the distance.

"Philip says history changing course in a moment is the exception rather than the rule. More often than not, forces—seen and unseen—operate for months, years, or even centuries to bring about the historic moment."

Cameron nodded. "Like winning the Kentucky Derby. Breeders sign up hundreds of promising fillies and colts as soon as they're foaled, but fewer than thirty will enter the starting gate, and only one will win. Folks like to credit the jockey or the sloppy track or something else, but the winning horse is the product of centuries of breeding and months of training by men with decades of experience."

Terrence smiled. "You lost me. What does winning the Kentucky Derby have to do with last night?"

"Well." Cameron frowned. "Nothing is ever as simple as it looks. Last night the race was run, but things around here have been building up to it for a long time."

"Exactly." Terrence nestled into Cameron's neck.

"Do you think Harold and Abigail exaggerated about what happened after we left?"

"No." Terrence shook his head. "Harold's not an embellisher. You know those cops trapped inside the club had to be terrified."

Cameron nodded. "I can't imagine the police are happy about the drubbing they took."

Terrence draped his arm across Cameron's chest. "We'll just have to wait and see what happens next."

"That's all we can do." Cameron frowned. "Besides worry about what Harold and Abigail plan to do to me."

CHAPTER FIFTY-THREE

Few things pissed Liana off more than getting called in on her day off. Not that she had any plans—a reality that irritated her at least as much as giving up her day off. But the sergeant didn't know she wasn't doing anything and hadn't bothered to ask when he'd told her to get her ass to the Precinct Six Station House.

In the months since she'd last had to wear her uniform, she'd gained a few pounds. Not much, really. On a taller woman, nobody would even notice. Whether the buttons on her shirt or the seam in the seat of her pants would last through the meeting was a big question mark. Unfastening her pants to sit took some of the pressure off the seam, but two of the buttons on her blouse were stretched to the breaking point, and she could think of no action to save them short of removing her top.

She'd heard through the grapevine the big boys up and down the chain of command and in city hall were not the least bit happy about New York's finest taking it up the butt by a bunch of fags. She snorted. Not that anyone had actually been fucked in the butt. Not any of the cops anyway, at least not as far as she knew.

She'd never seen so many angry cops in one place. Black, Italian, Irish, Polish…. Where they came from didn't matter. No self-respecting straight man, anywhere in the world, would ever let a homo get the best of him. Settling the score was a matter of pride.

The commander and his entourage arrived. He stood in the front of the room with his hands clasped behind his back. The buzz of conversations ceased. He glanced around and nodded, "Good evening, gentlemen."

Liana sighed. She never knew if the failure to greet ladies was habit or some kind of statement. Women had been part of the force for more than forty years but hadn't been permitted to take the sergeant's exam until this decade. Not that cops were sexist or anything. Much.

She was surprised when the commander introduced Chief O'Malley. She hadn't seen him come in and, as his presence at briefings was rare, hadn't thought to look for him.

He stepped to the front of the room and held up a handful of crumpled papers. "Do you know what these are?" He shook the papers and glared around the room. "Telegrams, from chiefs all over the fucking country, volunteering to rescue us from the faggots who kicked our butts last night."

The men around her hung their heads. From the other side of the room, somebody called out, "Sorry, Chief."

"Sorry?" He flung the telegrams to the floor. "The whole country is laughing at us and you're sorry?" He glared around the room. "Is that what you want me to tell the mayor?"

A burst of coughing and throat-clearing spread across the audience. Chairs squeaked as people shifted their position but nobody said a word.

The chief massaged his temples for a moment. His hand slid down his nose and he exhaled into his fist. "Things got a little ahead of us last night." He paused and took a deep breath. "We got caught with our pants down." He shrugged. "If we'd known the homos would go berserk, we'd have had more men on hand."

Liana counted at least a dozen women in the room. She wondered if the constant omission of any reference to the women on the force irritated any of them as much as it did her. She felt a tickle in her nose and held her breath for a moment, but the tickling persisted and built.

"Achoo!"

She watched in horror as a button from her blouse struck a gray-haired officer several feet away in the back of the head. His hand went to the nape of his neck. He glanced around behind him and bent down to pick up the button from beneath his chair.

Liana leaned forward, clutching her blouse closed with one hand and gripping her elbow with the other, and focused her attention on the front of the room.

"We increased foot patrols in the area this morning, and with queers flocking to Christopher Street all day, again this afternoon." Chief O'Malley looked around the room. "They think they've got us on the ropes." He nodded. "Last night made them think they can run all over us."

Every eye in the room was on him. Liana found one of the safety pins she'd dropped into her purse, just in case. She turned away from the victim of the flying button and pinned her blouse together. The result wasn't pretty, but prevented her breasts from falling out.

"But we're not going to let that happen again tonight," the chief continued. "Are we?"

"No, sir!"

"What?" He cupped his ears with his hands. "I can't hear you!"

"No, sir!" The walls shook.

"That's more like it. Now get out there and kick some pansy ass!"

LIANA JOINED a line of more than three hundred uniformed police spread out along Christopher Street. She and her comrades stood an arm's length apart from Waverly Place past the Stonewall Inn, almost all the way to West Fourth Street. Orders were to keep traffic flowing, and that meant keeping people out of the street.

She was sandwiched between Howard, a bear of a man from the ninth precinct, and Mick, a rookie out of the fourth precinct. Liana had more years on the force than the two of them combined and didn't have to ask to know they made more money than she did.

With the chief's words fresh on their minds, everyone was itching for a fight. The officers dispatched to the area earlier had done what they could to keep people moving and out of the street. But spectators had kept coming, converging from all over New York and the surrounding areas. By nine, people couldn't keep moving because there was no place to go but the streets.

The view from the front line was surreal. Just beyond the reach of their batons, men in dresses linked arms and kicked their legs high as they sang silly songs about underwear and pubic hair and taunted the police with slurs and vulgar epithets. Not that they weren't funny, but she didn't dare laugh.

Kids came out of nowhere, tossing bottles and hurling bricks before disappearing back into the crowd. The attacks were continuous, relentless, and unpredictable. Danger could come at any time, from any direction. Frustration and anger rippled up and down the line. The men and women in uniform brandished nightsticks, but the tactics deprived them of any targets.

A bottle bounced off Howard's helmet. He and the officer on the other side of him darted into the crowd and grabbed the first person they encountered—a waif of a boy with teased auburn hair—and fell on him with their batons. The idea caught on fast. Before long, officers up and down the line were beating randomly selected fags with their nightsticks.

Beating up the guilty was bad enough. Beating up innocent bystanders just to make a point sickened her. More than being at the wrong place at the wrong time, the victims were targets because of who they were. For the first time in her career, she wasn't sure if the police were the good guys or the bad guys.

CHAPTER FIFTY-FOUR

HAROLD AND Abigail had no trouble agreeing on a concept for Cameron's transformation. A natural flare for the dramatic, however, made deciding on the specific elements a bit more challenging. They had to keep reminding each other about Cameron's need to blend in rather than stand out from the crowd.

"Covering him up would be a lot easier in cold weather," Harold said as he browsed the clearance rack. He wanted something nondescript but not so ugly or dowdy as to attract attention—probably in black, gray, or navy. "Maybe we should reconsider the nun option."

Abigail giggled. "Creates more problems than it solves, remember?"

Harold sighed. Since putting the ensemble together around shoes that fit would be faster and easier than the other way around, they'd looked for shoes first. As expected, finding a pair they liked in a size big enough for him to wear had been a challenge. The elegant black pumps with sturdy low heels they'd decided on gave them plenty of wiggle room.

"Gloves big enough for Cameron's hands have to be special ordered." Abigail gnawed on her knuckle. "We've got to figure out a way to hide those monkey arms."

"What do you think about this?" He held up pink hot pants and a pair of white, knee-high go-go boots.

"With his furry legs?" Abigail shook her head. "And I thought we'd decided on the black pumps."

"For me, silly." He held the little shorts up to his waist. "To wear when we go out tonight."

She studied him for a minute. "Looks like they'd fit, and the boots are perfect for them. What kind of top?"

"I was thinking a white dress shirt, belted at the waist, and the hat you gave me for my birthday."

She smiled. "Perfect. I'm sure Marty will be impressed."

"I hope so." He scratched his head. "Now if we could just figure out how to dress Cameron."

As THE cab pulled away from the hotel entrance, Harold sighed with relief. A taxi waiting right outside the door spared them more of the kind of looks they'd received on the elevator and in the lobby. "Geez. I haven't been stared at so much since high school."

Except for his hat, he was dressed exactly like Abigail. The open-mouthed stares were not directed at her hatless form. Nor did he think the pink newsboy hat he wore drew their gapes.

"Let them stare," Abigail said. "We didn't dress to impress them, anyway." She glanced at her watch. "I can't believe it's already after ten o'clock."

The cab driver stared at Harold through his rearview mirror. If they hadn't been moving so slow, Harold would have told him to keep his eyes on the road. "Do you think Marty will be there?"

Abigail nodded. "I'm sure."

"But what if he's not?"

"Trust me." She patted his leg. "He'll be there." She leaned forward. "Excuse me, sir. Any idea why traffic is so heavy?"

"I got no idea." The cab driver shook his head and then shrugged. "Must be the heat. Weatherman says today was the hottest June 28th in New York history."

Harold could believe it. Despite the short-sleeved cotton dress shirt and hot pants, he was burning up, and his freshly shaved legs itched. The vinyl go-go boots didn't help.

"Gets worse the closer we get to Christopher Street." The cabbie spat out the window. "We're a few blocks away and haven't moved for five minutes."

Abigail dug through her purse and handed him some crumpled bills. "We'll get out here."

"Suit yourself." He took the bills and looked back over his shoulder. "If I can pull a U-ey, I'm gonna head back uptown. Maybe I'll get lucky and score an airport run."

Harold looked around as he stepped onto the sidewalk but saw no familiar landmarks.

"I know exactly where we are," Abigail said, standing beside him. "We're on Greenwich Avenue." She glanced up and down the street and then pointed. "Terrence's apartment is over that way."

"Oh yeah," Harold said, lying. He could remember what every person who'd passed them had been wearing since they'd exited the cab, along with at least one change he'd suggest, but he had no idea where they were or whether they were heading north, east, south, or west.

The longer they walked, the more crowded the sidewalks became. With few exceptions, everyone was headed in the same direction. Shouts of "gay power!" rang out and echoed up and down the street along with the occasional wolf whistle directed their way.

"Are we there yet?" Harold winced. "These boots ain't made for walking."

Abigail laughed. "You're such a pussy."

Drivers on Greenwich Avenue honked their horns in frustration. So many people had converged on the area that forward progress on the sidewalks had slowed to a crawl. When they reached Christopher Street, a human chain stretched across the intersection, preventing anyone walking or driving from entering.

Dwayne, the blond-haired boy with the bad haircut he'd seen with Marty, folded his arms across his chest and blocked their way. "Christopher Street is for homosexuals only."

Harold dropped Abigail's hand. He still hadn't figured out if he was gay or straight—labels he found as ill-suited for modern life as male and female. He liked to pick and choose from the available options, constructing an identity of his own design rather than jumping into some convenient but ill-fitting box.

"You." He pointed at Harold. "You can pass, but your fag hag stays."

"Fag hag?" Abigail stepped toward him. "I'm a lesbian." She put her hands on her hips and gave him a mean look.

He met her gaze, unimpressed. "I don't believe you."

She poked him in the chest. "Would kicking your pansy ass convince you?" She stood with her hands clenched at her side and glared at him, her nose inches from his.

He stepped aside to let them pass. "Okay, okay. You don't have to beat me up. Sorry."

She looked at Harold, indicating Christopher Street with the jerk of her head. "Come on! What are you waiting for?"

Harold looked at Dwayne and shrugged. "Damn lesbians. Can't take them anywhere."

Although they were still nearly two blocks from the Stonewall Inn, the scene on Christopher Street brought them up short. Buses and cars were trapped in a roiling sea of people. Burning trash bins at regular intervals on both sides of the street created an impression of order and celebration belied by the hundreds of protesters a block away, locked in battle with a cordon of two or three hundred baton-wielding police. Reinforcements had augmented the size of both forces, but in terms of numbers, the people in the street had a huge advantage.

The crowd chanting "gay power!" was two or three times the size of what Harold had seen the night before. People filled the street as far as he could see. Men held hands, kissed, and danced together all around him. "Where did all these people come from?" Harold said, scanning for Marty.

"I have no idea," Abigail said. "Feels like we're at the state fair, or maybe a carnival."

Harold nodded. "Except for all the cops." He couldn't say for sure but thought perhaps the police were trying to clear Christopher Street. They'd succeeded in front of the Stonewall Inn and appeared focused on holding the line, but all the way to Greenwich Avenue, the street was filled with people.

"Is the club open?"

Abigail craned her neck and squinted. "I can't tell. Maybe we should ask one of the nice police officers between us and the door."

Harold laughed. "By the way, that was a great performance back there at the roadblock."

She smiled. "Who said I was acting?"

"I know you better than just about anyone." He put his arm around her waist as they walked. "You're still you, no matter who you decide to fool around with. You became someone else—out of nowhere—and gave a very convincing performance."

"A pissed-off Kelsey was my inspiration. Do you think we'll see her tonight?"

"I don't know." He scanned the street but saw no sign of Marty, Kelsey, or anyone else he knew. "We'll never find Marty in this crowd."

Abigail shook her head. "Not with that attitude. Think positive!"

"Okay, I'm positive we'll never find him."

CHAPTER FIFTY-FIVE

PHILIP LAY across the bed, his head dangling off one side and his feet hanging over the other. George sat astride his back, massaging Philip's shoulders and neck. Philip moaned. "Oh yeah, right there."

"Here?" He kneaded each side, midway between his neck and shoulder.

Philip moaned again and nodded. "Yeah, just like that." The muscles in his neck and shoulders loosened in response to the firm pressure of George's hands.

"I've been thinking about Terrence wanting to go to San Francisco," George said as he worked on Philip's neck.

Philip raised his head up. "I still can't believe you made me promise to support whatever decision he made."

George put his hand on the back of Philip's head and pushed before resuming his massage. "You really have no choice."

Philip lifted his head again. "The hell I don't! He'll need the foundation's support."

George shoved his head down. "Maxine loves Terrence. If it came to a vote, I'm sure she'd want to continue investing in his future."

"And you?"

George continued his rubdown. After a moment, he said, "I'd rather change your mind than vote against you." He rubbed some more. "There you go getting angry. I feel you tensing up." Philip moaned as George's thumbs dug into the base of his neck. "Terrence does need to stay on track with his goals." He moved his thumbs farther apart and resumed the circular motion.

"Good." Philip nodded. "Then we agree. He's staying here in New York until he graduates." Philip groaned as George's thumbs moved closer to his shoulders.

"I agree Terrence needs to graduate." The heels of his palms replaced his thumbs, and Philip purred. "But he doesn't have to stay at Columbia." Philip tried to rise up, but George's hand on the back of his head prevented him from doing so. "There you go tensing up again. Hear me out."

Philip exhaled a deep breath. "I'm listening."

"The law schools at Stanford and the University of California, Berkeley may not be in the northeast, but they're on par with the Ivy League institutions. I know a few lawyers in the San Francisco area I could call, not that Terrence needs our help."

Philip sighed. "I'm so proud of him. I had high hopes for Terrence from the start, and since then, he's done nothing but exceed my expectations."

"I rest my case." George's hands crawled down Philip's spine and back up again. "Show him how much you believe in him. Let him make his own decisions."

Philip didn't even try to lift his head. "But what if things with Cameron don't work out?"

The massage stopped. George tugged on his shoulder and Philip rolled over onto his side. George slid in behind him until they were cheek to cheek and spooning. "I know how much you care, and that you don't want to see Terrence get hurt." He kissed Philip's brow. "But it's up to him—not you." He kissed him again. "Trust him."

"Terrence or Cameron?"

"Both." George smiled. "I have a pretty good feeling about them."

"Oh do you?" Philip snorted. "So now you're a matchmaker?"

"I didn't fix them up—they found each other." He shrugged. "And I trust Terrence. He's never given me reason to do otherwise."

"And Cameron?"

George stroked Philip's cheek with the back of his hand. "Cameron does what he's told. It's the only way he knows. That's how he lasted so long working for Frankie. He's a good kid, but he's going to need time to find out who he is and what he wants to do with his life." He chortled. "Unlike Harold, who knows exactly who he is and what he wants."

Philip nodded. "He sure put on the doll tonight for someone."

"Those matching outfits were something else." George shook his head. "The things kids will wear these days."

"Terrence says Harold found his tribe last night at the Stonewall Inn."

"Tribe?"

Philip smiled. "He had to explain it to me. The two of us are good old-fashioned homosexuals. Just being gay was tribe enough for us. Now they have flame queens, drag queens, leather daddies, hipsters, chickens, scare queens, chicken hawks, and various other categories."

"And to which tribe does Harold belong?"

Philip shook his head. "I can't remember. One of the queens."

"Let me guess," George said, rubbing his chin. "Terrence is a hipster."

Philip smiled. "Terrence claims allegiance to no tribe."

"Someday he'll be a great attorney, maybe even a politician." George kissed the edge of Philip's ear. "I hope we don't regret letting Harold and Abigail go back to the epicenter of last night's violence."

"I had to let them go." Philip shook his head. "I never would have allowed them to go last night—any of them, Terrence included—had I known what was going to happen." He turned to face George. "I hate that anyone got hurt, but I'm glad we were there—all of us—because after seeing what happened—the good and the bad—none of us will ever be the same."

George nodded. "I know what you mean. Know what impressed me most?"

"The police brutality?"

"No." George shook his head. "That's not news, but violence live and in person is far more disturbing than watching clips on television." He brushed his fingers across Philip's brow. "Seeing so many homosexuals in one place really impressed me. I know from our work with the foundation and the Mattachine Society that tens of thousands of homosexuals live in this country."

"Give or take a few hundred thousand, depending on what you mean by homosexual."

"However you define it, knowing in the abstract that thousands of homosexuals exist is one thing. But seeing hundreds, all in one place at the same time…."

Philip nodded. "I know. Powerful. I've never been ashamed of who I am." He stroked George's cheek with a knuckle. "But last night, for the very first time in my life, I was proud to be homosexual."

"For me," George said, "the experience wiped away any remaining vestiges of shame."

"I'd say, to varying degrees, Terrence, Cameron, and Harold experienced the same thing."

"I'd say so too. This trip—whether because of the solidarity he witnessed last night, finding his tribe, or something else—has been good for Harold." George chuckled. "I can see a difference in the way he carries himself." He ran a finger down Philip's nose. "Asking him and Abigail to transform Cameron was the pat on the back he's needed from you."

"He'll do a good job too." Philip squeezed his eyes shut and massaged the bridge of his nose. "I thought if I pooh-poohed his idea of skipping college long enough, he'd come to his senses." He shook his head. "His knack for always being right irks me. Despite my actions, I really do want what's best for him. Terrence too."

"I know." He kissed Philip on the forehead. "They know too. That's why they love you."

Philip turned around and snuggled up against George's chest until they were nose to nose. "You're supposed to be the brains behind the foundation—not the heart." He smiled. "Not that I mind getting all the credit."

"So if he decides to go with Cameron, you'll give Terrence your blessing?"

"Yes." Philip nodded. "And there's no 'if' to it. He's going."

George frowned. "Now you're going to make him go?"

"No." Philip closed his eyes and nestled into George's neck. "His desire to please me was the only thing keeping him here."

"Emotional blackmail?" George shook his head. "You should be ashamed of yourself."

"Your charge is rather harsh," Philip scoffed. "I may have induced a little guilt, but no harm was done." He shrugged. "Go ahead. Charge me with whatever you want." He chuckled. "My attorney will get me off."

CHAPTER FIFTY-SIX

THE CHENILLE house slippers Kreema had worn all day weren't nearly as pink as they'd been when she'd left Kelsey's apartment. She didn't care about their appearance. They were comfortable, and after an evening in heels, her tootsies needed the break.

She was glad she'd come to the park when she had. She'd run into people she hadn't seen for years. Everybody talked about the riot and wondered what the police would do tonight. The street kids bragged about the damage they'd done the night before and stockpiled bottles, rocks, and other throwable objects throughout the neighborhood. The old guard harrumphed that no good could come from so much violence. The queens were all pulling out their best drag and ignoring the three-garment rule. Whatever happened, everyone planned to be there. Kreema didn't want to miss a minute of the excitement, and her bench offered the perfect view.

But the growing police presence outside the Stonewall Inn and the aggressive way the cops confronted people had changed her mind. She didn't need a Magic 8 Ball to know the outlook wasn't good. The way things were shaping up, shit was going to hit the fan in a matter of hours.

She'd run to her little apartment, ditched the floppy hat, and swapped the slippers for her equally comfortable but far more practical steel-toed boots. She touched up her hair, redid her makeup, tossed back a few shots of whiskey, and packed her big black bag with everything she might need.

By the time she left her apartment, the streetlights were on. She heard an uproar coming from the direction of the Stonewall Inn and picked up her pace. She wanted to smoke, but a lady never walks with a cigarette in her hand, and she was too afraid she'd miss something to stop.

The closer she got, the more people she saw. The area around the Stonewall Inn looked like Times Square on New Year's Eve and, if you ignored what the police were doing to anyone who came within striking distance, was about as festive.

The scale was overwhelming. The vast crowd sprawled as far as she could see in any direction. There was just too much going on for her to take it all in. She dug through her bag for her cigarettes and lighter and looked for a spot with a good view where she could smoke.

She stood with her arms folded, puffing on her cigarette, as she tried to make sense of the chaos. Police fought to keep the sidewalk clear in front of the Stonewall Inn and along Christopher Street. She figured maybe three or four hundred cops held back a crowd of several thousand protesters and spectators, with resistance varying across the line. At the far end, near Waverly Place, trash-can lids, flung Frisbee-style, bounced off the policemen's helmets. Closer to where Kreema stood, they pelted cops with bottles. Right in front of the Stonewall Inn, a long line of high-kicking queens faced off with the police. They had their arms linked and chanted words she couldn't make out.

"Mm-hmm." She nodded and dropped her cigarette on the sidewalk. "What them bitches need is a leader." Extinguishing the cigarette with a twist of her boot, she headed for the dancing queens.

JOINING THE chorus line was the best idea she'd had since letting Harold and Abigail make her over. The roaring crowd and all the chanting brought out her inner cheerleader and her love for performing. If some in the throng had come to see a show, Kreema and her dance squad wouldn't disappoint them.

The girls welcomed her like she'd just won Miss America, crowding around her, blowing kisses, and hugging her neck. They put her in the middle of the line, and she nearly cried when they launched into Jackie DeShannon's "Put A Little Love in Your Heart." She'd never been so proud.

The biggest hit was a little ditty some of the girls had made up the night before, during Kreema's unfortunate incarceration. Since then, different queens had embellished the routine and the choreography had evolved. "We are the Stonewall girls, we wear our hair in curls. We wear no underwear. We show our pubic hairs."

Even the police laughed. Marty stuck to her like glue, looking back every thirty seconds and scanning the crowd. She knew who he was looking for. "Don't worry. He'll be looking for you too." She smiled. "And I bet if you stay here with me and dance a few more numbers, he'll find you."

The Stonewall Inn was open but had no booze, jukeboxes, or customers. She'd heard even the cigarette machine was gone. Employees came out onto the sidewalk half a dozen times and invited people in.

Although she was thirsty, she didn't go inside. The absence of a cover charge and the promise of free soft drinks weren't worth tangling with the heavy police presence outside the door.

The kick line was halfway through the crowd favorite when, out of the corner of her eye, she caught sight of Harold and Abigail. After finishing the number, she turned around and waved them over. Marty's face lit up like Santa Claus had arrived, his sled filled with presents just for him.

As bottles sailed over their heads and crashed on the street between where they stood and the police line, she hugged them both close. "I'm so glad to see you!" She looked them up and down. "Look at you and your cute little matching outfits!" She nodded. "Mm-hmm, as always, you look fabulous!"

Abigail smiled. "Thanks!" Then she whispered in Kreema's ear. "You won't believe who's next in line for a transformation."

She leaned back and studied Abigail for a clue. "Terrence?"

Abigail giggled and shook her head. "No, but you're close!"

Marty and Harold faced each other. Kreema couldn't decide who was more nervous. Harold studied his hands, while Marty examined the toe of his right tennis shoe. She looped an arm across each boy's shoulders. "Why don't you gentlemen see if you can find us some Cokes or sumpin'. I'm about to die of thirst." They looked at her like they'd seen a ghost. "Harold, you got money, don't you?"

He patted his pocket and nodded.

"Well, then, get moving!" She shooed them away. "Abigail and I will be over by the general."

Marty grabbed Harold by the hand. "I know where we can go."

Kreema watched as they ran off toward West Fourth Street. She turned to Abigail. "Miss Thing, let's see if we can't find us a bench. I want to hear more about this transformation."

CHAPTER FIFTY-SEVEN

As Marty led him through the crowd, Harold glanced back to see Abigail flash him a thumbs-up. He was giddy with excitement, thrilled to have run into Marty again, and anxious about going off alone with him. Just in case Marty deserted him, Harold tried to pay attention to landmarks rather than the people they passed and what they wore.

Disregarding orders to stick with Abigail worried him too. Philip expected a lot from Harold while making few demands. He didn't think he and Marty were going very far or would be gone for long. Until they got back, Abigail would be safe with Kreema.

The crowd had thinned enough for Harold and Marty to walk side by side. Holding hands in public attracted no more attention than his outfit did. He ignored the stares and comments they got from the people they passed.

Marty gave him a shy smile. "I was hoping to run into you tonight."

Harold squeezed his hand. "Me too." Their eyes met for a moment before Marty averted his gaze.

They walked along in silence. Harold tried to think of something clever to say but came up empty. He'd used up his weekly allotment earlier with his lesbian comment at the blockade. "I saw your boyfriend earlier tonight, over on Greenwich Avenue."

"Dwayne?" Marty shook his head. "He's not my boyfriend."

"Oh." Harold was relieved to find out Marty was unattached.

"Not anymore." He shrugged. "I hope I never see him again."

A thousand questions popped into Harold's head, but he didn't want to pry. He squeezed Marty's hand. "I'm sorry."

"It's okay." He stopped and turned to Harold. "He's history." He squeezed Harold's hand. "I'd rather talk about the future." Marty looked into Harold's eyes and, this time, didn't look away.

Harold's face grew hot, and he hoped Marty didn't notice his sweaty palm.

"Look, me living on the streets and doing what I do, and you being rich and everything… I know you're way out of my league." He sighed. "I'm not asking you for a handout or to take care of me or anything like that." He looked down at the sidewalk for a moment, then back to

Harold. "I was just hoping maybe we could hang out—until you go back to Washington."

Harold held his gaze for a long moment as he thought about what to say. The earnest, expectant look on Marty's face touched Harold's heart and made him feel good inside. Reassuring Marty, correcting his misperceptions, and explaining his feelings would take all night—if he could ever find the words. Marty's expression changed, and Harold knew his delay in responding was sending the wrong message.

The idea popped into his head out of nowhere. Having never done it before, Harold wasn't even sure he knew how. But he'd blown lots of kisses and figured it had to be the same, only without the hand. He leaned in and pressed his mouth against Marty's lips.

Marty sucked lightly on Harold's bottom lip. Harold reciprocated and then Marty pulled away. The whole thing lasted all of five seconds. Not long at all, but enough for Harold to know he wanted more.

AFTER HAROLD washed his face and brushed his teeth, he climbed into bed, put his hands behind his head, and smiled. He glanced at the clock. Almost four o'clock in the morning. He sank back into the luxurious bedding to again go over everything that had happened since he'd run into Marty. For the rest of his life, June 28 would mark the anniversary of his first kiss and his first date. "Are you awake?"

Abigail rolled over and faced him. "I was about to ask you the same thing."

"Was I wrong to kiss Marty on our first date?" He sat up and mussed his hair with his fingers. "I wouldn't want him to think I was fast."

She smiled and shook her head. "No. Not that Marty would care. He's crazy about you."

Harold squealed and shook his fists like an excited toddler. "I know!" He fell back onto his pillow. "I don't know what came over me."

"Oh, I do." She stood, leaned over, and kissed him on the nose. "And it couldn't have happened to two nicer guys." She slid onto the bed beside him.

"I feel bad for not inviting him back to our room." He sat up and turned to face her. "He doesn't have a home. His parents kicked him out two years ago, and he's been getting by however he can ever since."

"That explains why he left the way he did." She reached over and brushed the hair off his face. "He didn't want you to ask."

"Why not?"

"I'm just guessing, but if he really thinks you're out of his league, then he probably doesn't want to push his luck."

"Push his luck?"

She nodded. "He already knew he'd see you again. Kreema made sure of that."

"I hope you're right." Harold shook his head. "Meeting Marty helps me appreciate Philip that much more." He took Abigail's hand in his. "Poppa threatened to put me out several times, and would have if my mother hadn't intervened."

"Mom would have taken you in," Abigail said, squeezing his hand. "I'm sure of it."

"I couldn't do what Marty, Cameron, and Terrence have had to do to survive." He wiped a tear from his cheek. "They are so much stronger than I am."

Abigail stroked his brow. "You're about the strongest person I know. You've survived your crazy father, losing your family, life with that miserly foster family, and now, a riot." She grinned.

He shrugged. "You do what you have to do."

"Exactly," Abigail said. "And you never know what you can do until you don't have a choice." She stood and slid onto her bed. "There are different kinds of strength. Yours is the ability to hold on to who you are, no matter what." She turned off the lamp, plunging them into darkness. "For as long as I've known you, you went to school every day, without ever letting what the other kids said or did change you."

"I always knew they didn't understand."

"That's what I mean. Anyone else would have caved in."

Harold thought for a moment. He couldn't fathom changing a thing about himself because of what anyone else thought about him. If everyone thought the same thing, well, that was more about them than him. "Do you think Kelsey knows Kreema is hosting brunch for us at her apartment?"

"I doubt it. Kreema is house-sitting while Kelsey spends a few days with her girlfriend on Cape Cod," Abigail said.

"Do you think she knows we're coming to dig through her wardrobe for Cameron?"

"Her relatives keep sending her clothes she'll never wear. Kreema says the closets and drawers in Kelsey's spare bedroom are a dream come true for big girls like her. Kelsey seems to like Cameron, so I don't think she'd care."

"I hope we find something better for him to wear than what we found shopping. If not, somebody is in for an awful lot of shaving."

CHAPTER FIFTY-EIGHT

NOT SINCE Terrence had moved out of the shelter and in with Philip could he remember having spent so much time in bed. In his first few days in Philip's apartment, exhaustion had been the cause, and he'd had the bedroom to himself. This time, Cameron was the cause, and after nearly twenty-four hours, Terrence was exhausted and more than a little dehydrated.

Cameron leaned against the bed with his hands behind his head and his legs sprawled across the floor. "This place doesn't feel so cramped with just us."

"True." Terrence reached out and ran his fingers through Cameron's sweat-soaked hair. "But two people couldn't live in this little place. I feel cramped sometimes when I'm here by myself."

"Are you trying to tell me something?" Cameron reached up behind his head and stroked Terrence's arm.

Terrence laughed. "No, you haven't worn out your welcome. Far from it." He could look at Cameron in his white boxers all day. He'd look great in briefs too—or nothing at all. "Cooled off?"

Cameron nodded. "That little window unit makes a big difference." He turned around and slid into bed.

"Oh no." Terrence grinned, kissing him. "Not again."

"I don't know what you're talking about." Cameron leaned in and nibbled on Terrence's earlobe. "I just want to cuddle."

Terrence wrapped his arms around Cameron and pulled him closer. "I've heard that before, and I don't believe it's any more true now than it was then."

"This time I'm really sleepy," Cameron said, yawning. He snuggled into Terrence's neck.

Terrence rested his chin on Cameron's head, enjoying how he felt in his arms. Danny had been the last person he'd held this way. More than two years had passed since then. Where would he be today if Philip hadn't taken him under his wing?

Philip said somehow, some way, Terrence would have escaped the streets and made a life for himself. Perhaps. But he didn't think he'd be attending Columbia University and living in his own place in

New York. He'd have done well to pay for technical school, much less college—forget about Ivy League. Instead of pursuing his dreams, he'd have landed in some dead-end job he hated, living paycheck to paycheck until he died.

Getting noticed was the key to success. While his junior-high classmates had tried to blend in, Terrence had embraced the blond curls and feminine mannerisms that made him stand out from the crowd. If being different hadn't won him many friends, well, that was the price he paid for some kind of future.

His mother could never have given him much in the way of opportunity. She couldn't even provide basic needs. He didn't fault her for her helplessness, but he wasn't about to let her shortcomings hold him back.

Thanks to Philip Potter, Terrence had options he never even would have considered three years ago. Disregarding Philip's wishes for Terrence and his future for a guy he'd only just met didn't feel right. Philip deserved better than that. Besides, Philip wasn't telling him what to do so much as holding Terrence to the goals he'd set for himself.

"You sure got quiet," Cameron said. "What are you thinking about?"

He kissed the top of Cameron's head. "Nothing. I thought you were asleep."

"I bet it's that accordion knot thing." Cameron sat up. "I'm not going to beg you to come with me." He shook his head. "You know I want you to, but sooner or later, you'd resent me for giving up your dreams."

Terrence sighed. "I know." He pulled Cameron back down beside him. "That's why, barring some miracle, I don't think I can come with you." He kissed him. "But that doesn't have to mean the end of us."

"We'll be on opposite coasts." Cameron shook his head. "Flying across the country is too expensive to do very often, even if I could come back here to visit."

"There's the telephone." But Terrence knew as he said the words that neither of them could afford long-distance charges for more than the occasional short call. "And we can write letters." He tried not to think about his poor track record for keeping up with his correspondence with Harold and Philip.

They lay quietly for a long moment. The odds were against them. If Terrence stayed in New York, he might see Cameron once or twice a year and maybe chat with him on the telephone a few times. But with time, they'd get busy. Weeks without seeing or talking to each other would turn into months, and months into years.

Cameron peered into Terrence's eyes. "Until you and your friends came along, my life had been an inescapable nightmare."

Terrence took in the intensity of his gaze. He understood how Cameron felt. Terrence felt the same way about Philip for rescuing him.

"Maybe with your cherubic face, that curly blond halo, and those crazy sandals you always wear, you're really an angel." He smiled. "But an angel wouldn't worry about what Philip was going to do to him for abandoning Harold and Abigail."

Terrence laughed. "You wouldn't have to look far to find plenty of evidence that I'm no angel."

Cameron kissed him. "I don't believe the next few days will be the end for us." He shook his head. "Because I can't." He cleared his throat. "But if it is, I'll never forget you and everything you've done to help me break free from Frankie."

They kissed again. "I hate hard choices," Terrence said. "Instead of one or the other, why can't I pick both?"

Cameron raised his head up. "Yeah, that would be nice."

Terrence smiled. "No, that would be a miracle."

"Well, then maybe we ought to pray."

"What?" Terrence winced as he sat up. "I didn't know you were religious."

"I wasn't. Kreema converted me." Cameron smiled and kissed the tip of Terrence's nose. "And I don't think we'd be sitting here right now if I hadn't prayed for a miracle."

"You really believe all that stuff?"

Cameron shrugged. "Don't really know much about the Bible or any religion." He met Terrence's gaze. "I gave praying my best shot one time, and a few hours later, you were chasing me down the street." He shrugged again. "Now look where I am. I don't know if God had a hand in that or not. Can't hardly imagine, with all the billions of people on the planet, that he much cares one way or the other what I do." He smiled. "You either."

Terrence tilted his head. "I never thought about stripping away the bullshit and just going mano a mano with my creator."

"What have you got to lose?" Cameron stood and then kneeled by the side of the bed. "Praying won't hurt, and it just might help."

Terrence kneeled beside him and grinned. "This is the first time I've dropped to my knees for a man since I quit my old job."

CHAPTER FIFTY-NINE

Sunday, June 29, 1969

AFTER TWO hours on the front line, Liana Salvatore was about as tired as she could ever remember being. Everyone was. Beating up homos two nights in a row took a lot out of a person.

Not that she'd actually beat up any homos. She hadn't had anything to do with the crowd-control efforts the night before either. Had she been more involved with what was going on outside the club Friday night, perhaps she'd have had a better idea of what to expect tonight. Despite the chief's assurance, they had been caught with their pants down again. Nobody had been prepared for the size of the crowd or their angry reaction to the heavy police presence.

Nabbing innocent bystanders from the crowd and beating them up hadn't helped. The mob didn't appear to enjoy the sight any more than she did. Something about a man beating up a woman—even a man dressed as a woman—was hard to watch. Seeing defenseless little boys assaulted with nightsticks by big burly men in uniforms didn't sit well either. Every altercation angered the crowd more than the one before.

The most active participants in the protest were the drag queens and effeminate men who couldn't pass for straight if they had to. They figured out fast enough to use their biggest advantage: numbers. When Mick and his pal snatched a queen who had thrown a rock at them from the crowd, thirty or more nelly young men overwhelmed the nightstick-wielding cops to drag their friend back into the crowd. Mick gave chase, only to be rebuffed by a united front of fairies who took his blows without letting him through or giving up any ground. The same thing happened again and again, up and down the line.

But most of the people in the predominantly male crowd were much less flamboyant. Rather than homeless urchins and cross-dressing prostitutes, they looked the same as working-class men anywhere in America. They paid taxes just like everybody else and, it seemed to Liana, should be able to have a drink or dance without having to worry about getting arrested.

Last night's raid had ignited long-simmering hostility toward the police. Seeing the huge crowd before her gave Liana a better understanding of the predicament facing homosexuals. They weren't free to be themselves in straight establishments, and to be with their own kind, New York alcohol regulations forced them to seek out seedy Mafia-owned hovels.

Liana couldn't figure out why the police were even there. In her professional opinion, the heavy presence of law enforcement had caused the whole blowup. Watching the protesters engage the police gave the crowd something to do. If the cops had stayed away, the disgruntled fairies would have sung "Kumbaya" and "We Shall Overcome" a few times, and then gone on about their merry business.

The Stonewall Inn was open but empty, despite pleas from the owner and employees, as entering would mean crossing the line of baton-bearing cops. The police presence both angered and empowered the mob. The invasion by law-enforcement officers into a part of town long claimed by the homosexuals aroused their anger. The number of police on hand was a testament to how powerful and intimidating the homos had become. "Gay power!" reverberated through the crowd, ebbing and flowing but ever present and louder by the hour.

Once her initial adrenaline rush had worn off, holding the line became tedious. Liana's whole body ached. Her eyes wandered, taking in the spectacle farther up and down Christopher Street. The second time a flying object bounced off her helmet, Liana vowed not to let activities elsewhere distract her from what was going on less than a stone's throw away.

The arrival of the Tactical Police Force, better known as the riot squad, sometime after two in the morning, made things worse. The dancing queens, under the direction of the tall black man she'd had a run-in with the night before, shifted so the line spanned Christopher Street. The riot police, carrying clear plastic shields before them and standing shoulder to shoulder, advanced from Greenwich Avenue toward the line of high-kicking fairies.

Liana had never seen the Tactical Police Force in action. The phalanx of shielded cops marching lockstep was impressive. The street before them emptied, leaving nothing but open concrete between the monolithic TPF and the idiosyncratic chorus line. Step by step, the riot police advanced, but the dancers held their position, taunting the advancing cordon with obscene gestures, lewd names, and their high-kicking shenanigans as the crowd behind them cheered.

The contrast between the two sides was both striking and ridiculous— an army of masculine automatons versus an odd assortment of the girliest men Liana had ever seen. The police showed no emotion, while the homos looked like they were having the time of their lives. As the phalanx advanced on the revelers, Liana couldn't look away. The audacity of the queeny men impressed her almost as much as the zombie-like army approaching them.

As the wall of riot police advanced, Liana expected the dancing line to dissolve into the crowd. The closer the TPF got, the more certain she was the next step would be the one to send the queens running. She thought they'd bolt at twenty feet apart and couldn't believe they still held firm at fifteen feet. At ten feet, just when Liana started thinking maybe the queens intended to make the cops run over them, they broke and ran, laughing and carrying on like kids on a playground.

The wall of shields moved past her, and Liana saw the crowd had looped around the block and reformed behind them. Over the next half hour, the riot squad marched up and down Christopher Street. The protesters they herded out of the way darted down side streets, reforming behind the impassive line, only to be chased away again.

By three in the morning, both sides seemed to have tired of the cat-and-mouse game. But then all the bars closed, and a mass of newcomers came along to reinvigorate the crowd. Again, had there been no police, the new arrivals would have had no reason to linger. In the face of the TPF, the resistance didn't last long. By three thirty, the crowd had just about disappeared.

The police hadn't lost any battles, but they weren't winning the war. They'd held their line tonight, and she'd never felt as threatened as she had the night before when they'd been pinned inside the Stonewall Inn. But she didn't feel like the police, at any time, had ever really had the upper hand. They hadn't had their asses handed to them on a platter, but this night, theirs had been a hollow victory.

CHAPTER SIXTY

CAMERON HAD to admit the disguise Harold and Abigail had decided upon was brilliant. He didn't think he'd have any trouble playing the role. And if everything fit, he'd keep almost all his body hair.

Harold dabbed Cameron's brow with a sponge. "The worst is over. Waxing would have been faster than tweezing, but we couldn't find everything we needed. Sorry."

He hoped Harold was right about the worst being over but suspected Harold underestimated how uncomfortable Cameron was about wearing a dress. He squirmed in one of the folding chairs Philip had dropped by earlier, saying they were a late housewarming present. Cameron's feet soaked in a plastic washtub full of water. Terrence sat on the floor in front of him, razor in hand.

"Just up to the knee?" Terrence looked to Abigail for guidance.

She glanced up from the ironing board. "Shave to midthigh—so he can cross his legs if he wants."

"Yes, ma'am," Terrence said. He looked up at Cameron. "This is going to hurt me as much as it hurts you."

"Are you sure you can keep from nicking him?" Abigail asked Terrence. "I'd shave him myself if we had more time."

Terrence stretched his legs across the floor. "Go ahead. Run your hand over these gams." He ran his hand over his shins. "Smooth as silk and not a scratch on them."

"Not you, Cameron," Harold said. "Look up." Harold used his thumbs to spread whatever he'd been smearing on his neck, cheeks, and forehead under Cameron's eyes. Except for glancing down now and then to make sure the fly on his boxers wasn't gaping, Cameron did what he was told.

"I wonder who in Kelsey's family has the thing for gloves," Abigail said. "The selection in that bedroom beats what we saw at any store."

"I'm glad," Harold said. "Gloves work better and save us having to give him nails and a manicure and shave his arms."

"How was brunch?" Terrence smiled and lathered his hands with a bar of soap. "What did Miss Kreema cook up for you?"

"She went all out," Harold replied. "The first course was a bowl of cereal."

"Lucky Charms," Abigail said. "Because it was Harold and Marty's first real date."

Terrence dropped the soap into the water and turned to Harold. "Marty was there too?"

Abigail nodded. "He's such a sweetheart."

Harold's face turned crimson. He wiped his hands clean on a towel and picked up a small bottle. "Look down," Harold ordered. He pulled a little brush from the bottle and painted a cool liquid around Cameron's eyes.

The idea of Kreema cooking made Terrence smile. "What else did she fix?"

"Meatloaf, mashed potatoes, and peas," Abigail said.

Terrence looked at her, a hurt expression on his face. "And you didn't bring us any?"

"TV dinners," Harold said, opening another bottle and pulling out a small bristled brush. "There weren't really any leftovers. Look up."

Abigail laughed. "She dumped them out of the foil trays onto plates so we wouldn't know they were TV dinners."

"Yeah." Harold smiled. "Everybody knew but Marty. You should have seen the look on Kreema's face when he asked for seconds."

As Terrence soaped up his legs, Cameron thought about food he hated, nauseating smells, dead kittens, and blowing Frankie Caldarone—anything to keep his mind off the hands stroking his calves and thighs. He'd die of embarrassment if his hard dick poked through the fly of his boxers.

Harold rubbed something onto Cameron's eyebrows. "I haven't made anyone look older before." He worked on Cameron's face with a little pencil. "Took me a while to figure out to add the lines and wrinkles I usually try to cover up."

Abigail slid the black dress off the ironing board and onto a hanger. "You're doing a good job." She hung up the dress and folded the ironing board back into the wall.

Terrence finished shaving Cameron's legs and dumped the hairy suds down the toilet. When Harold finished the makeup, Abigail took over. She helped Cameron into black nylon hose, a garter belt, padded undergarments, and a slip. He stepped into the dress, slid his arms into the long sleeves, and adjusted the high collar around his neck as Abigail zipped him up.

The two of them hovered over him, adjusting the wig, tilting the hat at different angles, and fine-tuning the fall of the black beaded veil across his brow. They circled around him several times, now and then making an adjustment. Finally, they stopped, looked at each other, and nodded.

Terrence whistled. "Good job, kids."

Cameron gave him a coy smile. "Am I pretty?"

Terrence grinned. "For a stocky, aging widow, you're beautiful." He pointed to the bathroom. "See for yourself."

Walking in the shoes wasn't half the challenge he'd expected—the heels on his boots were almost as high. But the wig was hot, the high collar scratched his neck, the undergarments were tighter than anything he'd ever worn before, and the extra padding around his chest, belly, hips, and butt was uncomfortable.

He walked into the bathroom and stared at his reflection in the mirror. "Oh my God!" A gloved hand touched the face, and he realized both belonged to him. "I look like my grandmother."

BY THE time they exited the cab at Grand Central Station, Cameron was miserable. The shoes pinched his toes, his legs and arms itched, his ears hurt from the heavy clip-ons, and he didn't think he'd ever been so hot.

"We're almost there," Terrence said, walking beside him with a suitcase in each hand. "No need to rush, Grandma."

Cameron placed his gloved hand in the crook of Terrence's arm and squeezed. Hard.

"Our train doesn't leave for another hour." Terrence looked around the terminal. "Should we grab a cup of coffee or something?"

Cameron shook his head.

"What's the matter?" Terrence snickered. "Cat got your tongue?"

Cameron pinched Terrence's cheek and made kissing noises at him. "Don't make me punch you in the ribs," he whispered, the smile never leaving his face.

"Ouch!" Terrence rubbed his cheek. "It's not my fault you can't pee until we get to Washington."

Not by himself he couldn't, not with all the undergarments and padding. And Terrence going with him into either restroom would attract too much attention. He'd resigned himself to waiting until they got to Philip's apartment. Eight more hours wasn't that long. He'd relieved himself before they left the apartment, and if he didn't drink anything or think about it too much, he'd be fine.

They sat together on a bench near the gate for the outgoing train to Washington. "Philip and George are supposed to meet us here, but I don't see them. Do you?"

Cameron looked around the crowded terminal. He saw no sign of Philip or George, but two benches away, one of Frankie's guys sat smoking a cigar and browsing through a newspaper. He shook his head and whispered, "See the guy behind me reading the paper?"

Terrence glanced over Cameron's shoulder. "Older man smoking a cigar?"

Cameron nodded. "He works for Frankie," he whispered.

"Relax. Your own mother wouldn't recognize you." He adjusted Cameron's hat and tugged on the veil. "I have to admit, I'll never see you the same way again." He stood and winked. "In your day, I bet you were quite the looker." He glanced around the terminal. "I need to hit the bathroom. Will you be okay until I get back, Grams?"

Cameron nodded. He sat with his legs crossed and his hands folded on the purse in his lap, watching the people go by. Sensing someone at the end of the bench, he turned and sucked in his breath.

Frankie's goon sat with his arm across the back of the bench, smiling at him. "How you doing?"

Cameron gave him a weak smile and nodded. Then he opened his purse and pulled out a pack of cough drops. He popped one into his mouth, pointed to his throat, and shook his head.

He gave Cameron a sympathetic look and slid closer. "I'm sorry. Can I buy you a cup of coffee or something? A little hot liquid might loosen your throat up."

Cameron shook his head and waved his hand.

The man moved closer, sliding his arm along the bench behind Cameron's back. "You sure are pretty." He nodded his head slowly as he looked Cameron up and down. "I like a classy babe with a little meat on her bones." He smiled. "Takes a big woman to handle a guy like me." He winked. "Know what I'm saying?"

"Is this man bothering you, Grandma?" Terrence glared at the man. "We buried her husband yesterday."

He dropped his arm from behind Cameron and stood. "I'm sorry." He looked Cameron over again. "You live here in New York?"

"Not anymore," Terrence replied. "No point in her being alone here when she's got family who love her in Washington." Terrence touched Cameron's shoulder. "Right, Grandma?"

Cameron nodded.

"I'm sorry to have bothered you during this difficult time," the man said. "And I'm very sorry for your loss."

"Thank you for your concern," Terrence said. "Oh, look, Grandma. Philip and George are here." He looked at the man. "Cousins."

The man walked away, turning back to look at Cameron again, undressing him with his eyes. Thinking about the man's reaction if he could really see what was under the dress made Cameron smile, but the thought that he might be recognized scared the hell out of him.

CHAPTER SIXTY-ONE

Philip walked as fast as he could, but two heavy suitcases slowed his progress. He could go forty, maybe fifty yards before he had to stop, set the luggage down, and shake the blood back into his fingers.

"I told you I'd be happy to swap bags with you," George said. "Mine are smaller and not nearly so heavy."

"No." Philip shook his head and grabbed the handles of his suitcases. "I'm the one who insisted on bringing three times as much as I could ever wear. Perhaps the pain and suffering will help me to remember to pack lighter for my next trip."

"Oh my," George said. "There's Terrence and… er… his grandmother."

"In widow's weeds, no less," Philip said, stopping to allow the blood to flow back into his fingers. "I must say I never would have recognized… er… her."

"Me either," George said. "The veil is a nice touch."

Philip nodded. "Yes, and I don't believe I've ever seen a sadder looking widow." He wiped his brow with a handkerchief, returned it to his pocket, and picked up his bags again, determined to make it all the way to the bench where Cameron and Terrence sat.

"Terrence looks quite handsome in his coat and tie," George said. "Though I wish he had worn something other than those blue jeans and sandals."

Terrence jumped up from the bench and ran over to Philip. "Here," Terrence said. He took the suitcases from him. "Let me carry those for you."

"Thank you." Philip pulled a handkerchief from his pocket and wiped his face. He walked over and took Cameron's hand in his. "I'm so sorry for your loss." Then he leaned in and whispered, "It'll grow back."

They boarded, settled into their seats, and waited for the train to pull out of the station. Across the aisle, Terrence and Cameron held hands and peered out the window. George read the Sunday *New York Times* beside him as Philip attempted to solve the crossword puzzle.

As the train lurched into motion, Cameron turned to Terrence and smiled. George caught Philip's eye and held up crossed fingers. Philip wondered whether they'd really needed to go to so much trouble but accepted George's desire to exercise an abundance of caution. After all, he was an attorney. May as well follow his advice.

Unlike other excursions with George, this time circumstances had conspired to keep them busy with foundation work. They'd made dozens of telephone calls and met with several individuals to garner financial and in-kind support. Philip couldn't be happier with the way things were shaping up.

Although the getaway to New York hadn't turned out as planned, Philip was glad they'd come when they had. Witnessing what the newspaper referred to as the "Stonewall uprising" had moved him, and he was grateful George, Terrence, and Harold—all the men he loved—had been there too. Whether the uprising would change the world or not remained to be seen, but being there had certainly changed Philip.

Meeting Cameron had been a stroke of good luck. The sequence of events bringing Cameron and Terrence together had begun long before Philip's arrival in New York. He wondered how long he'd have been kept in the dark about the relationship had he stayed in Washington. When he did get around to telling him, Terrence could never have conveyed the way he and Cameron looked at each other and the ease with which they got along in his too-brief telephone conversations or rare letters. Seeing Cameron and Terrence together had spared Philip a lot of wondering and at least a few sleepless nights.

By phone or letter, Terrence would have had a heck of a time convincing anyone to come to Cameron's aid. The male prostitutes Philip had helped before had worked for themselves. Helping them was like rescuing orphaned puppies. Helping Cameron was more like springing someone from a high-security prison. Philip's willingness stemmed, in part, from Terrence's obvious affection for him. That the handsome, affable young man was polite, charming, and easy to like hadn't hurt.

He looked across the aisle and saw they'd fallen asleep. Terrence's head rested on Cameron's shoulder and served as a pillow for Cameron's head. Philip nudged George and pointed to the sleeping young men. "Too bad we don't have a camera."

George lowered his newspaper, glanced across the aisle, and smiled at Philip. "They've been through a lot the last few days."

Philip nodded. "Yes, we all have."

Thanks to George, Philip was okay with Terrence going with Cameron. Of course, he hadn't said so when Terrence told him he'd decided to stay in New York to finish his degree. George was still waiting to hear back from his friends in San Francisco. Rather than raising expectations and inviting disappointment, Philip wanted to wait until they'd worked everything out to say anything to either Terrence or Cameron.

The trip had also caused Philip to see Harold's career plans in a new light. The loneliness and isolation he'd experienced in high school had been difficult enough. Four more years in a conformist institution, enduring the taunts and stares of his classmates, wouldn't benefit Harold in the least. Philip couldn't blame him for wanting to be appreciated and valued rather than disliked and bullied. Never mind his obvious talent. He hoped the interview he and George had arranged went well, and the opportunity to work with such a talented artist would appeal to Harold and make it clear Philip supported what he wanted to do with his life.

Soon Philip would be living alone. Aside from the weeks between James's death and Terrence's decision to move in with him, he hadn't lived by himself for nearly ten years. Living with Terrence and Harold hadn't been easy. He'd often grown tired of picking up after them and dealing with the drama that goes with youth. But his pride in what they had accomplished and the young men they had become more than compensated for any hardship or inconvenience.

He pulled a handkerchief from his pocket and dabbed his eyes. Living alone wouldn't be so bad. Maybe he'd get a dog—a toy variety that would be content living in his small apartment. Philip would enjoy being welcomed home by something other than an empty apartment. A dog would be good company and a reason to walk more. He made a mental note to see what breed Maxine would suggest next time he talked to her.

CHAPTER SIXTY-TWO

HAROLD AND Abigail tidied up Terrence's place as best they could and, since the apartment would be empty for several days, carted all the perishable food to the trash. Harold slid the key into his pocket and bounded down the steps behind Abigail. Having promised at brunch to reconnect with Marty, they hurried to Christopher Street to find him.

"Wow," Abigail said, glancing around. "Look at all the cops."

Harold stopped and scanned the park. "At least they're not lined up shoulder to shoulder in riot gear." He looked around, shielding his eyes from the sun. "Do you see Marty?"

"No." Abigail stood beside him. "Do you think he'll be offended?"

"I hope not," Harold answered. "The haircut doesn't cost anything, so he shouldn't mind. Buying clothes might bug him, but I don't think he'll be too upset if we shop at the secondhand store."

"Shh." Abigail smiled and waved to someone behind Harold. "Here he comes."

Harold turned around, unable to keep himself from grinning ear to ear as Marty approached. He raised his hand to his shoulder and waved. "Hi!"

Marty waved back and came to a stop in front of them. "I've been watching for you."

"Sorry," Abigail said. "Making him stout wasn't as easy as we thought."

Harold nodded. "Getting the shape right and figuring out how to keep the padding from moving around took some doing."

A police officer walked over to them, his nightstick on his belt and his hands clasped behind his back. "All right, kids. No loitering. Move along."

"Come on," Abigail said, taking Harold and Marty each by the hand. "This way."

Harold would like to have held Marty's hand, but the heavy police presence deterred him. Besides, he and Abigail were on their own now, without Philip, George, or Terrence to rescue them if they got into trouble. Harold had decided to exercise, as George would say, an abundance of caution for the rest of their time in New York.

Marty glanced back. "The cops aren't going to let the crowd get ahead of them this time." He shrugged. "But I don't think they have anything to worry about tonight."

Abigail looked at Marty. "What makes you say that?"

"Sunday nights are always quiet because everybody works tomorrow." He shook his head. "And the vibe is different today—not as much anger on either side. Look how nice the cops are being."

Harold hoped Marty was right. Being part of what Philip was certain had been a historic moment two nights in a row was enough. Tonight he wanted to do what he'd come here to do in the first place: dance.

THE SHOPPING expedition had been enlightening. Marty's money sense had impressed Harold. He'd dickered back and forth with the thrift-store manager, bargaining and counteroffering until they agreed on a price a fraction of what Harold had been willing to pay.

Convincing Marty to come to their room at the Hilton had been the hard part. Harold worried maybe the reluctance had something to do with him having been so forward. After all, Harold had kissed him in the middle of the street. What might he do in the privacy of the hotel room? Harold assured him everything would be okay since Abigail would be with them, which didn't seem to help.

The three of them spent the rest of the afternoon altering the clothes they'd picked up at the thrift shop. Marty sat shirtless on the toilet as Harold cut his hair. They were alone, though right outside the bathroom, Abigail ironed the outfits they'd decided to wear and watched television.

"Turn this way a little bit," Harold said, gesturing with the scissors.

Marty complied. "You're probably wondering what happened between me and Dwayne."

Harold shook his head. "None of my business." He combed through Marty's hair, grasped a lock between his fingers, and snipped with his scissors. "Unless you want to talk about it."

"When you live on the street, being hungry is bad, but the loneliness is worse." He shrugged. "Dwayne kept me from feeling so lonely. I thought he really loved me, but he was just using me. He doesn't care about anyone but himself."

"I'm sorry." Harold combed through Marty's hair, checking his lines one last time.

"You're so lucky," Marty said. "Philip and George sound like great dads, Terrence is the coolest big brother in the world, and you couldn't ask for a better friend than Abigail."

"I know." He set the scissors and comb down on the vanity and brushed the hair from Marty's face, neck, and shoulders with a hand towel. "They're like family to me."

"I hope I can have a family like yours one day."

Harold studied Marty's face for a long moment and thought about what to say. He wanted to tell him how sorry he was for the hard times Marty had endured and that the foolish, willful acts of his stupid parents had nothing to do with him and everything to do with their own ignorance. He sat on the side of the bathtub, took Marty's hands in his, and looked into his brown eyes. "I don't know what's happening between us."

Marty's brow furrowed. "What do you mean?"

Harold took a deep breath and slowly exhaled. "No one has ever made me feel like I do when you look at me like that."

"Like how?"

"With your eyes open." Harold squeezed his hands. "Your expression doesn't matter."

Marty smiled. "I meant, how do you feel when I look at you?"

He paused for a moment. "I've never been interested in anyone before, man or woman." His face grew hot. "I thought the part of me responsible for falling in love was either missing or badly broken."

"Are you saying you're in love with me?"

Harold shrugged. "Everything has happened too fast for me to know. The whole experience—everything about it—is new to me." He met his gaze. "I like the way you make me feel, but I need to go slow. Maybe if I got to know you better…."

Marty squeezed his hands. "I'd give anything for the chance to get to know you better."

The moment had come. Harold feared Marty might get angry with him for even mentioning the idea. "Terrence and Abigail say I should talk to Philip and George about you."

"They do?" His eyes grew wide. "How do you feel about that?"

"I would have already, but I wasn't sure you'd want their help. Besides, I didn't want to betray your confidence."

"Do you really think they'd help me?"

The hopeful expression on his face touched Harold somewhere deep inside. He nodded. "They would."

CHAPTER SIXTY-THREE

Friday, July 4, 1969

TERRENCE WAS thrilled to again be celebrating Independence Day with Harold and Philip. For the third year in a row, they'd packed a picnic basket and arrived early enough to stake out a choice spot at the National Mall to watch the fireworks. Only this year, instead of just the three of them, there were five sitting on the blanket with their faces turned toward the Washington Monument, watching for the first burst of color in the night sky.

"George so wanted to be here," Philip said with a sigh. "He's gone to the annual Walker family reunion at a resort in the Catskills." He shook his head. "Roland, George, and the old man. Thank God he'll have Maxine to keep him company."

"What about the other Mrs. Walkers?" Terrence asked.

"Roland's wife divorced him after James's death, and the old man is a widower." Philip wiped his brow with a handkerchief. "He was too mean to die first, depriving his wife of her one opportunity for a few years of joy."

Philip got testy when family demands encroached on his time with George. Terrence didn't blame him. Spending the last few days with not one, but two sets of lovebirds probably hadn't helped.

"I'd hoped Kreema would get moved to DC in time to join us," Philip said. "But she didn't want to miss any going-away parties."

Harold nodded. "She's excited about being the housemother at the shelter."

"Good." Philip nodded. "I'm trying to make an honest woman out of her. She said she'd give it a try for six months."

Terrence reached over and mussed Harold's hair. "What did you two decide to do?"

"Well," Harold said, after a quick glance at Marty. "I'm going to work as an assistant in Vidal Sassoon's salon."

Philip patted Harold on the back. "He says you're smart, very talented, and will likely have your license in no time."

Terrence turned to Marty. "Are you going with Harold to New York?"

"No." Marty shook his head and looked at Harold.

"Me and Marty haven't known each other very long, and I've never had a boyfriend before, and… well, no offense, but we don't feel like we're ready to make any long-term plans together."

"Yeah," Marty said. "I mean, I'd run away with Harold today if it was the only way we could be together." He glanced at Cameron. "But I don't have to do that, and we want to be sure we're doing the right thing."

"We'll visit each other a couple of times a month," Harold said. "Marty wants to study business."

"Yeah, so I can manage operations and Harold can focus on his art."

The young lovebirds' decisions had Philip stamped all over them. Terrence guessed they'd heard "stay in the moment" and "if it's meant to be" a couple of thousand times in the last week. "So where will you live?"

"I'm going to live with Philip here in Washington for a while. He's going to help me with the GED."

"I don't think you'll have any problem." Philip patted him on the head. "You've been out of school for a while, but you were a good student."

"And I'm moving into Terrence's apartment," Harold said.

"You and Terrence are going to live together?" Cameron chewed on a blade of grass he held in his hand. "In that little apartment?"

"No," Terrence said, shaking his head. "I'm moving out."

Cameron looked at him. "First I've heard of this. You moving in with Kelsey?"

"I talked to her yesterday," Terrence said. "She doesn't want to come back to New York."

Philip turned to Terrence. "Because of the riot?"

He shook his head. "I don't think so. She and Carrie bought one-way tickets for the *Queen Elizabeth II* for an indefinite stay in Europe."

"So you're moving into her apartment until she comes back?" Cameron asked.

"Nope." Terrence struggled to keep his face serious.

Philip stroked his goatee. "Perhaps we should let Terrence's place go and see about subletting from Kelsey."

"That would be great!" Harold said. "Then Abigail could be my roommate. She's going to acting school and has already auditioned for several parts."

Cameron frowned. "Then where are you going to live?"

"In a 1965 VW Bus," Terrence said, with a quick nod.

"White over turquoise now, but I understand Terrence has plans for a custom paint job." Philip smiled. "The spacious vehicle is a gift from Maxine. She says it's the only way to see the USA."

Cameron scratched his head. "See the USA?"

Terrence nodded. "I got this little gig for the rest of the summer."

Cameron's face fell. "What kind of gig?"

Terrence placed his hand on Cameron's arm. "I've wanted to tell you, but there's never been a good time...."

Cameron looked like he might be sick. "Tell me what?"

Terrence glanced at Philip. "Well, this guy wants me to drive a friend of his to San Francisco."

"Drive? To California?"

"Yeah." Terrence smiled. "Says we should take our time and enjoy the scenery."

Understanding dawned on Cameron.

"I thought we'd swing down to Kentucky on the way so you could show me those horse farms you talk so much about." Terrence opened his wallet and held up an automobile club membership card. "And thanks to this, I've got these nifty little map books with campgrounds marked all along the route."

"But what about school?" Cameron sputtered. "I thought we agreed...."

"They have schools in San Francisco. It's too late for fall admission, but George has lined up an internship for me with a big law firm for the fall."

Rockets whistled and exploded into colorful starbursts over the Washington Monument. The crowd *ooh*ed and *ahh*ed as more explosions followed in rapid succession. Wisps of smoke filled the air as blazing red, blue, and green embers formed ephemeral shapes across the sky.

"Looks like we got our miracle," Cameron said, smiling. "When do we leave?"

"Whenever you want. The bus is parked at George's house, packed and set for the trip with a full tank of gas and all my eight-track tapes to listen to on the road." Terrence smiled. "I even bought a few country tapes, just for you." His camera, unfortunately, was also in the bus, so he couldn't capture the dazed expression on Cameron's face.

"I'm ready when you are," Cameron said.

"I was hoping you'd say that." Terrence stood up. "The sooner we hit the road, the more fireworks we'll see along the way." He offered his hand to Cameron and pulled him up. "No offense, Philip, but I couldn't sleep on your living room floor another night."

Philip stood and hugged him. "Send me lots of postcards." He pulled a handkerchief from his pocket and dabbed his eyes. "And be sure to call me when you get situated."

"We'll send you a postcard every day, I promise," Terrence said.

"I'll hold him to his word," Cameron said, extending his hand. "Thanks for everything."

Philip brushed his hand away and wrapped his arms around him. "I know you'll make us proud."

Harold got up and hugged Terrence, and he held his adopted brother tight for a long moment. "After we get to San Francisco, you'll have to come and see us." He glanced at Marty. "You too."

Harold nodded. "I'll write you every week." He gave Terrence a stern look. "And I hope you do a better job of answering my letters than you have since you left Washington."

Terrence mussed his hair. "I'll try."

"He will," Cameron said, hugging Harold close. "I'm going to miss you." He turned to Marty. "Good luck with school."

"If you're going to beat the rush, you need to get moving," Philip said, dabbing his cheek with a handkerchief. "Taxis will be in short supply when the fireworks are over."

Terrence kissed his cheek. "I love you." He turned to Cameron. "Well, cowboy, let's make like horse shit and hit the trail."

MICHAEL RUPURED grew up in Lexington, Kentucky, the thoroughbred horse capital of the world. In 1998, he moved to Athens, Georgia, home of the B-52s, R.E.M., Widespread Panic, and countless garage bands aspiring to make it big. He's an avid fan of SEC sports—especially Georgia football, Kentucky basketball, and women's gymnastics. Michael's personal involvement in sports consists of running, working out at the gym, and playing with his longhaired Chihuahuas, Tico and Toodles. In addition to "writing stories true enough for government work," he's on the faculty of the College of Family and Consumer Sciences at the University of Georgia. He's received numerous awards for financial education programs he's developed over the last thirty years for youths and low-income families and served in a variety of leadership roles at the state and national level. In 2015, he was named Postsecondary Educator of the Year by the Georgia Association of Teachers of Family and Consumer Sciences and the Georgia Association for Career and Technical Education. He joined the Athens Writers Workshop in 2010 and has since published three novels: *Until Thanksgiving* in 2012, *After Christmas Eve* in 2013 (rereleasing as *No Good Deed* in 2016), *Happy Independence Day*—a Rainbow Award runner up for historical fiction in 2014—and *Whippersnapper* in 2016.

Blog: ruptured.com

Twitter: @crotchetyman

Facebook: www.facebook.com/AuthorMichaelRupured

E-mail: mrupured@gmail.com

NO GOOD DEED

MICHAEL RUPURED

A Philip Potter Story

On Christmas Eve in 1966, Philip Potter, a kind-hearted Smithsonian curator, wraps up his last-minute shopping. Meanwhile, James, his lover of several years, takes his own life back in their home. Unaware of what awaits him, Philip drops off gifts at a homeless shelter, an act of generosity that will later make him a suspect in the murder of a male prostitute.

Following James's shocking death, two men enter Philip's life—and both drive yellow Continentals. One of them, though, is a killer, with the blood of at least six hustlers on his hands. And both are hiding something.

As Philip is about to discover, no good deed goes unpunished.

For more great fiction from

DSP PUBLICATIONS

visit us online.

WWW.DSPPUBLICATIONS.COM